H. R. F. Keating, a Fellow of the Royal Society of Literature, was the crime books reviewer for *The Times* for fifteen years. He has served as Chairman of the Crime Writers Association and the Society of Authors, and as President of the Detection Club.

He has written numerous novels as well as non-fiction books, but is most famous for the Inspector Ghote series, the first of which, *The Perfect Murder*, was made into a film by Merchant Ivory and won a CWA Gold Dagger Award, as did *The Murder of the Maharajah*.

A Detective at Death's Door is the fifth Harriet Martens novel.

He is married to Sheila Mitchell, the actor, and lives in London. In 1997 he was awarded the CWA Cartier Diamond Dagger.

A DETECTIVE AT DEATH'S DOOR

In her most personal case yet, Harriet Martens finds herself placed in grave danger at the hands of a cunning poisoner . . . Whilst relaxing with her husband at the Majestic pool one hot August bank holiday, Harriet does not expect the glass of Campari soda at her side to conceal a deadly drug. She awakes in a hospital bed, recovering from a near fatal dose of aconitine. Harriet knows she must find the person responsible, but no sooner has she mustered enough energy to begin making tentative enquiries than the poisoner strikes again. And this time he is successful . . . Will Harriet have the strength to find the murderer before he claims another victim and before the local population begins to panic?

Books by H. R. F. Keating
Published by The House of Ulverscroft:

THE MAN WHO . . .
A REMARKABLE CASE OF BURGLARY
BRIBERY, CORRUPTION ALSO
BREAKING AND ENTERING
A DETECTIVE IN LOVE

H. R. F. KEATING

A DETECTIVE AT DEATH'S DOOR

Complete and Unabridged

ULVERSCROFT
Leicester

First published in Great Britain in 2004 by
Macmillan
London

First Large Print Edition
published 2005
by arrangement with
Macmillan, an imprint of
Pan Macmillan Limited
London
and St Martins Press Inc.
New York

British Library CIP Data

Keating, H. R. F. (Henry Reymond Fitzwalter), *1926 –*
A detective at death's door.—Large print ed.—
Ulverscroft large print series: crime
1. Martens, Harriet (Fictitious character)—Fiction
2. Policewomen—England—London—Fiction
3. Poisoning—Fiction 4. Detective and mystery
stories 5. Large type books
I. Title
823.9′14 [F]

ISBN 1–84395–848–1

Published by
F. A. Thorpe (Publishing)
Anstey, Leicestershire

Set by Words & Graphics Ltd.
Anstey, Leicestershire
Printed and bound in Great Britain by
T. J. International Ltd., Padstow, Cornwall

This book is printed on acid-free paper

Author's Note

Admirers of the detective stories of Agatha Christie may be disconcerted to find mention in these pages of a book by her called *Twisted Wolfsbane*. Do not hurry to shop or library. The title is one I have had to invent in order to tell my story. I like to think of its presence there as a tribute to a writer whose sure hand with her narratives taught me more than perhaps even now I recognize.

1

Harriet, as she lay there, heard a voice.

'I think you can take it now that we've pulled you through,' it seemed to be saying.

Something stirring at the bottom of her mind told her that she knew the man who had spoken. He was — His name was . . . She had heard it. There was something . . . Something funny . . .

She felt herself sliding back into the semi-oblivion in which she had been lying, and with a jerk forced herself up from it.

Yes, I know. I remember. He's Mr Hume Jones. And, yes. Yes, this is it. I've got it. He called himself 'Hume Jones, no hyphen if you don't mind'. And he's been treating me.

Treating me? What . . . ? Why? Why am I being treated?

John. John's here. There, next to . . . To what's-his-name, Mr No-hyphen, if you don't . . .

Wait, I must think. Think why I'm here.

If I'm very careful, keep my eyes shut and take it slowly, I can think. Think it out.

One: I am Harriet Piddock. Two: John is my husband, John Piddock. And, three: I'm

Detective Superintendent Harriet Martens as well. Yes. And this must be a hospital. There's the smell. Sharp and sanitized, but lingering. The hospital smell. And up to my neck there's this stiff white sheet. My head on a starchy pillowcase. Yes.

So, four: I'm ill. In hospital. Very ill. But . . . But, yes, we've pulled you through. That was No-hyphen. And I — I sort of remember I heard him say that. Not now. Hours ago. Days ago? Yes, it could be some days ago.

The sod. We didn't pull me through. I came through. I pulled myself through. I refused to die. That's it. I was in danger of death, and I decided — somehow I decided I was not going to die. No, more than that. I decided I was not going to be killed. To be murdered. And . . . Yes, I was not going to be poisoned.

Right, it comes back. I was poisoned. What by? Don't know. But it's there in my memory. Somehow I drank poison. Enough to kill me. But I was determined not to be killed. By the poison. Oh, all right, be fair. I have been treated. By Mr Hume Whatsit. Treatment helped. Helped a lot. But if he thinks they've pulled me through, he's wrong. I came through. I've come through. I have.

She allowed herself to slip back into dulled nothingness.

It was morning. Pale dawn light behind the thin curtains in the window of the private room. The door had been briskly opened. The young Asian nurse who, as Harriet was vaguely aware, had been looking after her, went across and pulled the curtains fully back.

Harriet felt the stronger light as a blow in the face. She shut her eyes, turned away, felt injured and suddenly helpless.

'Mr Hume Jones says you can sit up today,' the nurse pronounced.

Harriet wanted to say, to shout, *Go away*. But she lacked the energy to utter even a word.

She found herself hauled up, and felt the pillows being rearranged behind her. And, yes, something metallic had been noisily pulled forward. She fell back on it.

Back-rest, yes.

But she was not to be allowed any peace. Bedpan pushed underneath her. A bed-table, she realized when she ventured to open her eyes again, had been efficiently slid in front of her and a faintly steaming basin of warm water was being put on it.

'Now you're so much better,' the nurse said, sharply enough, 'you can manage to wash yourself.'

A slimily soaped washcloth was put in her right hand. With firmness.

And, though the nurse had whisked away in a flurry of blue uniform, Harriet did as she had been told and sat dabbing at her face.

But before very long a hard little rebellious thought popped into her head. All right, I'll do it today. But when I'm feeling just a bit stronger, I'll bloody well wash when I want to wash.

She sat there with her hands resting in the basin and began to pull her thoughts together.

Right then. How did I come to be here? Because I'd been poisoned. Where? How? Yes, it was at the pool. The — I can get it — Majestic Insurance Company Sports and Social Club pool. Good. That's come back. I was there at the pool with John, Majestic Insurance high-up. It'd been hot, bloody hot. It was the bank holiday, August bank holiday Monday. I was in my two-piece swimsuit, the near-bikini I hardly ever wear unless it's really boiling hot. I was lying there, body well-covered with sunscreen, just beside the pool. And, yes, I'd drunk a Campari soda, a bright red, bubbles-tingling Campari soda, and poor John, because he'd said he'd be the driver, had had a bitter lemon.

And, yes, it's all coming back. I'd let John

4

get me a second Campari, and I'd had a swallow or two of it, that delicious sharp herbal bite, and then John got up from his chair, put down on it the book he'd been reading — yes, one of those Agatha Christies he relaxes with — and said something . . .

Yes. *I must go for a pee, shan't be long.*

And I let my eyes close, sort of dozed off. And there was something . . . something black and white. Don't know what. And then John was coming back. And I looked up at him and smiled. Pleased just to see him.

I lifted up that tall, cool glass and took another long swallow.

And . . . And something not quite right about the taste. My tongue tingling, pricking, and *God, I'm cold, freezing,* I said. And then . . . Then the next thing I knew was my head being held over a toilet bowl and, yes, John's fingers pushing hard into my throat.

God, I can suddenly feel them again. As if . . .

Am I going to puke? Into this basin of cooling soapy water?

No. Damned if I will.

★ ★ ★

John is here. The real John, not the John of those all too vividly re-experienced probing,

5

vomit-inducing fingers. And flowers, he's brought flowers. Can't remember what they're called. Deep sort of yellow colours. And lovely smell. One of my favourites. But I can't remember the name. Must ask him. Ask what's been happening to me, too.

Did that man, man in the blue woollen shirt open at the neck, beautiful soft blue, and the white coat just hanging from the back of his shoulders, with the long pale face, man-in-the-moon, did he really say he'd pulled me through? All a blur.

No, wait. Yes, Hume Jones, no hyphen.

'John. Hello. It's you, isn't it?'

'Yes, it's me.'

'John, were you standing beside — Man, doctor. No. Yes, consultant? Called, I think, Hume Jones. Said, 'We've pulled you through?' '

'Yes, I was. Three days ago, though.'

'God, as much as that? I — I must have been out, unconscious.'

'You were. You recovered, a bit. And then you had a relapse. And you've been unconscious or asleep ever since then. But that's a good thing. You're meant to get as much sleep as possible. You've had a pretty awful time, you know, though Mr Hume Jones is quite happy that, as he said a little too proudly, 'We've pulled you through.' '

6

Shouldn't mock really. He did a fantastic job.'

'I suppose so.'

'Oh, yes, no doubt about it. But you're going to find yourself very weak, and wandering in your mind most probably, for a good long time to come.'

'Yes. Yes, I feel as if I will be. But — but you can tell me things now?'

'Oh, yes. Anything you want to know. Hume Jones says it'll be the best way for you to get yourself together ag — '

'John. I've just thought. The twins. Did the twins come down to see me? All the way from university?'

'Of course they did. It was touch-and-go with you for days, you know.'

'And — this is right? — I was poisoned. Somehow poisoned?'

'You were.'

'And did you .. ? Did you have to make me vomit? I remember that. Or was that a hullu — Hallucin — No, wait. Hallucination?'

'No, it wasn't any hallucination. The moment I realised what might be happening, I rushed you off to make you spew up as much as possible. Turned out to be the best thing I could have done, according to Hume Jones, though if you'd swallowed one of the corrosive poisons it would have been the worst thing.'

7

A sudden rueful laugh.

'I was in a terrible dilemma at that moment actually. You see, I knew where the loos were; I'd just been spending a penny. And, without thinking much about it, I rushed you towards them. But when I got there I was confronted with two doors side-by-side. One sign had the figure with legs apart, and one the figure with the skirt. And I simply couldn't decide — only for an instant — which one to take you into, male or female. Both inappropriate in their different ways.'

Harriet found she wanted to laugh. Only she didn't know how to. Tears began to form at her eyes.

She saw the quick look of concern on John's face.

'Well,' he said hastily, 'I actually plumped for the Ladies', and there turned out not to be anyone in there. So that was all right. And then I had you whizzed off here. To St Oswald's. And Hume Jones saved your life, over the course of a week or more.'

'But, John, what was it that poisoned me? It was in that Campari soda, wasn't it? But how did you know what was happening?'

John's face lit in a broad smile.

'That was Agatha Christie,' he said. 'You know you're always knocking her for the way she gets her murders solved. Not exactly by

8

Greater Birchester Police methods. Well, you'll have to thank her for ever now for what she wrote in the book I was reading beside you, *Twisted Wolfsbane*.'

'Yes, I can see the book now. You put it on your chair when you went for a pee. *Twisted Wolfsbane* — odd title.'

'Oh, it comes from Keats. The 'Ode on Melancholy'. You must remember.'

He lifted up his head and quoted.

'No, no, go not to Lethe, neither twist wolfsbane, tight-rooted, for its poisonous wine.'

He looked down at her again.

'But do you know what comes from twisting, more or less, that root?'

'No idea.'

'Aconitine. The almost-always fatal poison that you swallowed with your Campari.'

'The second one, that I'd taken several swallows from earlier on?'

'Yes, I saw you doing that before I went off to the loo. So it was a wonderful piece of luck that I'd been reading the book immediately beforehand. Agatha Christie actually describes the symptoms — without going too deeply into unpleasant details, as was her way, bless her. But, yes, she wrote, and I'd just read the words, that the victim's tongue tingles violently, that they have a

9

sudden feeling of chill coldness, and then there's a painful burning sensation in the mouth. Just what you said to me.'

'Yes, I remember the tingling and the feeling of terrible coldness. But after that, not a lot. Except I've a very — what's the word? — *physical* recall of your fingers doing their life-saving work down my throat.'

'Well, life-saving only in part. Most of the credit ought to go to Mr Hume Jones. He and his team did heroic work once they had you here.'

'But, John, who was it? Who put aconitine — someone must have done — into my Campari? And why? Why, for heaven's sake?'

She sank back on the bed then, overcome by exhaustion. Through the haze, very faintly, the scent of John's flowers came to her.

Freesias. Yes, freesias.

2

The only visitor allowed was John. He came every morning and again in the late afternoon. On each occasion Harriet was able to say she felt a little stronger, though sometimes that was something of a lie. The weakness of will that seemed at every moment to be lying there deep inside her showed too often its morass-sucking power. Otherwise the days were marked by the regular rounds of Mr Hume Jones, different coloured soft wool shirt each day, accompanied now by a little band of nodding and grinning camp-followers. Early each morning, too, Nurse Bhattacharya swept in, firmly intent on getting the patient into an outwardly presentable state. A little later a paper girl appeared, and *The Times* and *Birchester Chronicle* were slammed happily down somewhere on the bed, John's order fulfilled. If to little purpose. Broadsheet newspapers can seem impossibly heavy.

Meals, which Harriet had little appetite for, were brought in with clockwork regularity: breakfast, lunch, supper, as well as cups of this and that which she did attempt to swallow, not always with success. And almost every day flowers arrived, with cards from friends and colleagues. Feebly she wished she could show more gratitude. The Chief Constable sent an enormous bunch of pallidly mauve Michaelmas daisies. His secretary contributed a pot containing a single African violet.

But on one of John's afternoon visits, just at the time his freesias were beginning to droop, he put, with evident caution, a question to her.

'Listen, do you think you might be well enough now to see your colleague, Detective Superintendent Murphy? He's the Senior Investigating Officer on your case.'

'My case?' Harriet said, struck by surprise.

'Yes, your case. After all, you're the victim of attempted murder. So no wonder Greater Birchester Police, for one of their own, are pulling out all the stops.'

'Yes. Yes, I suppose they will be. Somehow I haven't thought of myself as the central figure in a major investigation.'

John looked down at her with an expression of mildly pitying wonder.

'How well do you know Murphy?' he asked then. 'I don't think I've ever heard you mention him.'

'We've never had a lot to do with each

other, as it happens. But he's got a good reputation. Perhaps the best in the force. So I'm honoured, sort of.'

'I was certainly impressed when he interviewed me, as he did of course several days ago. He was tremendously thorough. Not that I was able to tell him anything relevant. Had I seen anybody suspicious near you? But what does a poisoner look like? A little malicious dwarf? An old, witch-like woman, evilly cackling? Or Claudius of Denmark, sneaking about with a phial of brightly coloured liquid, all ready to pour into the ear of the King, his brother? 'Upon my secure hour.' Think that's the words Shakespeare put into his Ghost's mouth.'

'John . . . John, I don't like this. I don't like it at all. I mean, I haven't up till now really properly thought about what actually happened to me. That — that someone actually crept up and put, put that stuff, aconitine, a deadly poison, into my drink.'

An onset of shivering passed along her body from ankles and calves right up to her forehead.

'Look,' John said, 'I think I've been premature in asking if you're ready to talk to Murphy. Let's leave it. Leave it for a day or two.'

'No.'

The word shot out with more ferocity than Harriet had meant it to have.

'No, John,' she said then. 'No, the case must be investigated. If someone has attempted to poison me — to murder me, damn it — then they must be apprehended, if only because they may go on to murder someone else. And if there's anything I can do to see they are apprehended, then I'm ready to do it. So tell Pat Murphy I'll see him just as soon as he likes.'

⋆ ⋆ ⋆

Detective Superintendent Murphy came into Harriet's room at exactly ten o'clock next morning. She had been told he was coming, and Nurse Bhattacharya had vigorously propped her higher on her pillows ready to receive him. The bulky shape of the man she had seen mostly at a distance came immediately into focus. His broad, floridly red face, the two sharply blue eyes in it, and, less well remembered, the white pelt of hair, hair that must once have been red or reddish. She recalled, too, his blue suit. She had never seen him wearing anything else, its cloth of a brighter shade than anyone she knew would have chosen, and the whole stretched at every seam by the powerful body underneath. She

14

remembered now the way that his tie, invariably of a plain, dull red and seamed with much knotting and unknotting, appeared to be always on the point of strangling the thick neck it encircled.

'Pat,' she greeted him. 'Hello.'

'Hello yourself. And how are you?'

She recognized the question had been asked out of more than everyday formality, if only because his lingering Irish accent emphasized not the *you* but the *are*, and she gathered herself up to answer equally truthfully.

'I'm not fit, Pat. Not fit at all. You know, I've been at death's door, all but finished so they tell me. And there are times still when I feel that door swinging open for me again. And I'm tired, utterly worn down. So don't expect too much from me, that's all.'

'I won't. So I won't. I'll just tell you now where we've got to so far, and then I'll maybe ask you a question or two.'

'Yes. Yes, I'll be ready. I'll try to be ready.'

'Well now, let me say first of all that we're keeping the attack on you under wraps for as long as we can. If we keep it that way, the fella who did it — or the woman, yes, the woman — may get anxious to know whether they succeeded, and if they try to find out we may get some sort of a line on them. I've a

15

WDC down there at reception tasked with keeping her eyes wide open, and you never know but that we may get something that way. Worth a try at least. So till I say. It's not a word.'

'Yes, I see. And you're right. Not that I can possibly tell anyone. My husband's the only person allowed to visit me, you know.'

'I do so. All right, now let me tell you that we've got the name of every single soul who was there round the pool at the Majestic Club at the time. They had security men on the gate, you know, two of 'em because it was a busy bank holiday. But there are altogether as many as a hundred and twenty-seven potential suspects, men, women and — God help us — children, and, worse, they were in every state of dress and undress. Sure, if our man was strolling about there in full evening kit, I doubt if anyone would have taken any particular notice.'

He sighed, or perhaps groaned.

'Whatever, they've all got to be interviewed. We're working away at that. Well down the list now, indeed. In theory anyhow whoever we're looking for ought to be there on that list, but we haven't had a smell of whoever it is so far. Your man's not one of the club staff, I can tell you that. I went well into where that drink you had came from, and I'm

16

one hundred per cent happy that the bottle of — what's it? Campari? — is in the clear. You were the only one to call for the stuff that morning, and they opened a new bottle.'

A sudden grin.

'Sure, and I can understand why no one else wanted it. I asked for a shot meself, part of my duties as you may say, and, by God, I've never supped anything so near cough-mixture in all me life.'

Harriet managed a pale smile.

'Yes,' she said. 'Not to everyone's taste. My boys call it cough-mixture, too. But in summer I like it.'

'You've every right, so you have. But let me go on. I got hold of the bottle of soda water they used to make that mixture, and the lab checked it for me straight away. Pure as a mountain stream. So there can be no doubt it was someone beside the pool there who put that deadly stuff in your drink. But which of them it was, well, to be frank, at this moment we've no more idea than the saints above. I had a fingertip search underway within an hour of — of it happening. Might have been something thrown down there. Even whatever the poison was in. But there wasn't. Twenty men and women, all in their white bodysuits, crawling about there in the hot sun, and finding nothing that meant anything. Not unless you count a sack full of fag-ends, sweet papers and ice-cream sticks, plus God knows what else.'

'I put you all to a great deal of trouble. I'm sorry. You know, I've never thought before about an investigation from . . . From what you might call the worm's-eye view. Makes me think.'

'Indeed it would. So can I ask the victim a few wee questions now?'

'Of course, Pat. Of course. If there's anything I know that's going to help, I'm only too willing to come up with it. If I can.'

'Right then. Your John — and there's a nice fella, if ever I saw one — he told me he found you asleep when he came back from taking a Jimmy Riddle. Is that so? You had gone to sleep when he left you?'

'Yes. Yes, I absolutely had. Or I'd dozed off, certainly. I'm not sure I was as deeply asleep as if I'd been in my bed at night.'

'Ah, I know how it is. You're lying stretched out there and the sun's nice and hot and you shut your eyes. And then you don't know if you're sleeping or waking. But did you see anything, see anybody, near you as you nodded off? Anybody at all? Anything at all?'

Harriet attempted to put herself back to that moment. But there was nothing. Nothing whatsoever. Almost everything had been

18

blotted out that had happened in the hour before that awful moment when she took a swallow of her half-finished second Campari soda and found its taste somehow altered. Mr Hume Jones, when she had managed to ask him about it, had told her that memory loss was common after a trauma. The events immediately beforehand might eventually come back, or they might not. He had flashed her then his smile and, followed by his cluster of acolytes, had moved on.

'No, Pat,' she said, trying to keep her voice steady. 'No, I really didn't see anybody, anything.'

'But you did see your John coming back? Or did he have to tap you on the shoulder to wake you? Were you that deep asleep?'

'No. No, I wasn't. As a matter of fact — I remember this now — I woke just before John came up to me. You know, there's sometimes something between people who've been married a long time. I don't know what. Sympathy, thought transference, something electrical. But, whatever it was, I woke when I somehow sensed John was coming towards me. He was five yards away, ten.'

'So he was. He told me you looked at him and smiled.'

'Pat, you old devil. That was a trick question, asking if I'd seen John when you knew all along I had.'

Pat grinned.

'Ah, it was that, so it was. But, you know, I'm needing to know how much I can rely on what you're telling me, poorly as you are.'

Now Harriet grinned, though with rather less vigour.

'What I ought to have expected after all,' she said.

'Well, I put your old man through one hell of an interrogation, wanting to get him to recall the least possible thing that might give us a clue. And it's you I'm going to ask again now. Was there anything, any little thing out of the ordinary, that caught your attention just after John had left you?'

'No. I said I couldn't — '

Then something seemed to fly past the very back of her mind. Come and gone in half a moment.

'Oh, there was something. No, it's gone now. It was . . . I don't know. All I can say is: it was something black and white. I don't know what. I don't know at all. It — it may have been nothing, something black or dark moving with something white. Someone's shirt, I don't know.'

'Well, don't fret yourself. If it's anything that matters, it'll come back to you sooner or later. And if it's nothing, then it's nothing.

But, if I'm not troubling you, there's one more thing I have to ask.'

'Go ahead, go ahead.'

'It's this. Just this. Enemies? Do you know of anybody, anybody at all, who might for some reason, or for no reason, want you dead?'

The thought came to Harriet as a bottomless shock.

Someone who wants me dead. No. Never. Why should . . ?

But, well, a police officer might, after all, have done something to a villain that rankled. Is there someone I put away? Someone who, over the years in prison, might have been thinking and thinking of that cow who . . ?

But, though she lay there attempting to pass her whole police life through her mind, no answer came.

'No,' she said at last. 'No, Pat, I really don't — '

And then, rising up like a waterspout from the heaving ocean, there came into her head something she had thought in the middle of the night, something perhaps she had dreamt.

She actually reached out and clasped Pat Murphy's big red hand as he sat there on the little hospital chair beside her.

'Pat,' she said. 'Pat, there's something terrible I've thought. Last night. In the middle of the night. I've been having terrible dreams, you know. Ever since I regained consciousness. Terrible. And there was this one, last night, or perhaps the night before. I get so confused. I've pushed it away. Pushed it down. But — '

She could go on no longer.

Pat Murphy looked at her, looked at the drained white hand that was clutching his own.

'Well now,' he said, 'how about telling me what this is all about?'

She took a deep breath.

'John,' she said. 'Could it have been John?'

Then a long gabble of ideas and suppositions came flooding out.

'Listen, what's the first action in any murder investigation? Look at the person who found the body, yes? And who found — found this body here? Or rather at the pool, beside the pool? Who did? John did. And most murders, what are they? Domestics. Domestics. Husbands kill their wives. They do. So it could be, couldn't it? You asked about enemies. But couldn't my husband be my secret enemy? My murderer?'

Pat Murphy looked at her.

'And just when did your John put that poison into your cough-mixture soda?' he said. 'Remember, he went away for his Jimmy

22

Riddle and you watched him go. You dozed off, and then what? You told me just now that you saw, or you sensed, him coming back towards you when he was — what? — ten yards away, five? And you gave him a smile.'

Harriet found she had loosed her grip on that big red hand.

'And then where's a fellow like John going to get aconitine?' Pat quietly went on. 'He might, of course, he just might. But it isn't so easy. I've been looking the stuff up. It comes from a plant called by some long Latiny name, but in plain English it's monkshood. Now where's John going to find monkshood, let alone boil it up or whatever? Have you got monkshood growing in your garden? Come on, now, answer up. Have you?'

And under this genial bullying all Harriet's night fears fled away. Things of the dark before the rising sun.

'No, Pat,' she said, 'we haven't got monkshood growing in our garden. I'd know if we had. And — And it's also called wolfsbane. John told me that. And — And — '

An uncontrollable giggle.

'And Agatha Christie told him.'

'So she did, so she did. He was after telling me about that book of hers. *Twisted Wolfsbane*. Wasn't that it? And didn't that come from some old poet? Keats. Yes, Keats. But I think I've been here bothering you long enough. Too long perhaps. So I'll be off. And you just forget about all that nonsense, lie there and take it easy. Get back to your old self. What they used to call you when you were over in B Division, the Hard Detective. Get yourself back to being the Hard Detective. That's who we want to see with us again.'

The door closed softly behind him.

Harriet lay there trying to get into some sort of order in her head all she had learnt from the man in charge of her case. But it was too much of an effort.

Have I got a headache, she asked herself.

And then, in a burst of self-directed fury, she thought, *Christ, I must know whether my head's aching or not.*

What a state I'm in. To be so feeble. All very well to say to John that if someone has attempted murder by poisoning they must be caught and put away in case they do it again, but what damn use can I be in helping to see that they are found and caught? None at all, none at all. But I must . . . I should . . .

Oh. Right, damn it. I have got a headache. It's getting worse by the minute. I need something for it. Hume No-hyphen said I could have something if I needed it.

Right, ring the bell, get Nurse Bhattacharya. Ask her for a pill.

Oh, God. The bell-push, it's too far away. I
can't get my arm to stretch that far. I don't
know how to get it to move. I can't. I can't.

3

Damn it, Harriet said to herself on the day that Nurse Bhattacharya seized hold of John's wilted freesias in one hand and gathered up in the other the Chief Constable's Michaelmas daisies, their foliage turned to a dry brown, to whisk them both off to the dustbin. Damn it, I am a detective. And not a bad one, even if that label, the 'Hard Detective' is only the half of what I can do. All right, I'm the victim, by some absurd chance, of an attempt at poisoning that only just failed to come off, and I ought to be able to see, if anybody can, how that case, my case, can be resolved.

Only I can't. I can't because the whole business is, so far as I can see, wrapped in what old Agatha Christie might have called impenetrable mystery. And I can't make even one step towards resolving the case because I'm stuck here in this hospital room unable to do anything. At the mercy of Nurse Bhattacharya. Deprived even of a telephone because a phone is thought to be too exciting for a patient who needs nothing but an existence of dead, featureless calm.

Right. Tomorrow morning when Mr Hume

No-hyphen Jones arrives with his simpering white-coated train I'm going to tell him it's time I went home.

★   ★   ★

That evening, one final supper, mostly pushed aside. One final cup of cocoa, sipped in spite of herself. The metal rest at the back of the bed clipped out of the way into its nighttime position by a nurse a little more human than the dread Bhattacharya.

And sleep. Broken sleep, of course, as it had been night after night ever since she had heard the voice of Mr Hume Jones proclaiming, 'We've pulled you through.' But, broken or not, sleep. Then the curtains flicked sharply back, she was heaved upright, and the thermometer, the bedpan and the washing bowl once more. But at last the door swept wide open and Mr Hume Jones, fine woollen shirt apricot-coloured today, white coat as far back on the shoulders as ever, was there in front of her.

'Good morning, Mr Hume Jones,' she snapped out quickly as she could, well knowing that the form was that the great physician should greet the humbly grateful patient and then receive acknowledgement of the dose of bedside manner he had bestowed.

'Well, we are on the mend, aren't we?' came his reply now, accompanied by a look that should have frozen the remaining flowers on the locker at the bed's foot.

'Yes,' she said. 'Yes, I think I am on the mend, as you put it. Certainly enough to be off home as soon as you give the word.'

The eyebrows at the top of the long man-in-the-moon face rose.

'Oh, no. I don't think so. I don't think so at all. Nurse, temperature chart, if you please.'

Chart reverently handed forward.

'Hm, yes. Yes, some change. But we're not out of the woods yet, not by any means.'

Why can't the bugger say what my actual temperature was this morning? Because it was down to bloody normal? Or at least somewhere near it. But, no, I suppose it's because I'm something of a prize patient. A prize specimen, the record salmon he's pulled from the stream. And he wants to keep me here to be gazed at.

But, give him the credit he deserves. He did pluck me back from the grave. He and his team really did do that.

'But, Mr Hume Jones, thanks to your care, I really do feel as if I'm almost completely over it now.'

A lie, of course. But I want to get home. To where I'll have a phone at my disposal and can at least make a few inquiries. Into the attempted murder of Detective Superintendent Martens, Greater Birchester Police.

'That's very good to hear, Mrs Piddock. It's a sign that you're recovering, almost as rapidly as we hoped. But I'm afraid I have to tell you that you've a long way to go yet. Let me see, you were admitted, as I well remember since I had to be called in specially, on the August bank holiday Monday, on the twenty-sixth that is. And today's date is — '

An abrupt check. Eyes swivelling round left and right. And no one able to produce the date, or not with printed evidence.

All right, I'll do it, Harriet thought. There's *The Times* halfway down the bed where the girl left it.

She heaved herself forward, extended her right arm. Her groping fingers fell just short. She scrabbled at the bedclothes.

But, no.

No, damn and blast it, I haven't got the strength.

But then one of the white-coated junior housemen managed to pull from his jacket pocket a much-folded gaudy copy of the *Express*.

'September the eighth, sir. It's the eighth today.'

'Of course. So, Mrs Piddock, you have been with us little more than a fortnight, during a good deal of which time you were undergoing very arduous medical procedures. Indeed, at one stage, let me tell you, you were in fact clinically dead. And you were also subjected, let me see, to no fewer than fifteen electric shock treatments. You're naturally in a state of physical and mental exhaustion, however much you feel you're better than you were. Look how just now you failed to get hold of the paper there, barely two feet away. You thought I hadn't noticed, didn't you?'

The smile flashed. White teeth.

'No, I don't think there can be any question of you leaving us just yet. Not for some considerable time to come, indeed.'

Harriet sank back on her pillows.

★   ★   ★

By the time of John's visit she had regained enough willpower to say to him the moment he came in — bunch of deep-red roses in his hand — 'John, I want you to do something.'

'Well, glad to find you want anything. A definite improvement.'

'Right, it's this. I want you to go to Mr Hume Jones and, hyphen or no hyphen, I want you to persuade him that I ought to be allowed to go home. This morning I asked the wretched man if I could go, and he produced a lot of poppycock reasons why I had to stay here. And, you know, really it's only because he wants to keep his prize patient as long as he possibly can.'

John looked down at her with an expression of mild interest.

'And what were those poppycock reasons exactly?'

Trust him to pick on the key point. And I know, all right, those reasons aren't total poppycock. But I want to go home. I must go home. If I don't, there'll be nothing at all I can do to resolve the murder, the attempted murder, of Detective . . . Superintendent . . . Martens.

'Well,' she said, feeling her way, 'he said it's been only a fortnight since I was brought in here and that wasn't long enough for me to be ready to go home. And then he claimed I was at one point clinically dead. But what does he mean by that? It's only some medical jargon. Must be. I mean, either I was dead — which plainly I wasn't — or I was alive. All right, if only just.'

'If that's all he said to you, I can tell you he spared you a good deal. There was an anxious hour or so when they thought you would have to have a temporary heart bypass. They'd have put you on a heart-lung machine, Hume Jones told me, and used a filter pump to clear out what they thought were still traces of aconitine in your blood.'

'Oh, John.'

She looked up at him, remorsefully.

'John, I've never really thought about what you must have gone through. I — I've been too wrapped up in myself and my ills. I'm sorry. You must have had a hell of a time, besides saving my life, you and Agatha Christie between you.'

'Well, she seems to have weathered it all okay.'

Harriet tried to laugh. She wanted to. But the mechanism defeated her. All she was able to manage was a come-and-gone half-smile.

'There was something else actually to Hume Jones's arguments,' she conceded then. 'He was just telling me exactly how short a time I'd been in here, and he wanted to know the date today. I'd reached out for *The Times* a little further down the bed and couldn't get to it. The bastard had noticed, and he chose to use it to prove to me, so he hoped, that I was still not fit to go.'

'I can see how you might have resented that. But, come on, was there anything more? Have you told me now everything he said to you?'

'Oh, all right, I haven't. Not quite. He also produced a lot of stuff about the number of electric shock treatments I'd needed. I think that was all, though listen to this: when he looked at my temperature chart he wouldn't say what my temperature was. And I bet it was normal, or almost normal. I feel as if it was.'

'I'm glad to hear that. But, you know, it's often policy in hospitals not to tell patients things like that, in case it makes you over-optimistic or plunges you into unnecessary gloom. Neither of which is good for you.'

'Yes, that's all very well. But I still want to come home. I feel as if I'd get on perfectly well there. And — And, well, at the end of a phone I could be doing something, something to find out who put that poison into my Campari soda. Or, as Pat Murphy very sweetly calls it, my cough-mixture soda.'

'Good for Mr Murphy. And good for him for another reason, too. It reminds you that in charge of the case of the poisoned police officer there's a detective with a very high reputation. He's someone as capable as anybody of finding out who that poisoner was. You should have experienced the going-over he gave me.'

'Oh, John, I know. I know all that. Of course I do. But all the same I must be somewhere where I'm not absolutely cut off from the whole business. You know, they won't even let me have a phone. I need to come home.'

John dropped down on the little metal chair beside the bed, still clutching his roses, and sat in thought for a minute, two minutes, almost three. Then he spoke.

'All right, I'll have a word with Mr Hume Jones, and I'll put your case to him. Then we'll see.'

* * *

Half an hour later John came back. Harriet, looking at him with a flick of over-sharp anxiety which she was unable to suppress, could make nothing of the expression on his face. But, as soon as he turned back from firmly closing the door, he smiled.

'All right, he's agreed. Took a good deal of persuasion and heaven knows how many promises, which perhaps neither of us believes are going to be strictly kept, but it's done. You can leave tomorrow, as soon as I can get an ambulance to take you.'

'An ambulance? But — '

'Oh, yes, an ambulance. No-hyphen — as I've heard you call him, most ungratefully, I may say — insisted on an ambulance, refused to have the hospital supply one, and warned me, with a certain amount of frigidity, that hiring a private one is an expensive business.'

'But, John, isn't an ambulance one of the promises you're not expected to keep? Surely it must be.'

'No, I don't think it is. Hume Jones said all the business of getting you dressed, getting you down to the car and driving you through the hurly-burly of the city could well be too much for you. He made an ambulance an absolute condition of agreeing to you going. Don't forget you were on the point of death not so long ago, and just this morning you were too feeble to reach for *The Times* there on the bed in front of you.'

'All right, yes, I admit it. It was a newspaper too far.'

She managed a small hint of a smile.

'Oh, and I admit, too, that I am in a bad state. Worse probably than I feel I am at this moment.'

'I'm glad to hear you've still got that much sense. So perhaps this is a good moment to put some conditions of my own, not insisted on by Mr No-hyphen.'

'Conditions? You're not saying you're going to impose conditions on me before arranging for that ambulance? John, you're not. I have to go home. Can't you see that? I must be where I can do something to tackle this person who put that — that aconitine into my drink. I must get out of here.'

'All right, calm down. Calm down, or you'll really make yourself too ill to leave tomorrow. All I said, you know, was that I have a condition or two you must agree to if I'm to have you at home.'

'No, sorry. Sorry, you're quite right. You've every reason to impose conditions. Once again, I haven't been thinking. Having me at home is going to make your life even more difficult than it has been since I came in here. I've never even asked you: how have you been managing at work? Does nobody mind that you've been taking time off, morning and afternoon, to come and visit me?'

'Well, they may mind a bit. But no one likes to say anything. And I've been getting through the work easily enough, after all. So you needn't worry your head about that.'

'But you've been at it every evening, and I dare say half the night, haven't you?'

'Okay, but what if I have? I'm happy about it. So long as you're getting better.'

'Right then, what are these conditions of yours? I'll agree to them. You've earned that.'

'We'll see when you've heard what I insist on.'

'No, no, I'll agree. I've said I would.'

'All right. Number one: you go to bed as soon as you arrive and you stay there till I say you can get up.'

'Agreed, agreed.'

'Two: you have daily visits from a nurse, National Health if they'll wear it, otherwise a private one. And the doctor, if needed.'

'But, John, the expense.'

'My condition.'

'Oh, all right, I'll agree to that, so long as it doesn't go on for ever.'

'I don't suppose it will be necessary all that long. So, condition three: all the time I have to be away at the office, or wherever, you have someone in the house with you.'

'Agreed. Sort of. I mean, won't the daily visits from the nurse be enough?'

'No, they won't. You must have someone there to see you stay in bed where you've been put, as well as to bring you something to eat every now and again and to fetch and carry.'

'I suppose that'll be all right. But it'll be more expense, and who are you going to get?'

'Oh, no difficulty about that. There's someone almost next door who knows all about the house, all the ins and outs.'

Harriet jerked up, and then fell back on the pillows.

'Mrs Pickstock,' she squawked. 'No. No, I

don't agree. I absolutely don't agree.'

'Now, now. You're not to get excited, remember. And there's nothing wrong with Mrs Pickstock. I know you don't much care for her, but — '

'Don't much care — . No. No, I'll be calm. But, John, your Mrs Pickstock is the most terrible interfering poke-nose imaginable. No, John, I won't stand for having her in the house all day. And what if you have to go away somewhere?'

'That's not at all likely, not at present. But, yes, Mrs Pickstock's my absolute condition. You must have someone there at hand, and, poor lady, she's the best solution. Besides, she's not all that awful. She's a great Christie fan, you know, reads a page or two of the autobiography every night before she goes to sleep. Just as if it was the Bible. She and I have had many a chat about *wonderful Dame Agatha* as she calls her.'

'I don't care how many chats you have. That woman — '

'And remember you owe wonderful Dame Agatha a great deal. Your life, if it's not stretching it too much to say so. Where would you be now if it wasn't for *Twisted Wolfsbane*?'

It was those words, *twisted wolfsbane*, that brought Harriet to her senses. Wolfsbane, monkshood, aconitine, poison. She was going to put all her efforts into helping track down the person who had twisted wolfsbane — if that was what they had done, in fact — to make the poison that had all but killed her. And who might, even at this moment, be targeting some other victim.

'Okay,' she said. 'I agree to Mrs Pickstock.'

John gave her a wry smile.

'That's the last of my conditions. I know when I've gone as far as I dare. I've met the Hard Detective before.'

4

Harriet lay in bed, trembling with exhaustion. Going from St Oswald's to the house had been every bit as much of a trial of her nervous strength as Mr Hume Jones had predicted, even though it had been in the expensive private ambulance.

Have I been stupid, she asked herself. It's true I'm nothing like as fit as I tried to convince myself I was yesterday. Perhaps none of the whole business was worthwhile. Am I really going to be able to do anything, now that I am here at home? For God's sake, how can I have expected to be able to add even the smallest fact to Pat's investigation?

She closed her eyes and let sheer weariness overcome her.

But after a little while — five minutes, an hour, five hours? — she found she was fully awake and had begun to think.

All right, on that sunny bank holiday — and the fine weather still seems to be here, if the glimpses I had of the outside world weren't a dream — I was lying beside the pool at the Majestic Insurance Club with John beside me. We had swum, energetically,

40

and I was pleasantly relaxed, well smeared with sunscreen, lying on one of the slatted wooden recliners. In my two-piece, which I think I can still get away with wearing even at my age. Just. John had got me a second Campari soda. And — always head in a book — he was reading. By a miracle of good luck, Agatha Christie's *Twisted Wolfsbane*. No, no, go not to Lethe, neither twist wolfsbane, tight-rooted, for its poisonous —

God, I've forgotten what. Its poisonous what? Poisonous . . . No idea, no idea. Yes, it's true, I can't rely on thinking properly.

She imposed on herself a few minutes' rest. Then her thoughts began to march forward again.

Right, I was lying there. John got to his feet, put his book on his chair and said he had to go for a pee. Off he went. I looked at the cherry-red liquid in my tall glass, the lazy bubbles rising up. I decided I wouldn't drink any more of it for a bit. I let my eyelids droop, drifted off.

And then . . . then, while I was asleep, half-asleep, someone . . . someone who for some unknown, unimaginable reason, was carrying about with them a dose of fatal aconitine, poured it into my glass. So when I sensed John coming back I opened my eyes, smiled at him, thinking yes, all's well with the world. Then I picked up that glass and took a good swallow. Something wrong . . .

And chaos. Chaos came.

But who? Who could possibly have done that? Poured the stuff into my glass? And why? Why? Why? Why would anyone want to murder me? Because that's what they must have wanted to do. To murder me, or perhaps — extraordinary though it seems — to murder just someone. Anyone. But why? Why?

There came a tap on the half-open door. A tap somehow announcing that it was being discreet.

Oh God, Mrs Pickstock.

Before Harriet could decide whether to call out *Come in* or to feign sleep Mrs Pickstock appeared, sturdy, perhaps overweight, aproned, grey hair in a cluster of neat curls.

'I've brought you up a nice cup of camomile tea, dear,' she said. 'It's very good for you when you're feeling out of sorts.'

Can I cope with this? Must make an effort, if only for John's sake. He's done so much . . .

'Oh, Mrs Pickstock, how kind . . . But, but you really shouldn't.'

'No, no. We must do all we can to get you on your feet again. Your hubby didn't tell me why you had to be taken to hospital so suddenly, but I do know you've been very ill.'

Oh Christ. Of course, the — what? — the attack on me is still meant to be kept under wraps. Pat Murphy's decision, and a sensible one even if it's not done any good up till now. But if Mrs Pickstock hadn't said that, I might have come out with it all. I don't have much control over my thoughts.

Fat lot of good I'm going to be making any sort of contribution.

'And, look, I've put two Rich Tea biscuits on a plate for you.'

'Oh, thank you. Thank you. Could you just put them on the table here?'

'Yes, yes. Where you can reach them quite easily. I'll just move the telephone down to the floor, so there'll be room.'

'No.'

It had been something like a shout.

Christ, if she puts the phone out of my reach I'll be just as cut off from everything as I was at St Oswald's. If I couldn't reach *The Times* yesterday to tell No-hyphen what date it was, I'm not going to be able to get the phone up from the floor. Not possibly.

Oh God, I'm so weak. So helpless.

She braced herself to make an effort to speak quietly.

'No, I like to have the phone here beside

43

me. I don't know why, but . . . yes. Yes, it's in case John rings up. He said he might.'

'Oh, if it's there for Hubby I won't move it. Not an inch. I can squeeze the biccies on to the table somehow.'

'Thank you. You're very good. And I will try to eat them.'

'More than try, dear. Remember you've got to build up your strength. Your hubby said he'd bring something for your supper. Otherwise I'd have got some nice strengthening thing from Organics 'R Go, my really favourite place.'

No.

No, no, no. I should never have agreed to this.

'Well, thank you again. And I think, when I've had that lovely camomile tea, I'll have another sleep.'

Will that chase her away?

'You couldn't do better, dear. You couldn't do better than sleep. But drink up all the tea first, won't you? It'll really do you good.'

And, at last, Mrs Pickstock left, creeping out on tiptoe in a way that sent Harriet's nerves screaming up and down some sort of mental scale.

★ ★ ★

She did sleep then, though she hadn't meant to. She woke when from downstairs she heard John ushering Mrs Pickstock away, even offering her the roses he had brought to the hospital the day before, and had, with a touch of meanness, or perhaps just good housekeeping, taken away with him in the ambulance.

I hope they don't die on the old girl before she's had some use from them, she thought.

Then John's sunburnt face was peering round the door.

'Hello,' she said.

'Ah, you're awake. Mrs P said you were having *a nice little sleep*.'

'Right, I was. If only as a way of getting her to go.'

'That bad, was it?'

'Oh, well, I suppose not. Not really.'

'So does that mean you survived the trip earlier on without having too much of a setback?'

'Yes. Yes, it does, definitely.'

Truth or lie, I mustn't admit that I may have asked to leave that wretched hospital room sooner than I ought to have done.

John came and sat on the edge of the bed.

'Well, if you really are feeling reasonably okay, there's something I've got to tell you.'

Harriet felt curiosity shooting up inside her. Much too violently, she knew at once.

But she managed to produce a decent semblance of reasonable interest.

'What's that?'

'It's this. Superintendent Murphy rang me just before I left the office. Some confidential news.'

She made herself draw in one long breath. 'Well?'

'Now, don't let it get to you. But well, there's been another poisoning. Aconitine. It looks as if it was from aconitine.'

'Who . . . ? Who was it? And are they dead? You said *poisoning*.'

'Yes, I'm afraid this time it was fatal. It was a young man, name of Robbie Norman. Robert, I suppose I should say. He was out drinking last night at a pub, the Virgin and Vicar. Down in Moorfields. I expect you know it. Know of it.'

'Yes. Yes, I do, of course. It's one of the places we keep a special eye on. It's famous for its striptease performances, and when the lads come out at closing time no young woman on her own is said to be safe. But, John, what does this mean? Two of us poisoned with aconitine. Are they sure it was aconitine?'

'Oh, yes, pretty sure. They've got to confirm it by analysis. But the symptoms, apparently, were all there. The chap had left his half-full pint somewhere and, according to witnesses, when he came back to it and took a good long pull all the same things happened to him that happened to you: the unexpected taste, the tingling of the tongue, the feeling of freezing cold. But with this poor chap the end came almost immediately, there on the spot.'

'The same person must have poisoned both drinks then. And . . . And . . . '

'Well, Pat Murphy is the one who can best comment on that. And, of course, he wants to come and see you. He says there may possibly be some link between you and this Robbie Norman, unlikely though it looks. So what do you feel about him coming to you again?'

'But he must. He must. I want him to.'

John picked up the phone from the bedside table and dabbed out the numbers.

★　★　★

Coming into the bedroom half an hour later, Pat Murphy looked even bigger, even more like a bull in a china shop, than he had seemed in the rather more bare room at St Oswald's. Bulgingly blue-suited and red-faced, he loomed over Harriet as she lay propped up in the bed wearing — Jesus, what will he think of me? — a lacy woollen bedjacket supplied with evident pride by neighbourly Mrs Pickstock.

'So, Pat,' she greeted him, 'there's been another case?'

'There has.'

'And John tells me you want to find out if that young man . . . What was he called? Rob something . . . Robert. I've forgotten. I can't remember a bloody thing for even five minutes.'

'So you can't,' Pat said, looking round for somewhere to sit and finding only the hard, little, drum-like, green-upholstered chair on which in normal times Harriet arranged her clothes for the next morning. 'And that's only natural. But I'm still going to ask you all the questions I have to. If there does turn out to be some sort of link between a detective superintendent of the Greater Birchester Police and Robbie Norman, young apprentice motor mechanic from the god-awful Moor-fields area, then we'll stand a chance, maybe, of finding your poisoner and putting them well away.'

'Yes, of course. But, though I've been thinking a bit since John told me, I can't for the life of me see there can be any link. But fire away, fire away.'

'I will so. Now, I take it that the name Robbie or Robert Norman doesn't ring any bell with you?'

'No. None.'

'And your car, have you ever taken it to the garage on the edge of Moorfields — Simpson's it's called — where the lad worked?'

'No. No, never even heard of it. When I need anything doing to the car I go to one of the mechanics I know at the police garage. But have you asked John this? He might have taken his car in there.'

'He has not.'

'Worth a try.'

'It was. So, now, do you have any sort of connection with anybody at all in Moorfields? Did you ever serve there?'

'No, thank goodness, I never had the pleasure, even when I was just a sergeant.'

'Do you ever go to any shops there? Anything like that?'

'Do you mean one of the sex shops? Hardly my sort of thing!'

'Ah, I didn't have that in mind at all, at all. But there might be some special shop you sometimes go to. I don't know. A halal butcher who sells better than average lamb? There're half a dozen Muslim places like that in Moorfields. Did you ever go to one?'

'Pat, you know the sort of thing people like me are apt to go in for all right. But, no, I've been about in Moorfields every now and again, but only on inquiries, and not all that often then.'

'You've not been to church there ever? For a wedding, a funeral, anything? Or to a cinema house? Only I think the one there is another of your sex places.'

'No, I certainly can't think of anywhere.'

'Well now, if you can't, you can't.'

'So it's the end of the line?'

'Not at all, not at all. You should know better than that, Detective Superintendent Martens.'

'You're right, I should. So there are other lines of inquiry?'

'Sure there are. All right, we've searched the whole of the striptease hall at the back of the Virgin and Vicar — and what a name that is; they should be ashamed — and haven't found the smell of a physical clue.'

He gave a rich guffaw of a laugh.

'Ach, you should have seen me there with the best of them, in floppy old white overalls and great flapping overshoes, peering and poking, and not at all knowing what it was we were looking for, a wee bottle, a test-tube, or any little squeezy class of a thing.'

'And there was nothing? Nothing at all?'

'There was not. Or, if there was something, we didn't know the significance of it. But there you are. And we're not beat yet. We've still got a few of the people with you at the pool not fully questioned, and now there's the whole lot from the pub.'

'I wish I could be there, doing my share.'

'But you can't be, not even if you were able for it. You're now our Victim Number One, don't you forget. It'd never do to have you giving evidence for the prosecution when we get the case to court. No, all you can do just at present, and it's asking plenty of you, I know, is to try to think if there's anything, any wee thing, you do know about the attempt on yourself. And there's one thing more: can you recall any young man who on any occasion did some odd job for you, say, at the house here? Or came calling for any reason whatsoever, offering to clean your car, anything? Take your time and think about it.'

Harriet did take her time. And thought hard, for a little. But then she found her slippery mind had wandered off elsewhere. There is, there must be someone, someone in Birchester, who has poisoned first myself and now this young motor mechanic, whom I know nothing about. So why has this person put aconitine into something each of us was going to drink?

Pat Murphy produced a noisy cough.

'Now, by the look of you it's wandering away you've gone. I can't say I blame you, not after what you've been through. But have you been able to remember any recent caller at the house?'

Harriet gave a deep sigh.

'No, Pat.'

The big Irishman heaved himself to his feet.

'I hardly expected there'd be anything,' he said. 'You don't get a piece of luck like that every day of the week. So it's back to questioning every friend and acquaintance that young man had and hoping one of them will know something that gives us a lead. And when we're done with that, questioning once more the people at the Majestic Club. One of them might remember that for some reason Robbie Norman had gone right across Birchester and visited the club. Asking for a Saturday job maybe. Something, anything. I don't know.'

He shook his head from side to side, like a frustrated bull.

'So now I'll be off. Let you get on with getting yourself on your feet again.'

He lumbered towards the door.

'Stop, Pat, stop.'

'Yes? There's something?'

'No, no, it's not that. Sorry I raised your hopes. It — it's just this. Pat, you will keep in touch with me, won't you? You'll let me know how it's all going? Please.'

'And why wouldn't I? When one of the best in Birchester CID is there to put in her thoughts.'

★ ★ ★

However, it was not the encouragement that sprang up from Pat Murphy's word of praise that buzzed and whirred like an angry bee in Harriet's head that evening. John had brought his supper tray up to the bedroom, set it down on the smooth, untousled half of the bed where he usually slept, transferred to his bedside table his glass of wine — one of the oversize ones the twins gave us, Harriet noted, and all right he deserves it — and had drawn forward the little green chair on which the heavyweight Irishman had earlier plonked himself down. All ready for a gentle chat. But what had set Harriet's anxieties swarming had been the not-so-gentle chat she had had earlier with Mrs Pickstock when she had brought up her customary cup of camomile tea with two Rich Tea biscuits.

'John,' she said to him at once, 'why was it me?'

John, looking cautiously at the sausages and oven-cooked French fries he had made for himself, spoke with deceptive calmness.

'Why was what you?'

'Why did someone attempt to kill me? John, you must have asked yourself that, too. Haven't you? Haven't you? So what answer have you got? Damn it, I've a right to know.'

'Darling, of course you have, and of course I've thought about it,' he replied, adding with a trace of bitterness, 'among other things.'

'Oh God, darling, I'm doing it again, forgetting about you, thinking about myself.'

She shook her head.

'But, you know, I can't help it. I can't do anything but think, think, think about the fact that someone tried to poison me. And I never find any answers to the questions that throb away in my head. John, can I tell you something that Mrs Pickstock said to me this afternoon?'

'Of course you can. What on earth can she have said that's put you into this state?'

'Oh, well, it was my fault really.'

'You haven't contrived to quarrel with the old dear, have you? I know she can be a bit of a busybody, but she means well. She really does. And, frankly, she's a godsend.'

'No, no. No quarrel. No quarrel at all.'

She took a sip of the cup of invalid's Bovril John had brought up on his tray.

'It was just that I allowed her to know it was poisoning I was suffering from,' she said.

54

'Oh, it was wrong of me, I know that. Pat still wanted it kept secret, certainly before we knew about this second poisoning. But the old bag — no, sorry, sorry. But your fellow Christie addict was going on and on about what could possibly have made me so ill, and how it must be because I'd been eating all the wrong things. And in the end I just burst out with it: 'No, it isn't lack of organic foods, it's aconitine. Aconitine poisoning. I was poisoned, poisoned on purpose.' And then — and this is what got to me — she told me that her beloved Agatha in her autobiography says that, when she was working in a hospital back in World War One, the chief dispenser there once showed her a piece of deadly curare he always carried round in his pocket because, she said, it gave him a feeling of power. And ever since I've been sort of obsessed with the idea. John, do you think that whoever tried to poison me, and succeeded in poisoning that young man at the Virgin and Vicar pub, did it just to prove to themselves they had the power of life and death?'

John, crouched there on his little chair, let his sausages grow colder.

'Well,' he said at last, 'fantastic though it seems, I suppose that is possibly what has happened. I should have thought of it myself.

I remember that passage in *An Autobiography*. Agatha Christie was deeply impressed by the incident. She even, much later, used the idea in one of her better books. And, you know, say what you like about her puzzles, she was a shrewd judge of human nature, and quite right to have her suspicions of that creepy hospital dispenser.'

'So you think that's what our man — perhaps I shouldn't say *man*, but an obsession with power is surely more of a masculine trait — that what he was motivated by was a lust for power, the power of life or death?'

'No, I won't be led into making assertions of that sort. We don't know anything like enough. But what you might call pure malignancy does undoubtedly exist. Read Shakespeare. Or, rather, now that I think where that diagnosis comes from, read Coleridge on *Othello*. He spoke of Iago's *motiveless malignancy*.'

Harriet stared at him.

'Look,' he said, 'would you like a sip of my wine? Might do you good.'

'God, no. No, I feel I'll never be well enough to drink alcohol again.'

5

'Oh, dear,' said Mrs Pickstock, bright in the morning. 'Friday the thirteenth. I sometimes wonder how I get to the end of the day when it's a Friday the thirteenth.'

'Oh, come on, Mrs Pickstock,' Harriet answered, managing to inject a touch of robustness into her words. 'If you think about it, nothing happens on that day more awful than on any other. You shouldn't let yourself be affected by superstitions like that.'

'But it's true. It is true. It was on a Friday the thirteenth, seven years ago to the day, that my poor hubby died. He was there with me in the morning at breakfast, and then, just as he was taking down the shopping bag from its hook to go to Sainsbury's for me, he dropped down dead. They said it was what's called Sudden Death Syndrome. Friday the thirteenth syndrome, I call it.'

Harriet felt a black cloud descend, obliteratingly.

She could say nothing more. The energy with which she had countered Mrs Pickstock's seemingly enjoyable pessimism had vanished. Gone as if it had never been there since the moment she had lifted that cherry-red glass of Campari soda and taken her one long, dreadful swallow.

She fell back against her pillows.

I'm as bad as I was in St Oswald's, she found herself thinking. Just as bad. I thought I'd been saved from the poison. But I haven't been. I'm going to die. In the end I'm going to die of it. I'll never do anything to find that man of — what? — motiveless malignancy. Never. I'm finished. Finished.

Through the bedroom's wide window she saw a sky of deep, unbroken blue. She shut her eyes against it.

Summer's not for me. This Indian summer's not for me. I'm going to die. I've been poisoned to death. Poisoned.

Mrs Pickstock was still chattering on, but she hardly heard a word. *Dame Agatha . . . Dame Agatha . . . Dame Agatha.*

Sleep then, mercifully, came clouding over her.

★ ★ ★

She lay asleep, if fitfully, till well on in the afternoon. When at last she realized she was fully awake she found Mrs Pickstock placidly standing beside her bed, a tray between her hands.

'Well, dear,' she was saying, 'I didn't like to wake you with your bit of lunch. You seemed to be so determined to stay asleep. But when I peeked in just now and saw you were stirring, I thought I'd bring you up something to have straight away. It's the really special soup I get from Organics 'R Go, Four-bean and Ginger. They say there's nothing like it for bucking you up.'

A waft of steam came to Harriet's nostrils. And at once she felt a rising wave of nausea.

But she heaved herself forward on her pillows while she tried to think what she could say. Sudden Death Syndrome, Sudden Death Syndrome, she could not help repeating to herself. How can I reject what I've been brought by the woman whose husband fell dead at her feet?

'Oh, Mrs Pickstock, thank you. That's so thoughtful of you. But, if you don't mind, I won't start on it just now. To tell you the truth, I'm hardly properly awake yet. But I'll have it before it gets cold, I promise.'

It seemed to be enough.

'Just as you like, dear. It keeps lovely and hot for quite a while. I think it must be the ginger.'

'Yes, I expect it is.'

'Oh, that's Hubby's car. I'll leave you then.

We don't want to come between husband and wife, do we?'

'I suppose not. So, goodbye. And thank you. I'll see you tomorrow.'

A few minutes later, while the soup was till faintly steaming, John came in.

'Has she gone?' Harriet asked in a whisper.

'Oh, yes. She was ready to go the moment I came in at the door. Hat on her head, plastic bag from that organics place in hand.'

'Thank goodness. I know she means well, but I do find her hard to take. Listen, could you put that bowl of soup away somewhere? I can't stand the smell of it.'

'Okay, I'll just pop it outside the door.'

'No, put it down the loo, for heaven's sake.'

'All right, if you want that.'

It was scarcely a minute before he returned. But during that time all she had felt when Mrs Pickstock had come out with what had happened to her husband one Friday the thirteenth came pouring back.

'John,' she said at once. 'John, am I going to die? Did they truly get rid of all the poison at St Oswald's? I — I'm sure they didn't. I feel so awful at times, I really do.'

John gave her a steady look.

'Yes,' he said at last. 'Yes, you are going to die. But not just yet. Probably in forty years' time, or even fifty.'

'Oh, John, don't be such a pig. But were you telling me the truth? I'm really not likely to die now from the effects of aconitine? They were right not to do that thing, put me on a heart-lung machine, back at St Oswald's? I won't — I won't have anything like Sudden Death Syndrome?'

'No more than I will, I hope. But, come on, you're just letting the black thoughts get to you. Understandable in your present state of weakness. Come to that, it's understandable for me, every now and again when I'm feeling low for some reason. How many times have I said to you that I think I'm suffering from cancer of the great toe?'

'Well, actually,' she said, unable to stop herself giving him a smile, 'I don't think you ever have, till now. Cancer of the great toe, indeed.'

'Well, if I haven't come out with it to you, it's only because I was being very brave about it.'

'All right, hero. And, John, when it's suppertime, I think I could manage some wine, half a glass.'

★ ★ ★

'Did you hear about that poor girl in City Hall Square?' Mrs Pickstock breezily asked as

61

she came in next morning after the nurse's temperature and blood-pressure visit.

Harriet looked at her.

'No, I don't think I have. Was it something on the radio? I haven't felt up to switching it on yet. There's only so much bad news I can take. Or good; come to that. So what is it?'

'It's in the *Chronicle* as well, though I did hear it on Radio Birchester first.'

Harriet felt a spasm of annoyance at this failure to produce the direct answer. She suppressed it and waited in silence.

'Why, it's that poor girl. Murdered, they said. Murdered. There she was — if the paper hasn't made it all up — lying asleep in the sunshine there in the square, and murdered. On Friday the thirteenth. Didn't I tell you something awful always happens if it's a Friday on the thirteenth?'

You did, Harriet thought sourly. You told me your husband died from Sudden Death Syndrome then, and I thought I'd so hurt you by saying Friday the thirteenth was just a silly superstition that I went into a black decline. And here you are talking about the thirteenth just as lip-lickingly as if the poor man's been dead not for seven years but twenty-seven.

'But tell me what it was they said in the *Chronicle*? I don't think they make things up there. Or not very often. Not like the *Evening*

62

Star. So what happened?'

'Well, as I said, there was this poor girl, Thomasina her name was. Only the paper said she was always known as Tommy. Tommy O'Brien. And in the sun — you know how hot it was yesterday, just like the height of summer — she fell asleep outside the City Hall, in the square. Sunbathing. You can catch some nasty skin trouble doing that, you know. And she had open beside her one of those plastic cartons of drink, the sort teenagers are always buying.'

A sudden dread struck at Harriet. A carton of drink . . . open beside her . . . and . . . '

'And what happened, Mrs Pickstock? What happened?'

'Well, this is what they said. Someone must have put something, something poisonous, into that carton. And when she woke up poor little Tommy took another drink from it, and before anyone could do anything she was dead. Poisoned. They said on the radio there was, well, sick all over the steps at the side of the square.'

★ ★ ★

It came as no surprise to Harriet when, just an hour later, Mrs Pickstock came plodding up the stairs again and announced that

Detective Superintendent Murphy wanted to see her.

'Tell him to come up, tell him to come up,' she said.

'But — But are you sure you're ready to let a gentleman come to see you? Would you like me to nip back home and fetch another of my bed jackets? I've got such a sweet one you can have, and the one you've got on is beginning to look a little the worse for wear.'

'No. No, Mrs Pickstock, it's a kind offer. But I really do want to see Mr Murphy as soon as possible.'

'Well, if you think so. He'll be here about little Tommy, I expect. After the way she's been poisoned, just like you were.'

'Yes, I imagine you're right.'

Pleased with her guesswork, Mrs Pickstock waddled out.

And, with a rush of heavy steps on the stairs, Pat Murphy came in.

'I hear you've been told,' he said. 'Victim Number Three. This changes everything.'

'Right, Pat. Sit down, sit down. True enough, there can't be any doubt now. Some sort of murderous maniac is roaming the city. Isn't that so? Me at the Majestic Club, that young man over in Moorfields, and now this girl outside the City Hall. Aconitine in all three cases. Yes?'

64

'You're right. It's been in my mind from the moment I heard how young Robbie Norman had died. That was why I tried every way I could to find some link between the two of you, to prove somehow it wasn't a random act. But, no, there can't be any doubt now. We've got what the papers call a serial killer. It's the class of thing I've prayed would never happen while I was still a detective.'

Harriet thought for some moments. Then she spoke.

'Pat. Pat, it's just possible, I think, that this is not a serial killer.'

'Not? But what do you mean?'

She bit her lip.

'Look, this may be nonsense. I may still not be thinking straight. But . . . well, I've sometimes in the past resolved a puzzling case by . . . all right, by a sort of leap of the imagination.'

'Sure, you have. Doesn't everyone in Birchester CID know it?'

'Okay, then, I'll tell you what I've just thought. Or, no, it's sort of what the lady who let you in, our neighbour, put into my head — Mrs Pickstock, a lady who seems to read nothing but Agatha Christies.'

Pat Murphy, almost obliterating the little green chair he had sat himself on, let a frown of incomprehension etch his broad forehead.

'Go on,' he said.

'Oh, Pat, I don't know whether this is sense or total nonsense. I'm not really fit to judge. But I must tell you. I must.'

'Then spit it out, there's a good girl.'

'I will. It's this. What are the names of this poisoner's three victims? One: Martens. Two: Norman. Three: O'Brien. Well, perhaps you don't know but Mrs Pickstock's favourite author once wrote a book called *The ABC Murders*, and — '

'Ah, I know it, so I do. I gave it a read years ago. Clever as can be, but altogether nonsense.'

'But is it, Pat? John was saying to me, just yesterday I think it was, that Agatha Christie was very shrewd. So she could be right. In the book somebody murdered a Mrs A, a Miss B and then a Mr C, just so as to conceal that the one they really needed to eliminate was Mr C. And our poisoner could have read that book, just as the two of us did once, and dreamt up the notion of doing the same thing. Only this time in reverse order. So he's murdered O, Tommy O'Brien, and N, Robbie Norman, just so that no one will think the one he wanted to eliminate was M, Detective Superintendent Martens, who perhaps got him twenty years a long time ago.'

6

Pat Murphy laughed. A gusty roar of rich laughter.

'Harriet, Harriet,' he spluttered, 'you've done it again. First it was your own John who was after murdering you. Then it was something about something black and white, or white and black. I could never make out what that was all about. And now . . . now you've invented some diabolical old Birchester villain who's gone about poisoning people left and right just so he can give Detective Superintendent Harriet Martens her comeuppance and get away with it. You ought to be a book writer, so you ought, though even Agatha Christie'd be hard put to have her murderer know that some girl sunbathing in City Hall Square, with a carton of drink convenient, happened to have a surname beginning with O.'

'Oh. God, Pat, you're right. How could anybody pick out a girl called O'Brien among all those half-naked bodies sprawled about the square? You're right. It was nonsense. Total nonsense. I suppose I still haven't properly realized what a state my mind's in.

But I'll get better. I must.'

'So you will, so you will. A week in bed here or maybe two, and you'll be as sharp as ever.'

'Jesus, I hope so. But tell me more about yesterday's business. The girl, Thomasina O'Brien, was actually asleep there in the square, right?'

'Right it is. You know how the youngsters flock there any time we get a bit of sun. Strip down as far as they dare, and lie soaking it up. Well, Thomasina was one of them. In her lunch hour. She worked at the City Hall, a telephonist. And beside her she had this big carton of blackcurrant drink. She'd drunk the half of it and left the rest on a step just beside her head. So then himself, or herself it could always be, comes along with that aconitine brew in some sort of container, and just tips it in. Easy does it. No one's to notice. No need even to touch the carton. So there's not even their prints on it. Our poisoner knows what he's about all right.'

'And no one saw them? Is that what you're saying?'

'It is. If all the questioning we've done of the bystanders — and of the by-lyers, if you like — means anything, nobody saw a blind thing. Most of them just as much asleep as poor Thomasina was. Still, we may find someone yet. There were plenty who hurried away when they saw or heard the girl spewing and vomiting the way she did.'

'Only not so effectively as John made me do, and not with the immediate action afterwards that Mr Hume Jones at St Oswald's was able to take.'

For a flashback moment she felt once more John's fingers pushing ruthlessly deep into her throat, as if they were there in reality once more.

'That's about the size of it, yes,' Pat said.

'So where do we, do you, go from here?'

'I wish to God I knew. We go through all the usual procedures, of course. Trace every potential witness, however long it takes. But that's a hell of a task. There's still people from the Majestic Club we haven't properly dealt with, and then there's all the youngsters from the Virgin and Vicar, most of them not at all willing to talk to police. And what am I to do, for heaven's sake, about this man or woman who's going about with a little bottle or chemist's phial ready to put more of the stuff into any glass or open carton or cup they fancy? If I had a hundred more officers to task, what'd be the use of having them patrol here and there just keeping their eyes open? They'd do no good at all, unless by a chance in a million they happened to see someone tilt something into somebody's drink.'

'And you've no other line?'

'Well, I've thought of trying to trace any monkshood growing in any gardens in the city. They tell me it's not so common, so we might get somewhere in that way. If I had enough officers to conduct a proper search. And the people at the university, the what d'you call 'ems, botanists — no, plant physiologists they are nowadays — they said monkshood will have finished flowering at this time of year. So how is anybody who's not an expert even to spot the damn things? Tell me that.'

'I wish I could, Pat. I wish I could. And I wish I was fit, and able to go out asking around myself, Victim Number One or not. But it's all I can do to get myself out of bed and inch my way to the bathroom when I need to, like some sort of blind beggar.'

'Ah, you stay where you are. I see you've got the phone there beside you, so I promise whenever I get a minute to myself I'll call you. Any ideas you have, I'd be happy to hear them. But I must be getting back to the incident room now. Something may have turned up in some report or other. Or maybe the hungry Birchester press corps will be there clamouring. And you watch out for them, too. We've named you now, of course.

But don't let a single one of those ravening eejits put so much as a foot inside your door. And, remember this, just as soon as you're able for it, there's nothing I'd like better than to have you, victim or no victim, on sick leave or not, sitting in the incident room beside me.'

Harriet lay there, thinking about what he had said, and occasionally breaking into surfacy giggles when she thought of herself as the corpse in the MNO murders. Good old Pat, too busy or too embarrassed to bring the invalid any flowers, like the ones the Chief Constable sent. But in the end giving me something far better than flowers that die. Giving me courage.

★ ★ ★

So next day, when the visiting nurse had taken her readings, asked her questions and pronounced her 'doing fine', she made up her mind. When John came to sit with her as he ate his Sunday lunch, the same sausages and oven chips that he had cooked for himself every evening in the week, she launched into her plan even before he had taken his first mouthful.

'John, listen. On Monday I want to go over to Headquarters and see the Force MO. I want him to pass me fit at least for light duties. He'll do it, if I make it plain to him it's what I actually want. I've known him for years now, and quarrelled with him more than once. He's a funny fellow, the world's greatest expert, he boasted to me, on mulligatawny soup. But he's also one of those medics who are in Chief Constables' pockets. When some officer has done something that needs to be quietly swept out of sight, he'll pass them as unfit, quick as you like once he's had the tip. That's what we clashed over in the past. But when he knows that I want quite the opposite of 'Unfit for duty', he'll play ball. I know he will.'

'All right, I dare say he might. But what about my conditions for snatching you out of the clutches of Mr No-hyphen? Number one was, I'll thank you to remember, that you stay in bed till I say you can get up.'

'But, John . . . Look, you know I'm fit enough now. You spoke with the nurse after she'd seen me this morning, didn't you? She said to me I was doing well. Don't tell me she said something different to you.'

'No, she didn't. And you are doing well, so far. But she didn't say you were fit to be on your feet, and I'd really be happier if you were to stay put, more or less anyhow, till the end of this week. You can go and see your

Medical Officer, not tomorrow but on Monday week.'

'John. Don't you realize there's a lunatic prowling the streets of Birchester? Perhaps at this very moment they're putting poison in someone's drink. I may not be able to do much towards stopping them, but I'll be better than nothing. Poor Pat Murphy's absolutely overwhelmed. The least I can do is to get up and go over to the incident room at Waterloo Gardens and take some of the strain. Isn't that so? Isn't it?'

John sat looking at her.

'All right,' he said at last. 'All right, if you'll spend the rest of today getting as much rest as you can, without thinking about your poisoner at all, I'll drive you over tomorrow to your MO, if he'll agree to see you.'

★ ★ ★

Harriet forced herself to move a little less like a blind beggar when she first got up at eight next morning. Even before John brought her up her breakfast — two thin slices of toast, no more — she found she was watching the clock in the radio flicking its way slowly onwards towards ten o'clock, the earliest she calculated that she could expect to find Dr Dalrymple in his surgery at Headquarters.

At last *10.00* showed on the green strip.

And she got the appointment she had half expected not to.

'Yes, yes, a terrible thing to have happened to you, Mrs Martens,' the mulligatawny soup expert concluded. 'A terrible thing. You were lucky to find yourself in the hands of Emlyn Hume Jones. I doubt if anyone else could have brought you through.'

'Well, yes, I was lucky. Very. And it's thanks to him, I suspect, that I feel I'm back to normal now, or pretty well back.'

A sudden shivering fit caused her almost to drop the handset.

'Are you indeed? I'd have hardly expected it after a poisoning of that seriousness. It's not much more than three weeks since it happened, isn't it?'

'Well, I was lucky in another way,' she replied. 'My husband spotted what the matter was and took steps at once to make me vomit. I suppose that accounts for my good recovery.'

But the feel, once again, of John's fingers deep in her throat told her, if nothing else did, that she was steadily lying.

'So,' she brought herself to say, 'can I come and see you, perhaps this morning? Perhaps you could certify me as at least fit for light duties?'

'Delighted, delighted, Mrs Martens. Shall we say twelve noon? Yes, I should be free about twelve.'

★ ★ ★

John drove her.

Flopping into the seat next to him, she thought how little capable she would have been of getting all the way across the city in any other manner. Even putting on clothes for the outside world had been more of a struggle than she had foreseen when, the night before, she had laid out on the green tub-chair her good linen jacket and the skirt that went so well with it. As well as placing ready on top underclothes not worn at all since the morning she had changed at the Club into her twopiece.

But before long she realized that the drive was not going to provide her with the period of rest she had hoped for, time to prepare herself for facing Dr Dalrymple. Tucked away at St Oswald's and in the quiet of her bedroom at home since, she had forgotten, it seemed, how batteringly noisy traffic was. But there was worse. She felt as if, every two or three minutes, some oncoming vehicle was about to smash straight into them.

She turned to look at John. He was sitting

there at the wheel, perfectly calm.

So why am I, beside him, flinching and flinching?

And it's not just the traffic. Everything I set eyes on seems to be, yes, menacing. The buildings loom down at me. The hoardings scream out. Too insistent, too bright, too yammering.

There. There. Huge red letters. *Total Stock Liquidation*.

Liquidation. The Stalinist word. And here in the city, there's the poisoner. Perhaps at this very moment making their way along the pavement just beside us. Set on liquidating their next victim.

What's that? What's that? I saw something. Something black and white. Out of the corner of my eye. And it meant ... it meant something. Something I ought to know about. But I don't. And it's gone. Gone, whatever it was.

And the appalling row is going on and on. The hooting, the roar and rattle of engines. Machinery. And, yes, now blaring music.

Where's that coming from, for heaven's sake?

Yes. Yes, that shop just there. *Sounds A Bell*. What a ridiculously silly name. A music place, I suppose.

'John, that shop where the music's coming

from — pouring from. Is it new?'

He turned for a moment to look and gave a grunt of a laugh.

'Good heavens, no. Been there for years now. Well, four or five at least. It's one of the Bell chain, owned by none other than Sir Billy Bell, last year's Lord Mayor of Birchester. You must know of him.'

'I suppose I do, though I can't remember a thing about him now.'

'No? Not about the big success story? Started with one shop, selling records, as I suppose they were then. He called it *Sounds A Bell* after himself, and it caught on. He opened shop after shop, here and elsewhere. In a very short time he'd got to be one of the city's richest men, and then he bulldozed his way on to the City Council and the Lord Mayor's chair. Now he owns one of the football clubs, don't remember which of them, and dozens of other money-making businesses. Oh, yes, including the *Evening Star*, bought from the Chronicle Group last year. You must remember.'

'But I don't. Not at all. And, you know, that's frightening. Forgetting facts I must have known perfectly well. Suddenly not to have them there in my head. It's awful.'

'They'll come back. Or that's what medical opinion in general seems to believe. In due course it'll all come back. All the trivia too. Won't you be pleased.'

They had begun to get to the outskirts of the city as John had talked, and Harriet found that, with the lessening traffic and her attention fixed on what he had been saying, she was feeling less fraught.

God, I hope I can keep myself this steady when Dalrymple takes out his stethoscope.

But now, suddenly, with John able to go a little more quickly, a fear that had occasionally touched her when being driven fast, rather than driving herself, filled and flooded her mind. The consciousness of how frail in reality a car was. The notion that one tiny miscalculation, one small internal fracture, would send them in an instant plunging to death.

An ambulance came hurtling along from the other direction, siren howling.

It was all she could do not to return scream for scream. Death at high speed filling her mind.

She made herself turn her head and pick out where the needle on the speedometer was pointing. Forty. Only forty miles an hour. And John totally in charge.

I must not let things like this happen to me. I must not. It's because I'm still far from normal. I'm weak. Physically, a certain amount. And mentally a hell of an amount. Which I must not let Dr Dalrymple see. At any cost.

★ ★ ★

'No,' said Dr Dalrymple, wobbling cheeks, red mulligatawny-soused wattle ears, stethoscope dangling on lurching paunch. 'No, my dear, you're nothing like fit enough, not even for light duties. You ought to be in bed, lying flat on your back. You should hear the beat of your heart. It's in a thoroughly bad state. I wonder you even managed to get all the way here.'

'My husband drove me,' Harriet replied stiffly.

'I hope he's a good driver to take you back, that's all. Any sudden emergency might have you suffering a cardiac arrest.'

'Well, we got here.'

'You were lucky. I mean that. I've half a mind to order an ambulance to take you back to St Oswald's. Heaven knows what Emlyn Hume Jones would say if he heard you'd been gallivanting all over the city.'

'Oh, come. I've not exactly been gallivanting. And this morning I was feeling almost back to normal.'

All right, I'm lying. But surely he's making

too much of it all, the old fool.

'Well, you're in nothing like your normal state now, I can tell you that.'

'Oh, you're right, I know, Doctor. The trip across the city did take more out of me than I expected. And, if you think I should, I will go back to bed again. For a day or two.'

'My dear lady, you must have complete bed-rest for much longer than that. I don't think you can have the least idea what a major trauma such as you have suffered does to the body. It's going to be three months at least before you're completely right. Three months.'

7

At home, defeated, Harriet was glad to tumble into bed and, with the words *three months* echoing and echoing in her head, to fall into a deep sleep. She was woken by the shrilling of the phone at her side.

Muzzy-headed, she eventually got the handset the right way round and muttered, 'Hello?'

'Harriet?' It was Pat Murphy's Irish-laced voice.

'Yes? Yes, it's me, Pat.'

'You sounded three parts asleep.'

'I was. I am. What time is it, for God's sake?'

'Let me — Yes, half eight. I couldn't find a minute to ring before. Harriet, there's been another one.'

'Aconitine? Another aconitine poisoning?'

'Just that. This afternoon. At a place out in Boreham, a tea shop, I suppose you'd call it. Mary's Pantry. And the lady who's dead fits the place to a nicety. A fifty-year-old widow, Mrs Sylvia Smythe, Smythe with an e.'

Harriet's head was clearing.

'Yes,' she said, 'as different as can be from

Robbie Norman down in dirty Moorfields. And from snoozing-in-the-sunshine Tommy O'Brien. Or, come to that, from Detective Superintendent Martens, asleep in the sun too, if in rather more classy circumstances.'

'Ah, you're right so. And, besides adding a dozen or more witnesses to be questioned to the hundreds we've already got, it confirms, if confirmation's needed, that our poisoner is altogether roaming round seeking like a roaring lion whom he may devour.'

'True, Pat. And you're right to be quoting the Good Book. This is not far short of evil, pure evil.'

'And you know what the public of Birchester is going to make of it, aided by the TV and the *Evening Star*. There'll be panic, fearsome panic from one end of the city to the other. We've got to catch this maniac before it gets even worse than that. So, listen, Harriet, I know it's too soon for you to take any active part, but will you think about it all? Think as hard as you can, and come up with something. Because I'm damned if I know what more I can do. I'm down in the incident room seventeen or eighteen hours at a time, the Chief calling every five minutes to tell me the citizens of Birchester are *wrapped in fear*, his words. And so far I've got nowhere, nowhere at all.'

'Pat, I'll do my best. I really will.'

And what good will my best be, she thought, dropping the phone on its rest. Wasn't I told just this morning that I'll have to wait three months before I'm fit to go back to work? Three months. Three months when I won't be able properly to get my head round any problem at all, least of all the problem of finding who, among the half-million inhabitants of Birchester, is seeking to administer aconitine to as many individuals as they take it into their head to do.

Bloody Dr Dalrymple was right about one thing. I really should stay in bed a little longer. God, that trip across the city really took it out of me, and the trip back was nearly as bad. But that means I'll be here, stuck here, and not even really able to find out what's going on. Yes, there's Radio Birchester. Must start listening to the news every time it comes on. And the *Evening Star*, that rag; I suppose I'd better order that, too. Me, with the *Evening Star*.

And then what? Sit here, or lie here rather, and hear about murders number five, six, seven, eight, right up to infinity?

★ ★ ★

It was in the middle of a restless night, wild with frightening dreams — too much daytime sleep — that Harriet abruptly thought how after all she might play a part in tracking down the poisoner. But it was not until early in the morning that she was able to look properly at the idea and decide whether or not it was some small-hours fantasy.

What had come into her head then was the recollection of a lady with the unusual name of Earwaker.

Miss Earwaker had, years ago, been a teacher at the twins' primary school, where, of course, she had been known to the kids as Miss Earwigger. Can it be, Harriet asked herself now, that she actually was in those days a Botany teacher? Surely not. Even twenty years ago teachers in primary schools were class teachers, Year One, Year Two, whatever. No, a Botany teacher is a throwback to my own eight-year-old self, sent away to boarding school.

But whatever had been Miss Earwaker's actual designation, she had been an expert on wild flowers. They had been her hobby, even her main interest in life. She used, yes, to take parties of the children off on expeditions into the countryside to identify and collect wild flowers. Even now I can see the exercise books the twins had, with alternate blank and lined pages and the pressed flowers they had stuck on the plain sides, with often only a yellowing inch of sticky tape still in place.

So, isn't it likely, more than likely, that Miss Earwaker will know everywhere round Birchester where monkshood grows? And didn't Pat mention to me — don't know when — that the forensic lab had reported that the aconitine they had subjected to analysis, perhaps even some of what came from my own body, had been from poorly processed *Aconitum napellus*? Yes, and Pat had added, characteristically, 'Monkshood, if you speak God's English.'

So is it possible — yes, Miss Earwaker's still about, I've seen her in Sainsbury's — that she could tell me where to find the monkshood plants from which the poisoner may have obtained new supplies? Supplies to add to what, according to Agatha Christie, they may have been carrying about, like that lump of curare she was once shown, to fondle in pocket or purse.

Miss Earwaker. Yes, Miss Earwaker. And she could well be at the end of the telephone.

What's the time?

Christ, only six thirty. I can't call an old lady at half-past six in the morning. But I could ring at — what? — nine. No, she'll be up early; she was the sort of person who

85

started her day promptly, if I'm right in what I remember of her. Chirpy. Always busy. No, I could ring her at eight, even at a quarter to.

It was just a few minutes after half-past seven that Harriet, hearing John's car drive away, went cautiously downstairs to consult the telephone directory. She was relieved to find she was better now at getting about. The groping, blind beggar banished? Three months, she thought with a dart of contempt for puffy Dr Dalrymple's warning. I'll be a hundred per cent fit long before that.

By the time she had riffled back and forth through the E section of the big, floppy directory she was not feeling quite so pleased with herself. However, she managed at last to focus enough on the small print to find Miss Earwaker's number. Glancing at the clock on the wall, she saw it was still only twenty to eight.

Patience, she said to herself. Patience. It'll be a test of how much in control of myself I am to wait till exactly seven forty-five before I tap out the number. No, till seven forty-six.

She succeeded, even if her finger had stayed poised over the first digit for almost two minutes before she let it jab down.

The distant ringing. Once, twice, three times.

God, have I woken her up after all? She

won't be any too pleased.

'Hello?'

The hesitant voice. Hesitant and distinctly elderly.

Is she going to turn out to be too old for any trip to whatever part of the countryside where she remembers monkshood growing? Will she even remember anything about it now?

'Miss Earwaker?'

'Yes?'

'I don't know if you'll remember me, but I'm Harriet Piddock, the mother of a pair of twins you used to teach.'

'Graham and Malcolm. Nice boys, though naughty at times of course.'

'And on the point of leaving university now and going out into the world, still nice, I hope, and still occasionally naughty. But how are you, Miss Earwaker? I caught a glimpse of you in the supermarket the other day and you were looking well.'

'Oh, I'm not so bad, though I am in my eightieth year, of course.'

Her eightieth year. That's seventy-nine. Seventy-nine but jumping the gun a little. And game. Game. Nothing wrong with her memory, too. Instant recall of Graham and Malcolm. Yes, I can put my request to her. Though, if she says yes to hunting for monkshood all over the countryside, will it be me who turns out not to be up to it?

'Miss Earwaker, there's something I want to ask you. You've heard about this maniac who's roaming the city looking for people to poison?'

'Ah, now I know what it was I was trying to think of. You must forgive an old lady's memory. As well as being Mrs Piddock, mother of those two boys, you're Detective Inspector Martens as well, aren't you? So important to have ladies in the police, I always say.'

'Yes, though I'm actually a detective superintendent now.'

'Oh dear, I am sorry. I find I don't keep up with things nowadays, not the way I used to.'

'But you remembered the twins, and got their names right in a moment.'

'Well, you know, the past is often more vivid to me than what happened just yesterday. But — but didn't I read in the *Birchester Chronicle* that it was you who was the first person to be poisoned? Before that girl lying sunbathing in City Hall Square? And there's been a young man as well. But you? How did you manage to survive? Did you reject whatever had been put in what you were drinking?'

'Yes, I was the first victim, or so we

suppose. But I survived because my husband, sitting beside me by the pool at the Majestic Insurance Club, was actually reading the Agatha Christie murder mystery that describes the poisoning symptoms. And he acted with wonderful quickness.'

Once more she felt, almost as if it was happening at that very instant, John's fingers pushing and pushing down the sides of her throat.

'*Twisted Wolfsbane*,' Miss Earwaker jumped in. 'So that's what the poison is. Aconitine. The paper has never said, you know, or I don't think so. The poison from monkshood. Dear John Keats' wolfsbane. The 'Ode on Melancholy'. So beautiful. So sad. If, I always think, a little difficult properly to understand. 'No, no, go not to Lethe, neither twist wolfsbane, tight-rooted, for its poisonous wine.' Though, of course, the poison is chiefly in the tuber, not the root. But the poet must be allowed his licence, mustn't he?'

'Yes, Miss Earwaker, you're quite right. And this brings me to what I want to ask you. You see, we in the police are inclined to believe that the poisoner used to carry about with them some aconitine, probably obtained from monkshood, in a small container of some sort. It was to give themselves a feeling of power, the power over life or death.'

'Oh dear me. Not a very pleasant person, not a pleasant person at all. And you in the police believe, is it, that once this person had fallen into temptation and used their long-kept supply, they must have taken it into their head to do it again and again? And so they've dug up tubers from monkshood plants somewhere and made more of the poison?'

'Yes. Or at least we think that's possible. But is it? The plant physiologists at the university tell us that monkshood is over by September.'

'Oh, yes, it is. It will be. But, you know, even when the plant has finished flowering — such beautiful flowers, deep blue usually, even purple, and standing up so proudly — the tubers will still be there, just under the ground. Like potatoes, if it isn't awful to say so.'

'So then, Miss Earwaker, do you know anywhere round the city where monkshood is likely to be found?'

'Oh, yes, of course I do. You see, once it's established anywhere it will come up year after year. And monkshood in flower was one of the things I often took my children on an expedition to find. So nice and easy for them to spot. The littler ones always like that, to be the first to point it out. But, of course, I had to warn them never to touch even the leaves. They're poisonous, too, you know, though nothing like as poisonous as the tubers.'

Harriet took a deep breath.

'Miss Earwaker, could you take me on . . . on an expedition?'

'Do you mean . . ? I'm not quite sure what you're suggesting, Mrs Piddock.'

The puzzlement came down the line as strongly as if it was making an electronic buzz.

Harriet nerved herself up to give Miss Earwaker an explanation that would convince her.

'It's like this,' she said. 'The police are absolutely at full stretch trying to trace the poisoner, as you can imagine. And they are checking gardens inside the city to see if they have monkshood growing. But they won't have any officers to spare to go hunting for monkshood plants all over the countryside. But you, Miss Earwaker, are perhaps the person in all the city with the best credentials for locating it. So if you and I could find where this poisoner dug up their source of supply, then we might just possibly be able to tell my colleagues how to track them down.'

'Oh, I see. Yes, I see now. And I believe I could lead you to some of the places within reach of the city itself — well, perhaps really to all of them — where you could find monkshood. If it helps to catch this dreadful murderer before they . . . well, before they pounce again, then I must do it. Certainly I must do it.'

8

The monkshood search did not take place as soon as Harriet might have liked. Miss Earwaker, with a flurry of apologies, had produced a long catalogue of distress about her 'dear little Honda' being in the garage for 'some repairs they said the poor thing must have'. So it was not until the following Friday that she arrived at the house, at exactly the agreed time of two o'clock. Harriet had been pleased in the end to have had the extra days to regain more physical strength. But, even after the lapse of time, getting dressed in denim jacket and jeans had been a much more laborious business than she had counted on. Nevertheless, well before the appointed time she was on the watch at the narrow window beside the front door.

But when she saw the battered little car draw up in the road outside she felt at once a lurch of dismay.

Am I going to be able to cope, she thought, with another journey through the rackety, oppressive streets of the city? Was John right, when I told him about Miss Earwaker, to oppose the outing so strongly? And was I right, was I sensible, to say that I really did feel much better?

And did he realize I was lying? He almost certainly did, knowing me as he does. So was he right, guessing I'd had to kid myself into feeling just fit enough, to give his reluctant agreement?

From outside there came a single little discreet toot of a horn.

God, right or wrong, I've got to go now. I mustn't keep the old dear waiting so long that she feels obliged to come and ring the bell.

She swept the front door open, strode out.

'Good afternoon, good afternoon.' Miss Earwaker, tiny, bespectacled, her much wrinkled face pink-cheeked with enthusiasm under a stiff blue cotton sunhat, poked her head through the car's lowered window.

Harriet advanced.

'My dear,' Miss Earwaker continued, 'I cannot tell you how much I'm looking forward to our little trip. I haven't been out flower-hunting for . . . well, it must be two or even three years. I'm getting on, you know. In my eightieth year. And I know we shan't be able to find monkshood in bloom, those wonderful spikes of deep, deep blue. But I'm sure we'll spot lots of other things. We may even find the sweetest of all autumn flowers, Bouncing Bet. Or soapwort as it's more often called. Not at all a pretty name for a pretty little pink flower.'

Harriet felt a jab of dismay.

Christ, am I going to go all through this and end up looking at some wretched pink flower? And be expected to enthuse about it? Can I . . ? Yes, even now I could say I'm actually feeling worse. As I am. I could postpone the trip. Cancel the whole idea.

No. No, I won't. There's little enough I can do. But what I can do, I must

She walked round to the far side of the car, opened the door — she found it tended to stick — and manoeuvred herself into the passenger seat.

With a horrendous jerk, Miss Earwaker put the little Honda into motion.

'My dear,' she said, almost immediately, 'I've just realized you haven't brought a hat. In this sun, you know, it's really quite a mistake to be out of doors without one.'

God, Harriet thought, are we going to have to turn back? I couldn't bear it, not after I've managed to take the plunge and set off.

'Oh,' she said, a liar once again, 'the sun never seems to bother me. I haven't worn a hat for years, except when I'm in uniform of course.'

She gave a little hysterical laugh.

But, as they travelled on, she found the

traffic was less oppressive than on her trip with John across to Dr Dalrymple's surgery. Mercifully, too, Miss Earwaker, crouching over her steering wheel, was soon too rigid with concentration to be able to chatter.

For twenty minutes and more while they negotiated the crowded inner-city streets, not without causing some furious hooting from drivers who felt put in peril by Miss Earwaker's unorthodox choice of direction, Harriet contrived to fight off the pounding noise that, out with John, had seemed to pierce right to her inner self. Now the tangle of blazing advertisement hoardings and the multiple rattle and roar of the traffic did seem to strike her less forcibly.

I am better, she said to herself. I was right to tell John I was, even if at the time I thought I was putting on an act.

And then, ironically, as they reached the less traffic-ridden suburbs, quite abruptly her old fears came flashing and smiting back.

God, this woman's a bloody maniac driver. We won't last another half-mile. We'll run smack into a big bus, like that one there. And why did I think it was quieter today? It's not. God, that's a road drill. Incessant. An incessant torment of noise.

Can I ask her to stop? Give me peace for a moment? But she won't She won't. Look at her, face set, hands clamped to the wheel, willing herself forward. Plunging onwards. Plunging to death. Yes, to death. I can't even move —

'My dear, you're suddenly looking quite ill. I think we had better come to a halt. I'll see if I can spot somewhere to have a nice cup of — Oh, look. Look, there's a place. What they call a coffee shop, I think.'

With a wild swerve that set Harriet's heart thumping once again, Miss Earwaker brought the battered little Honda to rest alongside the kerb.

'Come along, dear. Some good strong tea will soon put you right. It's what I used to give myself in the staffroom if my class had been more than usually disruptive. You know, towards the end of my teaching days I did begin to find the children worse behaved. I don't know whether it was a sign of the times — too much television too late in the evening — or whether I was beginning to lose my grip. But there were certainly days when I thought the bell would never go for the end of a lesson. And, of course, I was getting a little deaf even then.'

Which accounts, Harriet thought, feeling less panicky now the car was stationary, for the way she drives. She's deprived of much of her sense of hearing.

But some sort of a reply was needed. Miss Earwaker ought at least to be assured it cannot have been her fault if she had found it harder to keep discipline in the last of her teaching days.

But where is the energy to produce such an assurance?

Curse the individual who, from out of nowhere, took it into their head to pour that foul stuff into my Campari, she thought in a swirl of viciousness. Curse them, curse them, curse them. She pushed open the car door. A passing motorist let fly with a volley of horn blasts.

And curse him too.

She half-flung herself out into the roadway, staggered round the back of the car, patting at it with a pawing hand, and at last managed to follow Miss Earwaker through the coffee-shop door.

Inside, she turned and dropped into the first chair she saw at the nearest vacant table, leaving Miss Earwaker to come trotting back to her when she realized she had been deserted. She set her large handbag squarely down on the table.

'My dear, you are in a state. Now, you just sit here, and I'll fetch us tea. Well, no, perhaps in a modern place like this they don't have tea. Or if they do, it will be perfectly horrid.

So, I'll get us coffees. Is that all right?'

'Yes. Yes, thank you, Miss Earwaker. I — I'm sorry to be such a nuisance, but I'm suddenly feeling ridiculously weak.'

'No, no. Not at all. After all, you have been seriously ill, poisoned. But I'm sure a nice strong cup of coffee will put you on your feet again in a jiffy.'

She trotted resolutely off towards the tall counter where a young Italian-looking man presided over an array of shining silver machines backed by a long, glass-fronted display case with above it a list of the varieties of coffee on offer.

Harriet sat where she was and allowed her eyes to close.

Eventually she became aware that the invigorating aroma of freshly brewed coffee was not wafting up to her. Surely it should be? By now?

She made the effort to lift up her head, open her eyes.

A scene seemed to be taking place at the counter, very discreetly on the part of Miss Earwaker, volubly on the part of the Italian-looking young man.

And, yes, he is actually speaking Italian, or what sounds very like it.

She listened with more attention.

Ah, got it. It's his list of the various kinds of

coffee available, and rippled out at top speed. *Espresso, cappucino, caffè latte, mocha, caramel macchiato, americano, espresso macchiato, espresso restorello, caffè italiano realmente.* And evidently being rippled out not for the first time.

'Espresso? Cappucino? Caffè latte? Mocha? Caramel macchiato? Espresso restorello? Caffè italiano realmente?'

Plainly he's under the impression that the only way to make a *stupido* English woman understand is to shoot out his questions each time louder and louder.

And quite as evidently Miss Earwaker is not understanding a thing.

Oh God, I'll have to go and rescue her. Or could I leave her there till she gives up? And goes right out of the place? Or I could get up myself and go out and stand by the car. Say I must go home. But, no. No, I mustn't give up. I won't. I got hold of this ally of mine and I must stick by her. Till we have found the monkshood the poisoner may have been digging up as, if I'm right, he will have had to do.

She put both hands flat on the table, heaved herself to her feet, managed to make her way over to the counter without swaying or stumbling.

'Miss Earwaker, let me help.'

She took a look at the long list above the glass display case.

'Two caffè lattes,' she said.

'Beeg? Sma?'

'Big, big. As big as you've got.'

Back at the table, after another short bout of complication over paying, Miss Earwaker was a mass of apologies.

'You know, I really couldn't understand a word that young man was saying. So stupid of me. But, well, he really was speaking very fast. And rather loudly. People must have been listening. It was . . . it was most embarrassing.'

'Don't worry about it, Miss Earwaker.' Harriet sipped greedily at her coffee. 'It wasn't your fault at all. He should never have been put behind the counter if he couldn't speak some sort of understandable English.'

She found that with each sentence, each new sip of coffee, her mind was becoming clearer.

Yes, I'll be ready when she's finished her cup. Perhaps I shouldn't have got her a *beeg* one. But I'll be ready then to sit in that car, to be driven, however erratically, to wherever she thinks monkshood was in flower a month ago. And then . . .

'Well,' Miss Earwaker was softly twittering, 'I know places like this are very popular

101

nowadays. But, really, I must say, I do prefer the good old-fashioned tea shop, where one used to be served by — perhaps I shouldn't say this — by ladies. And where you could always rely on the tea. Where there was a little vase of flowers on the table, even if, as was sometimes the case I admit, the blooms were past their best. You know, there used to be a very nice place not far from here called Mary's Pantry. When I was taking one of my parties of children to swim at the public baths nearby I used to go there for a cup of tea, and sometimes a cake, a homemade one, after I had handed my charges over to the men at the baths. They were excellent fellows, and the bath itself was always very well kept. So I knew I could safely trust them, as I really had to do since I never learnt to swim myself. But, of course, nowadays they have to shut the baths on September the first. Too costly, they say, to keep them open.'

She gave a little ladylike snort of derision.

But Harriet had hardly been listening.

Over at the long, shelf-like table fronting the shop's windows a tousle-headed young man, perhaps a student of some sort, was sitting on his high stool, reading a book placed flat on the narrow table. Not so much reading it as poring over it, deeply abstracted. At his side his smart-looking mug of coffee

— *Espresso? Latte? Americano?* — was totally neglected. And, in a lightning flash of revelation, she had seen how simple it would be for someone — a man, a woman — to walk quietly past that bent, studious back and tip into the mug from some small container a quantity of liquid. Then, a moment later, after the heavy glass door of the shop had swung itself quietly closed, death would come. Loudly. The sharply tingling tongue, the feeling of overwhelming chill, and the vomiting. The vomiting not violent enough to avert the death soon to follow.

I must go. We must get into the countryside and find, if it's at all possible, the clump of dried-up monkshood the poisoner has dug at.

'Miss Earwigger,' she asked, 'are you ready?'

And then she realized what she had said. Miss *Earwigger*, the name the twins had always used at home about the old teacher.

Oh Christ, will she be offended? Will she say she thinks, really, she will not go hunting for monkshood after all? Have I lost my one real hope?

'Miss — Miss Earwaker, I'm sorry. I shouldn't have . . . I mean . . . I — '

'My dear, that's quite all right. You don't think I didn't find out years and years ago that the children liked to call me that behind

103

my back? I rather cherished the name, you know, and had a little laugh to myself if I ever overheard it. And, yes. Yes, I'm quite ready now to set out again.'

★ ★ ★

The search for any last remains of tall-flowering monkshood was, however, a failure. Harriet had tramped for what seemed hours over the scrubby stretches of uncultivated land which Miss Earwaker had declared were 'just the sort of place dear old monkshood loves' but they had found nothing. At last Harriet knew herself to be so exhausted that she had to cry off.

'Never mind,' Miss Earwaker said, with a cheerful determination that scraped against every nerve in Harriet's head, 'We'll go again another time. Yes, I shall be free on Sunday afternoon, two o'clock sharp again. Have a good sustaining luncheon, and we'll try Halsell Common. Do you know, I think that's where we should have gone first of all. Yes, Halsell Common, quite the likeliest place.'

A good sustaining lunch? Plainly this ancient tiger I've set on the trail doesn't want to have another long coffee-shop halt. But isn't there something . . . ? Something to do with that place that I ought to remember?

Not my vision there of what could so easily happen, at any moment, at any coffee shop, or any pub, or any café or restaurant anywhere in Birchester. But something else. Something . . .

No, it's gone, whatever it was. I dare say it wasn't at all important. But . . . Oh, well, forget about it. God, I shall be glad to get back home. Bed. No supper, nothing. Just bed. Bed and sleep. Sleep, sleep, sleep.

9

Next morning, when Harriet came to tell John the story of her outing, with certain omissions such as their sudden necessary visit to the coffee shop, she got a considerable talking-to.

'Now, listen, it's time you paid some attention to what people who aren't suffering from post-trauma exhaustion tell you. Three months, that's what Dr Dalrymple said you'd need before you were properly back to full health. And you should have seen yourself when you came home yesterday afternoon. It was a good job I'd got back early. I don't think you'd have got upstairs if I hadn't been there to heave you on. It's not as if I didn't warn you when you told me about your silly plan to go prowling all over the countryside with that old woman.'

'It wasn't a silly plan. It was the one chance I had to do something about this maniac creeping round the city poisoning people. Poisoning me. All right, I lied to you a bit about how much better I was feeling. But I had to go. You do see that, don't you? I had to go.'

'Yes. Well, I do see it, I suppose. But, darling, you really must think before you go leaping into things like that.'

Harriet looked at him.

'I have thought,' she said. 'A bit.'

'Thought about what, for heaven's sake? You're not planning to go off again on some — I nearly said *fool's errand*. But I grant you that whatever you have in mind won't be that, or not exactly. But you're not planning another outing just yet, are you?'

'On Sunday.'

'Tomorrow. But that's much too soon, much too soon. And where are you thinking of going, anyhow?'

'To Halsell Common. Do you know it?'

'I do, as it happens. I know just where it is, and it's miles out of the city. Are you intending to go out there with your Miss Earwaker again?'

'She's coming to collect me at two o'clock.'

'Oh, is she? And here's another thing. I'm quite likely not to be here tomorrow evening to pick up the pieces. There's a damn silly affair I've got to go to at the Sports and Social Club. A prize-giving for some competition we're running for something or other. Bit of publicity, I think. It's Buggins' turn, and I'm Buggins. I have to be there before six, to see that everything's in order. Prizes to be presented by Sir Billy Bell, no less.'

'Oh, yes, former Lord Mayor, isn't he? You were telling me about him for some reason.'

'Because you complained, when we were on our way to see Dr Dalrymple, about the noise pouring out of one of his *Sounds A Bell* shops.'

'I remember.'

'Well, that's a good sign at least. You said then in the car that you'd never heard of him. So your memory is gradually coming back.'

'Which means, with you at home or not when I return, it's perfectly all right for me to go out again with Miss Earwaker. You know it is, John. And if I do come back totally washed-out, Miss Earwaker can always go round the corner and ask Mrs Pickstock to come in for a few minutes.'

John made a face.

'All right,' he said. 'If you can cheerfully suggest having Mrs Pickstock come in, you can't be quite as bad as I'd thought. But take care tomorrow, won't you? Be sensible.'

'Yes, yes, I will be. Truly. Because out at Halsell Common I may actually advance the poisoner investigation. Miss Earwaker said that, after all, it was the likeliest place outside the city for anyone to find monkshood.'

★   ★   ★

This second monkshood hunt turned out to be very different from their first venture when hours of leaden-footed tramping had produced not a single find. Again, it was almost heatwave hot. And again Harriet had failed to provide herself with a hat. But now, when after a quiet Sunday afternoon journey Miss Earwaker brought her little Honda to a sudden jerking halt at the end of a rough track leading into the common, Harriet found her full of confidence.

'Yes, yes,' she said. 'Yes, we really ought to see the dear things in just ten minutes' walking. This was where I often used to take my class. There's a bus that stops just a few yards along there. So convenient with the children. Off we go.'

And, after perhaps a few more minutes than ten, they came to the first clump of monkshood. Or what Miss Earwaker declared was monkshood. To Harriet the clump looked like nothing so much as a bundle of withered and forlorn-looking stalks, and there were certainly no signs that anybody had been digging nearby. Yet Harriet felt somehow that this had to be a good omen. As apparently did Miss Earwaker.

'So silly of me,' she said. 'I knew perfectly well that Halsell Common was the best place. But somehow I got it muddled up with where we went before.'

'Very natural. It's hard to distinguish between the look of things there and the look here. I can easily see why you got them mixed up. So where do we go now?'

'Oh, not much further. Can you see some smoke rising up at the other side of the ridge here?'

'Yes.'

'Well, I rather think we shall find two or three good specimens on the far side. Of course, it isn't at all likely that they'll be in flower, but if we're lucky you'll be able to see the spikes looking much more erect than these ones, poor things.'

They set off again.

'But, goodness, isn't it hot?' Miss Earwaker said before long. 'Really, it might be July. And you still haven't got a hat.'

Harriet, hardly listening to this chirping, felt the beginnings of jubilation pulsing up in her. Somehow, with reason or against reason, she felt this was going to be the moment she would see for the first time monkshood in its full glory. And, if her luck still held, there would be a clump of it with at its foot plain signs of disturbance to the ground. Disturbance caused by the poisoner seeking a fresh supply of the deadly stuff that was obsessing them.

Almost leading the way, all signs of fatigue banished, she strode up the gentle slope. Five minutes' more brought them to the crest.

'Look, look,' Miss Earwaker cried. 'Look, there it is. Standing up like a trooper. The dear old plant.'

Harriet looked in the direction in which Miss Earwaker was pointing, but could see nothing. Only bare brown grass, a few haphazard wind-bent trees, a patch of gorse still in brilliant yellow flower, and further away an ugly heap of discarded scrap metal.

The countryside, the beautiful British countryside, she thought with an excess of bitterness.

But Miss Earwaker, tiny and determined, was tripping down the far slope. Harriet set off behind her, and in hardly more than a minute was able to make out in the direct line they were taking three tall brown spikes rising up against the greenish tan of the distant grass.

Two minutes later they were standing there side by side, both puffing and panting, looking at the gaunt stems. In a moment Harriet saw that on the shortest of them there were three — no, four — dried-up bell-shaped flowers, still with traces of deep-blue colour.

No, not bell-shaped, she said to herself.

Hood-shaped. Monk's hood-shaped.

'Mrs Piddock, Harriet,' Miss Earwaker broke in. 'Why are you staring at the dead flower-heads? Look at the ground behind. Look at the ground.'

Harriet looked.

The ground in the rear of the clump showed clear signs of having been recently, even freshly, dug at.

'Miss Earwaker, do you think . .?'

'Yes, I do. Someone has been digging at the roots of the clump. And, yes. Yes, look at this.'

In a moment she had knelt beside the freshly turned earth and, without actually touching anything, she was pointing with her thin, old woman's finger at what Harriet saw as just a patch of dirtyish white.

'A tuber,' Miss Earwaker said. 'Someone has wrenched off the better part of one of the tubers here. I do hope they took care to wear gloves. What's inside is really a very dangerous poison.'

'I know,' Harriet answered, with a laugh that had a trickle of hysteria in it. 'I swallowed some not so very long ago.'

Miss Earwaker looked at her.

'And do you think, Harriet,' she asked almost tremulously, 'that it was from here, from this place exactly, that the poisoner got the material for aconitine?'

'I can't be certain, of course,' Harriet replied, calmer now, the police officer coming back. 'But it's a possibility. It must be. The thing is, though, could anybody have seen who was digging here?'

'Yes, well, someone might have done. There are some cottages just down there. You can't quite see them because they're in a little dip where there's a stream. I seem to remember that they're no longer inhabited, because they're so out of the way. People nowadays, you know, like to be where they can see other people, get to the shops and the cinema. But that smoke we saw. It just might be coming from there. The best thing would be to go back up the ridge for a little and look.'

Harriet did not wait for more.

'I'll go,' she said. 'And you stay here, Miss Earwaker, if you will.'

'Yes, yes. On guard.'

Harriet found that to get a proper view she had to go further up the ridge than Miss Earwaker had indicated. But in four or five minutes, reinvigorated by what they had discovered, she reached as far as the top. The first thing she actually saw, however, was down on the opposite side. A group of youths on cycles were clustered round Miss Earwaker's battered little car. She could hear, faintly, shouting and laughter.

Up to some mischief, she briefly wondered.

But she had more urgent business. She wheeled round and looked to see if the smoke was still there. And, yes, from the chimney of one of three ruined cottages she could see now a rope of dull grey smoke was lazily rising.

She hurried back down and then, barely stopping to tell Miss Earwaker that there was a sign of life, she plunged onwards.

It did not take her long, with Miss Earwaker eagerly coming along behind, to reach the little row of cottages overlooking a tiny stream. She could see no sign of there being anybody inside the one, a little less dilapidated than the other two, from which the smoke was coming. But without hesitation she lifted its rusty iron door-knocker and gave it two or three vigorous bangs.

There was a long silence. A bird was singing somewhere.

Could it be a lark? Would I know if it is?

Then at last came the thump of heavy footsteps from inside.

The door was pulled open. The man standing at it looked to be about seventy or even eighty, though by no means stringy with age. But his eyes were a bleary blue and the close-cropped hair on his head and bristling

114

at his cheeks was washed-out to the palest of greys.

'What you want? Can't a man get his sleep of a Sunday afternoon?'

'I'm sorry if I've disturbed you,' Harriet answered quickly, doing what she could to infuse her voice with friendliness. 'But we're wondering about the place just over there where there's been some digging.'

'Wolfsbane,' the old man grunted.

'Yes, yes. You're quite right. Someone's been digging at the wolfsbane there, the monkshood.'

'What if there was?'

And then Miss Earwaker, hovering in the background, broke in.

'But it's poisonous, you know. Deadly poisonous really. It isn't safe to touch, not unless you're very careful.'

'Know that, don't I?'

Oh God, Harriet thought, don't let him lose whatever sympathy he has for us.

'What we were really wondering,' she said, 'is whether you happened to see who it was who was digging there?'

'Saw him, didn't I? Told you that.'

He had not. But Harriet answered as if she believed his every word.

'Yes, yes, of course.' With a pulse of effort, she made herself sound enthusiastic, even

115

admiring. 'Was it someone you knew? Or was it a stranger? Can you tell us?'

'Can't.'

A sulky silence.

'But you did see them. Can you describe them at all? What sort of age were they?'

'How'd I be able to tell that? Only saw him through the window. Had on a grey suit and a weskit. And he had a tie. A tie.'

'And what sort of height was he?'

'Saw him through the window, didn't I? How d'you expect me to know that?'

Harriet felt misery creeping up through her veins. All right, if she had been thoroughly fit, she would have known how to wheedle, and if need be bully, out of an obstinate witness like this what she wanted to discover. But now it seemed as if the old man was a mountain blocking her way, there and unclimbable.

She looked at him, fighting to push down her rising blackness. In the doorway he stood, simply looking back.

But then, for no reason, he spoke, or growled, again.

'Little feller. Like one o' they pet rabbits, the white 'uns.'

Then a new silence.

The bird, lark or not, had stopped singing.

Harriet puzzled over the curious description the old man had at last produced.

Like one of those pet white rabbits? What could he mean? No doubt the man digging had reminded him of a rabbit, for some reason. But it seemed impossible to fathom his train of thought.

What on earth could she ask that might lead him to expand on that description?

She glanced quickly at Miss Earwaker in the hope that the words had meant something to her. Plainly they had not. She seemed as baffled as she had been when the young man at the coffee shop had poured out his stream of Italian information.

But then, from far away on the other side of the ridge behind them, there came, suddenly distinct in a puff of breeze, the sound of voices raised to a peak of noisy excitement.

Miss Earwaker's car, Harriet thought. Won't it, somehow comical as it is, have roused the nastiest instincts in a group of feckless youngsters? Which was what I thought of them, without much taking it in, when I looked down the far side of the ridge not a few minutes ago.

And does Miss Earwaker, so willing to put herself out for me, deserve to get back to her beloved little Honda to find . . . what? The tyres let down? Paintwork scratched or scrawled over with obscenities? Perhaps that sticking passenger-door forced and things taken?

No. No choice.

If I leave the two old people confronting each other here, will Miss Earwaker learn something more? But, whether it's yes or no, I must go. At once.

She whirled round and set off at a loping run up the ridge. But now, knowing she was leaving that tiny spring of hope behind, each stride took more and more out of her. A fierce stitch soon made itself felt. She gritted her teeth, fought her way onwards.

At last, the top. She stood for an instant, sucking in air, feeling the sweat suddenly burst out. And, yes, there, as she had feared, was the cluster of youths, banging now on the Honda's top like so many demented drummers.

The booming sound, distorted and ugly.

One last strangled breath, and she set off again towards the white-surfaced track Miss Earwaker had driven her along. Leaping bounds, careless of roots that might trip, holes that lay in wait.

Uncannily soon, she was within shouting distance of the drummers on their bikes.

'Stop that. Stop it.'

Her voice, she could not think how, had penetrated the cracked thunder from the car's roof. It tapered away into silence.

She took a step or two further forward.

'Get away from that car,' she barked, sucking in a breath.

'Go and stuff yourself, old bag.'

She wasn't able to see which of them had shouted. But it hardly mattered. The same look of ruffled hostility was on each face.

Stiffening every sinew, she marched forward down the gentle, tussocky slope.

'Police officer,' she snapped.

I've handled worse. I've handled worse. The phrase repeated itself in her head, mantra-like, struggling against the jelly feebleness she felt within.

'Oh, Miss Plod, we been naughty.'

She singled out the jeering speaker leaning on his racing bike as the likely ringleader. Short, dark-haired, muscular, a bright red jersey, smooth-shining grey trousers tight to the leg, taut over the buttocks.

'Detective Superintendent Martens.' She sent the name and rank, a pistol shot, out towards him.

'Oooh, oooh, it's the big boss.'

Red Jersey unimpressed. As yet.

'Right, names,' she snarled, thrusting a hand into the top pocket of her denim jacket.

Only to realize that, being Mrs Piddock setting out with her sons' former teacher to look for wild flowers, rather than being Detective Superintendent Martens always on duty, she had neither warrant card nor notebook with her.

Then her scrabbling fingers touched in the pocket something smoother than a notebook. And, yes, she remembered. A slim tin of waterproof plasters. I put it there one day when we were going to the beach somewhere. Years ago.

She pulled it out, cupping her hand round it. At this distance, would any of them see it was not a notebook and that she had nothing to write on it with?

'I said names,' she barked again, raising the thin tin to a point where she would have written on it, had it been a pad, and shaping her other hand as if it were holding a ballpoint.

'Oh, piss off,' Red Jersey shouted.

But he had wheeled his bike round and he set out now with the stones from the white track spurting under his back wheel.

And the whole little mob of them followed.

Harriet stood where she was until they were out of sight. Then she lunged out towards the car, reached it still on her feet, sank to the ground and sat there, head bowed.

After a long while, it seemed, she heard

Miss Earwaker's chirpy voice, and looked up.

'My dear, I couldn't at all make out where you had got to. Are you all right? Not another of those nasty mental attacks?'

'No, no,' she managed to say. 'I'm perfectly all right actually. It was just . . . well, when I was up on the ridge the time before, I saw a group of youngsters surrounding your car, and then while we were talking to that old man I heard a lot of noise and shouting. So, I thought I'd better just go and take a look. And actually I saw the boys drumming on the car roof. So I went down and shooed them off.'

'That was very good of you. I'm afraid, though, you tried to do too much. In your state of health, I mean.'

Harriet was about to deny this. But then she realized she had in fact *done too much*. It would be all she could do to get to her feet again.

'Yes,' she said, 'I think perhaps you're right. John warned me about over-exerting myself, but I rather ignored it. He's really a bit of a fuss-pot. So, yes, I think I'd like to go back home now.'

'And so you shall,' Miss Earwaker said, extending a frail hand. 'Ups-a-daisy.'

Harriet did, however, manage to push herself to her feet unaided, and then made her way, step by step, to the far side of the car. Miss Earwaker, she found, had failed to lock the sticking door.

If those louts had only known . . .

But, once sitting inside, a small rash of doubts invaded her.

'Miss Earwaker, did that old man say anything more to you after I'd left? We . . . we didn't get very much out of him.'

'Well, I don't think he would have told us any more however long we'd stayed there. The disagreeable old fellow just stepped back when you went, and, well, he slammed the door in my face.'

'Oh, Miss Earwaker.'

'But we did learn something, you know. He did tell us that the person who was digging there wore a suit, with a waistcoat. A grey suit, and a tie. And you know what that means, don't you?'

Harriet did. She had stored away the implication in her mind the moment the old man had mentioned the suit and tie. But she thought she ought to let Miss Earwaker have a little triumph.

'No,' she said.

'It means, my dear, that the digging man came from the city. By the bus, I expect. A grey suit with a tie. It can hardly mean anything else. But . . . I'm not sure what we can learn from what he said about one of those pet rabbits. Did it mean something to you?'

'No, it hardly did. But I'll remember it.'

10

When Miss Earwaker had seen her indoors
— she had managed not to ask her to fetch
Mrs Pickstock — once again it was all Harriet
could do to climb step by step up the stairs
and at last to fling herself down on the bed,
still in jacket and jeans. She had just a
moment before sleep overtook her, deep as if
drugged, to think what luck it was that John,
safely at the Club prize-giving, was not there
to see his warning to her justified.

At least, she had thought leadenly, I got a
description, of sorts, of the poisoner.

Or of someone else altogether..?

★　★　★

The ringing of the phone woke her.

God, what time is it? It's dark. Where's
John? Why doesn't he answer it? Still at the
Club? A few drinks?

She heaved herself into a sitting position.

'Hello. Hello.'

'Harriet?'

Pat Murphy's voice.

She tried, with blinking, sticky eyes to see

the figures on the bedside clock.

'Pat. What time is it? I've been asleep, and I've no idea.'

But she did not wait for Pat's answer. Her head had been clearing, and she abruptly realized she had been so stupefied when she'd got home that she had failed altogether to pass on to Pat that she and Miss Earwaker had discovered the dug-at monkshood, and to give him her description of the digging man.

'Listen, Pat, I've got something to tell you.'

'No, it's me that's got something to tell you, Harriet. Harriet, there's been another one. Another poisoning. And it was the Big Fella, Sir Billy Bell himself. Over at the Majestic Club.'

Harriet sat, holding the handset, dumbstruck.

'Harriet?'

'Yes, yes, Pat, I'm here. But John? John must have been there. On the spot. Is he all right?'

'He is so. He was the first man among them all with the sense to ring and report it.'

'Oh yes, he would be. But . . . but tell me what happened. When was it?'

'No more than fifteen or twenty minutes ago. It seems they were having some drinks after the prize-giving, whatever, had finished. There was quite a crowd of them. And, well, you can guess what happened. Suddenly Sir Billy was violently sick, and then . . . well, then he was dead. I'm going now to catch up with the team I've sent. Should have left already. But I thought you ought to know, specially if your John doesn't get back till God knows when.'

'Yes. Thank you, Pat. Thank you.'

She felt incapable of any coherent thought, and, after sitting hunched-up there for three or four minutes, she decided the only thing to do was to take off her clothes and put herself properly to bed.

* * *

When John had come in, much later, he had woken her. But, even more muzzy-headed than when Pat had rung, she had just muttered, 'Tell me in the morning,' before thrusting herself once more into the pit of sleep. So it was not until nearly nine o'clock, over a late breakfast, that she heard his full account.

'It was all a bit odd somehow,' he said. 'I mean, there we all were on the platform in the Club hall and there were people who had come to watch the ceremony still milling about down below. Up at our end there was champagne, courtesy of the Majestic

126

Insurance Company, needless to say. I imagine one or two of the more fly among the spectators may have seen the chance of getting a free drink and had come up for a crafty mingle. It's easy enough to reach the platform, just a couple of steps at each side. And then ... well, then there was the unpleasant sound of somebody coughing and spluttering and then being comprehensively sick.'

'Sir Billy?'

'Yes, Sir Billy. He'd been swigging away at the champagne, hard as he could go. Typically, from what I know of him. A reputation for enjoying life to the full, or, depending how you look at it, for making a pig of himself.'

'I get the picture.'

John was silent for a second or two.

'I don't know,' he said. 'I wonder if I've given you the right impression. I said the whole scene was a bit odd, but I rather doubt if I've managed to make it clear why I felt that.'

'Odd?' Harriet repeated, with a prickle of curiosity.

John shook his head in some bewilderment.

'No,' he said, 'I shouldn't really have mentioned it. It was just that . . . no, I don't know. I just felt it all was somehow not quite as I'd have expected. It was . . . well, I'll tell you one thing. It wasn't like it was with you at the pool. I don't know. If he hadn't vomited in that way, I'd have thought he'd just died of a heart attack. But it was only a momentary uneasiness I felt. Take no notice of it.'

But Harriet had taken notice. Her mind was in a whirl. A hundred and one notions of what could have been odd about Sir Billy's death surfaced and sank again.

With an effort she pulled herself together.

No. I'm letting my uncontrolled mind get out of hand once more. It's the *John was my murderer* nonsense all over again. The MNO conspiracy. All those idiot ideas good old Pat's shot down for me.

'Look, the real point,' she said, 'is that Sir Billy was poisoned, suddenly. That's why the poisoner is so terrible. What was it you said to me when I was still in St Oswald's? I've remembered it off and on ever since. Shakespeare, 'Upon my secure hour'. And, you know, that somehow makes a difference, death coming at a time you feel everything's going right. An enormous difference really. I mean, if Sir Billy had died of natural causes one day, after years of self-indulgence, you wouldn't feel it was particularly awful. Or those of us who know him only by reputation wouldn't. I suppose it'd be different for, say,

128

his wife. If there is a Lady Bell.'

'Oh, there is. Former dancer in musicals, I believe. But luckily she wasn't there last night. Don't suppose she much cares for social events of that sort, and she may be fed up with seeing Sir Billy being Sir Billy.'

'One good thing, she didn't have to watch him die. But, tell me, what were the exact circumstances? Were you too far away to see?'

'Yes, and no. I was quite near him, but I was busy keeping an eye on the trays of champagne. If no one does that, they tend sometimes to get delayed off-stage, delayed and depleted.'

'Dear old human nature.'

'Yes. So all that I saw really was that Sir Billy was taking yet another glass, just as soon as he'd swigged the one before. But I didn't properly see the one that poisoned him, though, now you remind me, I did just notice Sir Billy pull a face when he put it to his lips. But then the stupid fool — oh, I know *nil nisi bonum* and all that — instead of putting the glass aside, he took a really big gulp. I actually turned away then, didn't want to look at him.'

'And then you heard the spluttering and the vomiting?'

'At the very next moment. I looked back in time to see that great fat body of his go thudding to the ground. Of course, I knew at once what had happened. Everybody there must have thought the same thing, the poisoner being so much on everyone's mind.'

'Yes, of course. You know, here safe indoors all day I don't feel it quite as strongly, especially as I rather discourage la Pickstock's gossiping. But, of course, everyone in the city must be thinking at every minute: *Will I be the next? Will it be me, out of the blue?*'

'Exactly. You should have seen the reaction all round when it became clear Sir Billy had been a victim. Frankly, there was plain relief on every face. *Not me. Not this time.*'

'Yes. And . . . and I suppose it's possible that one of those faces was deliberately putting on that same look of relief. To cover up. The poisoner.'

'It could have been, certainly. But equally whoever it was could have slipped away the moment it was clear that from the expression of distaste on Sir Billy's face that he had taken at least some of the aconitine. Once the proceedings started there was no one there on the door to look at invitation cards.'

'And Pat hasn't got anywhere, as far as you know?'

'No. He was on the scene quickly enough, and his team had had all the exits stopped in minutes. Then they started the questioning.

None of us was allowed to go until they'd seen everyone.'

'So it was very late when you woke me last night?'

'It was today, in fact. Early morning today. I didn't quite know what to do, but I thought you might have been worrying. So I woke you. Not that you were worrying as it turned out.'

'No. I was so knocked out by my trip with Miss Earwaker that I just wasn't in a state to do any worrying about anything.'

John gave her a more authoritative glance.

'I doubt very much if it was the trip alone that exhausted you,' he said. 'You're still under doctor's orders, don't forget. You're still ill. I should have put my foot down more firmly yesterday about you and your wretched Miss Earwaker. It was a nonsense you going out like that. You've a long way to go, a very long way, before you're back to anything like normal. And you've got to remember that.'

'Oh, John, don't preach. I know all you said's right, and I will try to take it easy. I really will.'

'I hope you do. You know, if you go on the way you've been doing these last few days, you'll do yourself some permanent damage. And I'll find, instead of being the supportive husband of senior police officer Detective

131

Superintendent Martens, I'm being sick-nurse to bed-bound Mrs Harriet Piddock. If not worse.'

★ ★ ★

Whatever feelings of remorse Harriet had been left with were to be put under severe strain before Monday was much older. Scarcely had she finished the long process of choosing what to wear and getting herself dressed — she was determined at least not to endure compulsory bed-rest — than Pat Murphy rang.

'Harriet, something new. And hopeful, at last. We've got a witness to your poisoning.'

Into her head, as she sat there on the edge of the bed, there came again that flash of thought saying somehow *black and white*. For a moment she was thrown by it. What exactly was it? It was nothing like an image of anything black and white, more just a single thought attached to nothing. And it vanished as quickly as it had arrived in her head.

But it had stopped her properly listening to Pat.

' . . . or at least it looks as if we've got one.'

Was he saying that? He must be.

'But it's not . . . not certain about this witness?' she asked clumsily.

'It's not certain to me, that's for sure. But maybe it's because I've yet to see the fella. He was one of the two security men on the gate at the Club when it happened to you. Name of Bruce Grant. But that's about all I know.'

'So how did you get to hear?'

'Ach, the fella went sailing into his local PS — it's the station out at the Meads — just last night. Happy as Larry he was. 'Yes,' he said at the desk, 'I saw the woman do it.' '

The woman. Then that old man out at Halsell Common must have seen someone else altogether digging beside that monkshood plant. The man in the grey three-piece suit with the tie must have been someone quite innocent. Perhaps the tuber there was broken months ago.

'A woman?' she said slowly. 'You know, I've been trying to keep a woman in the frame, in my mind's eye, all along. Assuming nothing. The good old rule. But somehow I never really thought the poisoner could be female.'

'Woman's point of view. No, tell the truth, I had the same trouble as yourself. And even now I'm not quite happy with the notion of the poisoner being a female. But then I'm an old-fashioned family man, I suppose.'

'Family man, yes. But old-fashioned, I don't think so.'

'Well, that's as may be. But what I want

from you is not your half-arsed compliments, but yourself sitting here, out of sight if you like, while I get my teeth into this fella Bruce Grant.'

'Pat, I can't. John gave me such a lecture half an hour ago.'

'Telling you you've got to look after yourself, is it? Well, if you can't, you can't.'

'No. No, Pat, I'll come. I'll come. If the poisoner's to be caught, and if your Bruce Grant saw him — saw her. Her. Her. Then if my being there when you interview Grant will be any help, I'll be there.'

'Good girl. Half-past two, here. But take a taxi, mind. We don't want you back in St Ozzie's again.'

11

I'm back on the job, back in the Job, Harriet thought with emotion bubbling hard, as having changed into the grey pleated skirt and the white shirt she generally wore for work, she sat in a tiny cubicle next to Interview Room One at the central police station. Perched up in the corner above her there was the blue-lit monitor screen with its camera focused on whoever might occupy the interviewee's chair at the bare square table next door.

She waited.

In two minutes or perhaps three, she said to herself, Pat Murphy will lead in this man, Bruce Grant, who says he saw who put aconitine into my Campari soda. All right, if I observe anything useful, I shan't, as the poisoner's victim, be able to appear in court. But, never mind that, this is police work and I am engaged in it. This is no longer pussyfooting around with a retired primary school teacher hoping to find a monkshood plant from which the poisoner may have dug up its deadly tuber. This is it, the real thing.

The blue screen above her showed a sudden movement. The door of the interview room had been thrust wide open. Pat Murphy's burly, bear-like form appeared, guiding in, hand on elbow, Bruce Grant.

He seemed to be in his late thirties, thin face dark with indifferent shaving, sleepy-eyed, ganglingly tall. He was wearing, surprisingly, the uniform that Majestic issued to its security staff. Perhaps, she thought, he hopes it will add to the authority of what he is going to tell Pat.

So who is the woman he's going to describe? The woman he saw dropping something into my tall, half-empty glass as I lay there in the sun, vulnerably all but naked? Will I recognize her as someone I've seen before? Be able to put a name to her?

But forget speculation. Pat's seated himself. He's going to begin.

'Well now, Mr Grant, they tell me at the Meads police station that you saw who poisoned the lady at the Majestic Sports and Social Club on August bank holiday Monday. So just what was it you did see? Did you actually notice someone putting something into the glass of bright red drink which Mrs Harriet Piddock had beside her?'

'You trying to say I didn't?'

Pretty truculent that. What's wrong with

136

the fellow? But perhaps Pat was being a bit impatient.

'Not at all, Mr Grant, not at all. So, why don't you just tell me in your own way what it was you saw?'

Ah, that's better. Grant looks more co-operative now.

'Saw a woman, didn't I? Old woman. Saw her go creeping up to where that lady was on that recliner, and then I did see her pour something liquid into that glass. While Mrs Whatever-you-said was asleep.'

'So, can you tell me what this old woman looked like? Were you at your post on the gate when you saw her?'

''Course I was. Never leave it, do I? What I'm paid for. I'm on duty there, see. Never mind how bloody boring it gets I gotter stand there.'

'Right you are. So this woman you saw must have come past you earlier on. Did you take note of her then?'

'No, I didn't. Lovely sunny morning like it was bank holiday, you get 'em streaming past by the dozen, all talking and yapping. Girls a sight to see, too. It takes us all our time to check they got their membership cards.'

'So you and your mate were busy men, though you did have time to look about and see this old woman go creeping up to where the lady was stretched out there?'

'Yeah, 'course I had time. It slackens off after a bit, you know. Slackens off. And that's when I saw her creeping up to where that Mrs Piddock was lying. And then I saw her put that stuff into the drink. Definite.'

'All right, you saw her. So what did she look like?'

Bruce Grant seemed to be having some difficulty in producing an answer.

Okay, he doesn't seem to be particularly intelligent, Harriet thought. He may just be having trouble getting the words right.

'Looked like an old woman,' Grant said at last. 'Sort of bent and creeping, like I said.'

'Well now, that's not a great deal for you to have noticed. You'd been watching her, hadn't you, watching her while she crept up and then put something into that drink?'

'I told you.'

'You did, you did indeed. But you haven't managed to tell me just what she looked like. You know, if we're going to catch her before she poisons any more people, we've got to have the best description we can get.'

Bruce Grant, there on the screen, shifted about a little on his chair opposite Pat.

'It's hard to think,' he complained.

'But try, Mr Grant. Try.'

'Well, she had on a sort of . . . I dunno. A

sort of cloak thing.'

'Right. A sort of cloak. Colour?'

A momentary hesitation.

'Green. Yes, green.'

'Light green or dark?'

No hesitation now.

'Oh, dark. Yes, dark green.'

'And what else besides the cloak?'

'I dunno. I mean, when you see someone, old woman like that, all bent over, pouring something into someone's drink, you don't go thinking about what clothes she has on. Do you?'

'I dare say you don't. But what about her face? Did you see her face while she was pouring the stuff in? How far, now, would you say it was from the gate to the pool?'

'I was near enough. I saw what I saw.'

'So how much did you see of this old woman's face? If we're to get our useful description, that's what we really need, what her face was like.'

'Yeah, yeah. Her face. She was old, like, wrinkled and, yeah, with a hook of a nose. And . . . and her hair was sort of whitish, and long and straggly. And she looked evil. Just evil.'

Evil? For God's sake, what sort of a description is that? If he can't do better than this, Pat's never going to get any further forward. He can hardly have every police officer in the force going about with eyes skinned for a bent old woman who looks *evil*.

★ ★ ★

By the end of the long session they were, in fact, a little further forward, if only a little. Pat, Harriet thought, had been wonderfully patient with the stupid man on the other side of the table. But he had been able to do no more than screw one or two more details out of him. Yes, he had not thought much about that bank holiday happening, not until he had chanced to read a copy of the *Evening Star* — all that about poisonings — then he had remembered. No, he hadn't seen the old woman leave the club. But then a lot of people had begun to go, and it wasn't his duty to take any particular notice of them.

No wonder, Harriet thought. If the guests at the Majestic Insurance prize-giving had made their hasty exits when Sir Billy was so tumultuously sick, then there would have been a good many people at the pool that holiday Monday who would have thought it best to leave when John led me off at top speed, already beginning to spew out that poison, to — which was it? The Ladies or the Gents? I forget what he said.

140

And dumb Bruce Grant had managed to add a long skirt — 'grey, I dunno, yeah, sort o' greyish,' — to his description of the woman who had, it seemed, poured out that aconitine. The poison she might have carried round with her for years, if Agatha Christie's dispenser was anything to go by, waiting for the moment of life or death. My moment of life or death. But why did she choose that particular moment? Why did she choose me? Did she somehow know who I was, an authority figure, a senior police officer? Right, a crazed old woman, if that is what Grant's poisoner is, may well have nurtured some hate of that sort. Or was it simply that, lying there wearing only my minimal bathers, I looked particularly vulnerable? Somehow temptingly vulnerable?

Pat Murphy, his witness disposed of, came in.

'So, Harriet, what did you think?'

'I don't know, Pat, I really don't know. I mean, he was firm about seeing what he did, so he must have seen something, somebody, even if it went out of his mind almost straight away. But why, when you did all you could, didn't he give you a better description?'

'Well, the fella was a fair distance away. I've just taken a quick look at the plan the Scenes-of-Crime people drew up. It's all of thirty yards, or metres as they will call them nowadays, from the gate to the place where you were lying. More even. So he mightn't have seen all that much.'

'No, I suppose not. But he was quite detailed about her pouring the stuff into my drink.'

'He was. And I'll tell you what I'll do, soon as I get a moment. I'll have a bit of a reconstruction. Not with you, not with you. I don't want to put you back in hospital. But I'll have a WDC get into her swimsuit and lie there, and I'll have a constable at the gate, someone about the height of that long streak of a fella. And we'll see what he can see. That should tell us just how much anyone could observe, one way or another.'

'And in the meanwhile..?'

Pat heaved a huge sigh.

'I'll be seeing Grant's mate on the gate there,' he said. 'Might get some corroboration out of him. And then each of the female witnesses at the pool will have to be interviewed once more to see if any of them fits at all your man Grant's description, or if anyone saw an old woman who does. And more than half of the hundred and twenty-seven we've got are women. Then, if we get no luck, we'll have to tackle all the men again, the men and, damn it, the boys.

142

As if my resources aren't stretched enough as it is.'

★ ★ ★

Harriet, suddenly so tired she could hardly walk, had gone home then. Luckily, censorious John was still at work. All right, she thought, I'll tell him all about my afternoon. One day. When this nameless old crone that dismal Bruce Grant saw has been caught. And from now on I really will take things quietly. God, I feel dopey enough now, and all I've done is to take a couple of taxi rides and sit watching that monitor screen while Pat attempted to squeeze information out of Grant.

But why was Grant so unforthcoming? All right, he's not the best communicator in the world, and it could be that the right words just elude him, have never before entered his head. Yet I feel something was wrong about him.

Wrong? No, call it *not quite right*. I couldn't pin it down as I watched from the cubicle, the way I had to concentrate with all the force that's left to me. But —

No, wait. Here's one thing. Grant mentioned me, lying there on the recliner, and he described the mysterious old woman, if not in detail, at least moderately clearly, her hooked nose, her straggly white hair, the cloak, the skirt. But he never described with a single detail the person he saw being poisoned. Me. And me, not dressed in any ordinary way. Far from it. Me, lying there in the bikini I put on only when it's so hot I feel I must have maximum exposure to whatever wafts of breeze there are. The almost naked me.

And Grant's a man, isn't he? Didn't he comment on *girls a sight to see* going past him through the gate? He must have had some reaction to me, even if there was a lot of so-called talent about. But he didn't. He never indicated in any way that the victim of his old woman was almost naked.

I wish I'd realized this when I was discussing Grant with Pat. Call him now? But is my near-nakedness much of a fact for his files? And won't he, in any case, have spotted the inconsistency for himself? And perhaps he didn't quite like to mention it to me. Pat, the decent family man, God bless him.

So, no, leave it, leave it. If only because Pat's stretched to the utmost. Under maximum pressure. And there'll be another opportunity at some time. Plenty of them.

But now, if not bed, I need at least to lie down on the sofa, and sleep. I need to. I need to.

12

For all her determination not to be stuck day after day in bed, Harriet realized next morning that she did not in the least want to get up. And when John poked his head in at the door to say he would bring her breakfast before he left for the office, she succumbed. And then ate scarcely any of the little rack of toast he left her with, and failed to finish her coffee.

She lay there vaguely cursing herself for her lassitude. A relapse? All right, I suppose I might have expected something like this. But why did it have to happen when, with a description of the poisoner secured, however sketchy, things seemed to be going well at last? Answer? Because things were going well.

And then oblivion again. Until Mrs Pickstock tapped on the door and, neat head of grey curls half-in, half-out, said brightly, 'Hubby thought you were a bit off-colour today so he asked me to keep a special eye on you.'

So it was Four-bean and Ginger soup again.

One good sign, Harriet thought, as,

watched at every spoonful by the proud shopper at Organics 'R Go, she actually managed to finish the bowl. I'm obviously better than I was last time I was presented with this appalling stuff. So progress. I'm making a little progress.

She found, though, that she had no inclination to test this by getting up and getting dressed. Then later Mrs Pickstock came positively barging in holding the newly delivered *Evening Star*.

'Look, look,' she jabbered out, voice squeaking with excitement. 'They've found who it was who poisoned you. A Majestic Insurance security man saw her. It . . . it was a woman after all. It's all in the paper. I took a peek as I came up the stairs. A wicked-looking woman who crept up to where you were asleep, dear, and poured that terrible poison into the drink you had there, the Camp-something. And then . . . then she just crept away and no one stopped her. I must say I think they ought to — '

'Mrs Pickstock, do let me see it,' Harriet managed to say quite calmly, despite her rising exasperation.

'Oh, yes. Yes, dear, I quite forgot you won't know anything about it. Here you are then. Here you are. Yes, you'll be in the news again today. I wonder if we won't have more of those reporters banging on the door, not that you knew anything about the first lot. Hubby said you mustn't on any account be disturbed by them. Perhaps now we'll have the television, too. But I'll chase them away. Don't you worry.'

Ignoring the bright babble, Harriet saw that almost half the *Star* front page had been devoted to a full-colour picture of the familiar dimly dark face of Bruce Grant, the man who had identified 'the Poisoner'. The *Star*'s capital *P* positively leapt from the columns.

She looked again at Grant's full-colour face.

Familiar, yes, yet not quite familiar. All right, it may be because all I've seen of him is on that monitor screen that I'm missing some subtle diff — No. No, I've got it. In the photo here that permanently sullen look I saw has gone. Instead, plainly now I've noticed it, there's an expression of self-satisfaction. Yes, that's it. The cat that's got the cream. A real cliché expression illustrated.

So what cream has the cat got?

In a moment she knew.

He's got attention. He's someone now, getting his picture in the paper. As if he's a star footballer. At one bound he's left the dull routine of a security man, stuck all day or all night at whatever post he's been assigned to, and he's a celebrity. Someone who'll be recognized in the street. He's famous, or so he thinks. And, yes, didn't he say to Pat in the interview room that it got bloody boring standing at the Club gate all morning? So . . . so, can it be that he thought eventually, in that slow way of his, that his life would be set glowing with excitement if he had actually seen the Poisoner that the *Star*, as well as Radio Birchester and Birchester TV and even the more sensational of the nationals were headlining?

But what does that mean? Can it . . . can this be right? Is it possible that Grant made up the story he produced at the Meads PS?

But, if he did, why did he invent that particular woman? Can he have seen someone somewhat like her at the pool? Have even seen them come near to me there? And based his firm identification on them? Is that possible?

No. No, I won't pass this idea on. I'd better not. It may be, for God's sake, just another of those hit-or-miss fantasies I plagued Pat with earlier. Thinking, when I was at my most feeble, that John had put the poison in my drink, then believing because of a coincidence in the surnames of the next two victims, MNO, that the whole thing was an Agatha Christie conspiracy against me.

But I'll still keep it in mind. I'll go over the idea again.

When I feel my head is clearer.

★ ★ ★

But before she had come to feel her mind was in less of a state of fluffy confusion she was subjected to a new shock. The phone beside the bed shrilled out, waking her from a restless half-sleep. It was Pat Murphy. But she found she could respond only listlessly to his first anxious inquiries about her wellbeing. 'Yes, I'm okay, Pat, more or less, thank you.' And, in the relapse into weariness which she now seemed entrapped in, her energy was slipping away yet more rapidly as she waited for him to tell her why he was calling.

'Listen then, Harriet, there's something you could maybe help me with. We've been working away again at the witnesses round the Club pool, in the light of Grant's evidence. So this is what I'm doing. I've tasked my lads and lasses with getting just two answers from those people, by phone if they can: Did you see last bank holiday Monday an old woman in a green cloak-like garment with straggly white hair and a hooked nose? And for such female witnesses that they do have to go and see: Does the

149

person you are addressing fit that description, taking into account she may be wearing altogether different clothes? Well, so far we've got no answers to question number one, and we're well through the list, phones here in the incident room going like crazy. No one, so far, has seen Grant's bent old woman. Doesn't necessarily mean she wasn't there, of course. If she's the sneaky creature Grant made her out to be, she could have crept in somehow, round the back or something, right?'

'Yes, Pat. I suppose so.'

'But now,' Pat's voice came ringingly in her ear, 'what we did get was one response to question number two, or a sort of response. But we need only the one if it turns out that this is our woman. Though, I may say, that doesn't look too likely. The lady, name of Dora Long, Mrs Dora Long, elderly widow of a former Majestic director, has got the long white hair all right and, according to the DC who saw her, she's even got a bit of a hooky nose and she's certainly arthritic. So she may go about — Grant's words — bent over. But the DC was a fella, and not too good on describing females. Well, I'd like, of course, seeing how it just may be the big breakthrough, is to go and have a look at Mrs Long meself. But you know the pressure I'm under, Harriet. A hundred and one priority tasks. Here from six in the morning, and it's past midnight before I've done writing up my Personal Record.'

Harriet, by now, knew what was coming.

She was going to be asked to interview Mrs Long. And she quailed at the thought. What if that tentative identification turned out to be good? Am I going to come face-to-face with the woman Bruce Grant saw creep up to me and put aconitine into my Campari soda? If he did.

All right, I was asleep when it was done, but I may not have dropped off altogether when she began to approach. I may have seen her, though I've no recollection of it. Except perhaps, just perhaps, those flashes of something black and white are linked to something I saw as I lay there on the recliner before sleep descended?

Can I do this? Can I face it? Oh God, I feel so tired.

She must have failed to reply to whatever final question Pat had asked, because she heard him saying urgently *Harriet? Harriet?*

'Yes, Pat, yes.'

'Ah, I knew you would. I knew it. It's a lot to ask, but I knew you'd say yes if you could do it at all.'

Oh my God, he thinks when I said yes I

wasn't just acknowledging that I was hearing him. He thinks I've agreed. I've agreed.

Well, haven't I really after all? It's something I must do. Something I ought to do. It may all come to nothing. But Pat's relying on me. And if anyone has a duty to assist to the utmost in the hunt for the *Star*'s capital-P Poisoner, it's their first victim, the survivor.

'Yes, Pat, I'll go and see her. When do you think I should?

★ ★ ★

By next morning at eleven, the time Pat had arranged for her to see Mrs Long — her house, it turned out, was only some five minutes from Harriet's — she felt she had enough energy to walk the short distance. She had said nothing about what she intended to do to stern John, and she had done no more than leave a note for Mrs Pickstock, safely banging about in the kitchen.

She still felt a knot of anxiety at the prospect of just possibly coming face-to-face with the woman who might have poisoned her. But she had thought out the situation carefully, and had come to the conclusion that, if there was to be any more to the interview than simply checking a rather too hazy identification, Pat would not have suggested it was something she could do for him. No doubt he had reckoned that a gradual return to proper police work, even if it was unofficial, would be good for her. And rid her of such wild notions as the MNO murders.

But, she thought now, what if my idea, not mentioned to Pat, that Grant has fabricated his description of the Poisoner is really just another of my wild, brain-fuzzed notions? What if Grant, as far as he could, has accurately described my would-be murderer and the DC who saw her has truly identified her?

She came to a sudden halt, there where she was, feeling herself locked rigid with something like pure fear.

She fought against it. And after perhaps a minute found she was able to go forwards again.

Three minutes later, when Mrs Long opened her door to her ring at the bell, she knew that at least she was not face-to-face with the old woman who, according to Bruce Grant, had poured poison into her Campari. Yes, this elderly woman, dressed in a well-cut pale blue suit, did have long hair, though it was pale grey rather than white. But it was carefully combed into a neat chignon. And,

153

yes, though she was holding the upper part of her body at a slight angle, the result most probably of arthritis, she could hardly be described as being *all bent over*. And, yes, again, her nose, which was small, could just be seen as hooked. But the whole was so far from Grant's witch-like picture that the DC who had sent back that report really must be too gullible ever to rise from his present humble rank.

Still, an interview had been arranged and must be conducted.

Conducted it was, over coffee and a plate of wafer-thin ginger biscuits, though Harriet, still feeling nauseous after her moment of panic on the way, could not bring herself even to try one of those.

'Oh, my dear, so it was you who was poisoned at the Club,' Mrs Long exclaimed when Harriet had told her, with all the tact she could summon up, that it had been thought she fitted a description of a woman seen, apparently, putting something into her Campari.

'Yes,' she said, 'it seems I was the first victim of this Poisoner who's been roaming the city. Only, by a wonderful piece of luck, my husband recognized the earliest symptoms and took immediate action.'

Yet once more she felt John's probing

154

fingers in her throat.

Will I ever banish this awful physical throwback, she asked herself unable to check a shudder.

Mrs Long must have seen her look of distress because she immediately led the conversation in a new direction.

'And you say that this security man — whatever was his name? I read it in the paper yesterday — actually claimed to have seen me pouring something into your drink?'

'No, no. He didn't go so far as to describe someone precisely like you. No, he gave us in fact a description of someone who was hardly the sort of person you would expect to find at the Majestic Social Club, a sort of ugly old crone dressed in some sort of green cloak.'

'Well,' Mrs Long said, with a smile, 'I really think I am not quite like that. And neither, for the matter of that, did I see anyone at the pool that morning who looked at all like it, though there were one or two rather odd people in the crowd there.'

'Odd people?' Harriet asked, with a sudden stir of interest.

'Well, perhaps I'm being a little censorious. But people at the pool this summer have often been not quite the sort who used to come when my husband was a Majestic director. I even wondered, when there's been a bigger crowd than usual as there was on the bank holiday, whether the men on the gate are as conscientious as they ought to be in examining membership cards.'

'Yes,' Harriet said. 'Yes, Mrs Long, I think that's something I should bring to the attention of Detective Superintendent Murphy, the Senior Investigating Officer for the case. Thank you very much.'

★ ★ ★

It was early next afternoon, however, when the *Evening Star* was sent rattling through the letterbox, that Harriet's ideas about Bruce Grant and the old crone he had, by dribs and drabs, described, took on a more solid shape. The paper's front-page picture was devoted once again to the Poisoner. This time it was not a colour photo of Bruce Grant looking pleased with himself, but an artist's full-colour impression of the person Grant had described. It was based, so the caption below said, *on an extensive and searching new interview with Bruce Grant (see p. 2).*

Looking at it, Harriet realized that the artist must have got from Grant much the same basic details as Pat Murphy had squeezed out of him. There was the straggly whitish hair, the strongly hooked nose, the deep wrinkles and the dark-green cloak just visible round the shoulders. But now the eyes were shown as a glittering green and, on a noticeably pointed chin, there were distinctly three curling black hairs.

It was these romantic additions that finally gave it to Harriet. She was looking at nothing less than the picture of a witch. A picture one might have found — had the artist? — as an illustration in an old-fashioned book of fairy stories, though perhaps made a little more evil-looking.

Yes, surely Bruce Grant saw nothing at all of whoever put poison in my Campari soda. He invented the whole thing. He did.

She dropped the paper to the floor at her feet, strode out of the hall and into the sitting-room, picked up the phone and punched out the number for Pat Murphy's mobile.

'Pat, your Bruce Grant made the whole thing up.'

There was a moment's silence at the far end.

'Did he now? You know, I'm not surprised to hear it. But what makes you say so?'

'Have you seen today's *Evening Star*?'

'I have. You mean the picture on page one? It's pretty much the old harridan Grant described to us. So why do you say he invented her?'

'Oh, I do, Pat. I do indeed. You see, that picture is not of anyone who could possibly have been at the pool that day. It's a picture out of *Grimm's Fairy Tales* or any cheap children's book, or even from a comic based on those. It's the picture of a witch, and nothing else.'

'You're right about that. By God, you're absolutely right. You know, every time I had occasion to mention that description I got out of Grant, the word *witch* would come floating into my head, and I, like an eejit, did my best not to use the word so as to keep that description as factual as I could.'

A rueful chuckle came down the line.

'And, you know what,' Pat suddenly bounced out, 'if this is right and Grant concocted his whole story, something I see as distinctly possible, then, damn and blast, we're looking for just anyone once again. Just anyone at all, man or woman.'

'We are, Pat. We must be. We're right back to the beginning.'

She checked herself.

'Or,' she said cautiously. 'Or perhaps not.'

'What's this? Another one of your wild ideas?'

She thought for a moment.

'No, I don't think this is. For one thing I'm not the only one who came across this.'

'All right. Was John the other one? If he was, I'd be altogether more inclined to go along with it, whatever it is.'

Then she realized who it was she was going to have to name as backing her up. Not solid John, but twittery, eighty-year-old — no, 'in my eightieth year' — Miss Earwaker.

'Listen, Pat, and don't jump down my throat when I tell you.'

'Would I do such a thing now?'

'All right, I'll trust you. Pat, there's a lady I've been talking to recently. She once taught the twins at their primary, and she was a great expert on wild flowers. Her name's Miss Earwaker.'

'Earwigger? Did you say Earwigger? Now, Harriet, I promised to let you have your say, but I warn you, you're getting near the edge. Very near.'

'Now, calm down, Pat. Calm down. I did not say *Earwigger*. I said — listen — Earwaker. It's an odd name, but there are a number of Earwakers about. And this is the point. I thought of asking Miss Earwaker where in the countryside within reach of the city monkshood might be found. And — '

'Yes, that's not a bad idea. Inquiries at city gardens have got nowhere. Tell your old girl to keep at it.'

'Pat, she has. She took me to two possible sites, and at the second one, Halsell Common, on a rural bus route from the city, note, we found not only some monkshood plants, but a monkshood plant where someone had been digging at the roots and had located a tuber.'

'A tuber?'

'Like a potato, Pat, for heaven's sake. And it's the really poisonous part of the plant. And, more, we got a description from an old man out there of a person he saw digging at it.'

'A witch-like old woman?'

'Not at all. A man. And, more, a man wearing a grey three-piece suit and a tie. In other words, as likely as not, a man straight from the city here.'

'For God's sake, Harriet, when was this?'

'It was just before our friend Bruce Grant stepped into the police station at the Meads and announced he'd seen on old woman poison me. Which is why, until now, I've said nothing.'

'Afraid crass old Pat Murphy would — what was it you said just now? — jump down your throat?'

160

'Well, yes. Yes, that did hold me back as well.'

'All right, from here on out I'll listen to your every word, however damn nonsensical. But now, tell me, what's the name of your witness there out at Halsell Common? Name and address?'

It was then that Harriet had to confess to the debacle that had occurred when she had seen a group of hooligans on bikes attacking Miss Earwaker's precious Honda.

Pat was understanding, and eventually agreed there was probably not much to be lost if he sent a reliable detective out to question the old man more thoroughly.

'If he gets something out of your obstinate old devil,' he said, 'then I'll forget about setting up my reconstruction to get proof Bruce Grant's a liar. But when we have the handcuffs on the Poisoner, I'll give Grant a talking-to he won't forget in a hurry.'

★ ★ ★

But that moment of dizzying hope was to fade. Pat Murphy rang and told her that out at Halsell Common one of his most experienced detective sergeants had interviewed the old man at the half-ruined cottage, Ernest Brown by name. And he had

161

been no more successful than Miss Earwaker had been. The door had not been slammed in his face, but he had been able to learn nothing more about the digger at the monkshood plant beyond that he was a small man and that he was wearing a grey suit with a waistcoat and a tie.

And somehow that unexpected disappointment seemed to have plunged the whole inquiry into the doldrums. None of the outstanding interviews of the witnesses at the pool or at the club hall where Sir Billy Bell had met his end had produced anything at all worthwhile, let alone the few remaining uninterviewed youths from the Virgin and Vicar or the youngsters who had seen poor Tommy O'Brien die in City Hall Square. So Pat's officers were left drearily to patrol the streets, to go into the pubs and the coffee shops, and even into Birchester's smart restaurants, all on the faint chance that they would catch either a crone-like old woman or a small man in, possibly, a grey three-piece suit in the act of tipping something into someone's drink.

The days passed, too, mysteriously without the dreaded news of a sixth poisoning. And, as if in sympathy, the prolonged Indian summer came to an end, not with the bang of a gigantic thunderstorm but with the whimper of continuous soft rain. Day after day it rained. Rained and rained with hardly a break. Pat, still at the central police station at almost every hour that passed, was becoming in his regular calls to Harriet more and more depressed.

Every day, with no news of another poisoning to report, Birchester Television and the *Evening Star* found inaction almost as good a stick as action with which to belabour Detective Superintendent Murphy's broad back. The *Star* stuck firmly to its unmasking of the witch-like old woman as the Poisoner, while the TV havered between her and a mystery man. Pat, too, was stalled, if for a different reason. He was unable to disprove with a reconstruction Bruce Grant's identification because, in all the misty rain, he could not reproduce the sun-sweltering conditions when Harriet, on the point of death, had been rushed away to St Oswald's.

'Sure,' he said once, 'I'd have a WDC in a bikini the like of yours out there in two minutes, naked to the rain, if I thought visibility on a desperate day like this would still nail your man Grant. But it wouldn't, so I won't.'

Harriet, feeling herself almost hour by hour more ready to take a part in the investigation, could only agree. She felt able now to take short strolls morning and afternoon, drizzle or no drizzle, into the nearer streets of the city in the hope that it might be she who saw what none of Pat's officers had seen so far: a hand hovering over a cup or glass about to pour something in. In fact, when she peered into the few coffee shops and the occasional pub in her residential area all that she saw was hands kept flat over the tops of cups or mugs, or newspapers laid over beer glasses that were, even for a few seconds, not under their owners' eyes.

On Sunday morning, over the breakfast croissants John had got from the shop in smart Aslough Parade which prided itself on selling them fresh from the oven, she even found herself wanting to have a look at one of the bulky newspapers he was speedily flipping through, leaving on the floor underneath him a messy heap of discarded advertising brochures and unwanted supplements. She realized that this was the first time she had felt that much curiosity about the goings-on in the great world, aside from her duty-urged reading of any news or half-news about the Poisoner in the *Evening Star*.

'When you've finished with that one,' she said to John, 'you might pass it over.'

'Well, who's back to her old self?'

'I wouldn't say that, quite. But, yes, I don't

feel as awful as I did a week ago. I might even have a go at the garden later on, if the rain eases up. If I give the seed-pods on the sweetpeas a good picking-over we may yet get a final batch of flowers.'

'Well, if you feel up to tackling forty-odd Sunday morning pages of mostly guff, you have to be fitter than you were, by a long way. Look at this. Big page one headline: *Gays on the March*. And what's it all about? Nothing. Just that there's going to be, later on today, a demo down in London, a few hundred gays and lesbians having a bit of a parade.'

'At least they'll be having a good day for it. The radio said this morning it's going to be hot and sunny down there.'

'Rather them than me, though. I'd had enough of the heat before it came to an end.'

'Yes, indeed. But nothing in the paper about the problems of the fair city of Birchester?'

'Not a thing, unless I've missed a paragraph tucked away on an inside page. But I suppose, with nothing new having happened since poor old Sir Billy's death, the story's gone dead as far as they're concerned down in the south.'

'I imagine so. And when is the story going to break into life again here?'

13

Eerily unsettling as the inexplicable lull in the Poisoner's activities had been, it did not last beyond the next twenty-four hours. As Harriet lay, on Monday morning, trying to decide if it was time to get up or whether she could allow herself another quarter of an hour in bed, she heard the phone.

She began heaving herself up to answer. But after just two rings it ceased. She realized that John must not have left the house, and sank back on her pillow.

Then, some three or four minutes later, she heard his hurried steps on the stairs.

What? Who ..? Why? Why, if it was for me, isn't he just calling to me up here?

She felt her heart at once beating too fast.

Before she had managed to control it John came in.

'Bad news,' he said. 'Nothing to worry about, not the twins or anything. But not good all the same.'

She pushed herself up into a sitting position.

'It was Pat Murphy, of course,' John said. 'To tell you it looks as if the Poisoner has struck again now. But this time in London.'

'London? He's sure?'

'Oh yes, almost certain. It happened there yesterday, and now, all bar the final tests, it's been confirmed as poisoning with aconitine. It can hardly be a coincidence.'

'No, I should say not. But do you know any more?'

'Yes. You remember I said something yesterday, while we were reading the Sundays, about a Gay March down in London? Well, apparently, one of the marchers, a lesbian by the name of Margery, or Marge, something-or-other, was offered a can of drink — it was a fiercely hot day down there — by someone watching the show from the pavement. And the lady took a big swig from the already opened can. And . . . well, we both know what must have happened then.'

'That twitch at the hint of a bad taste. The tingling and pricking on the tongue, that feeling of freezing cold . . . ' She could not check a sudden shuddering. 'And then, what you saved me from with your pushing and probing fingers, the vomiting that's violent but not violent enough.'

'Exactly.'

Harriet felt then a prickle of unease at the back of her mind. Was there something wrong about that list of her symptoms? Something she ought to be able to lay a finger on? Not to do with Margery or Marge down in London, but wrong in some other way?

But no explanation came to her.

She shook her head.

'And does Pat know any more than that?' she asked.

'He certainly does. Just before he rang he'd been told that the National Crime Squad is taking over the whole investigation. Their team will be arriving in a few hours.'

'Yes. I suppose that's to be expected. It's become a nationwide affair now. I can't say I'm sorry either. A poisoner who poisons at random and seems never to leave a clue; it's become too much for a single police force to deal with. Not that Pat hasn't been doing everything that's there to be done. And I dare say it'll be too much for the NCS, come to that. But at least there'll be more personnel available.'

'Yes. But there's something else I've got to tell you.'

There was a plainly anxious note in his voice.

'What? What is it?'

'Just this. Pat wants you to come down to the incident room as soon as you can.'

'Did he say why? Why now?'

'He didn't actually. He just said he

wouldn't have asked unless he felt he had to, but that he'd like you to be there before the National Crime Squad team make their appearance. Which will be first thing this afternoon. But I did learn from him, incidentally, that Mrs Piddock took it into her head the other day to resume her existence as Detective Superintendent Martens and interview a witness, one Mrs Dora Long. All without saying anything about it to her anxious husband, at the time or afterwards.'

'Oh God, yes. Yes, well, I'm sorry. But, well, I knew you'd kick up a fuss if I told you, and so . . . I thought what you didn't know wouldn't do you any harm.'

'Did you indeed? So what are you going to do if I say to you now that, however much better you think you are, you're still under medical advice to take things quietly and that you oughtn't to be going over to Waterloo Gardens?'

Harriet sat there in her rumpled bed and tried to think what her answer should be.

'All right,' she said at last, 'you know perfectly well that I am going to go, and I know perfectly well that in an ideal world I'd stay lolling about at home. And, yes, I know that's probably what I ought to do if I don't want to risk my head or my health being permanently damaged by what the

Poisoner did to me.'

'Well then,' John said, 'I'll run you over there as soon as you're ready.'

She felt a rush of affection for the understanding man she'd married all those years ago. But all the reward she felt capable of offering him at this fraught moment was a small smile.

★ ★ ★

'Harriet, thank God.' When Pat Murphy's warm exclamation came to her ears she felt such a jolt of pleasure that tears almost came into her eyes. I'm wanted, she thought. I'm here in the incident room and Pat, the Senior Investigating Officer for perhaps the most serious crimes that have ever occurred in Birchester, is plainly glad I'm here.

'So,' she said, by way of finding out why Pat had asked for her so pressingly, 'we're about to be privileged to have the mighty National Crime Squad coming up from London.'

'A privilege I'd rather not have been offered, so I wouldn't. The high-and-mighty interfering buggers. That's why — I'm not ashamed to say it — I'm wanting a kind of angel hovering near.'

170

So, that's my answer.

'Well, yes, Pat,' she said. 'I know what you mean. Those people are going to be critical, whether they show it or not. The *we know best* mob. Yet I suppose, in a way, it's a good thing to have as much backing as possible. If the hand-picked Londoners can advance things even a little, there's more hope of catching this man. Or this evil woman, if we're to believe fantasist Bruce Grant.'

Pat had opened his mouth to reply when, with two crashing thumps, the double doors of the room banged open and in strode an officer in uniform with the insignia of a Metropolitan Police commander at his shoulders.

Early. An altogether unexpectedly early arrival.

'Rance,' he announced. 'You'll know the name.'

Commander Rance was, Harriet took in, a man of just below average height. But he was holding himself so erect that he seemed to be as tall as Pat Murphy himself. A thin face. A strip of narrow moustache above tight-set lips. Two sharply piercing grey eyes.

At once Pat strode over towards him, a grizzly bear poised between bun-hungry friendliness and long-clawed aggression.

'Detective Superintendent Murphy,' he said.

'So the National Crime Squad has come to the rescue.'

Harriet, taking a step backwards out of the way, could not help allowing herself an inward smile at the manner in which Pat had managed to imbue the words with neither a trace of irony nor a hint of subservience. No fool at all, Pat Murphy, despite his lumbering appearance.

Behind Commander Rance as he stepped further into the big room there came a dozen other Squad members, in an array of smart suits rather than in the uniform their leader had chosen to wear.

'Yes,' Rance snapped. 'The NCS, here to see what's to be done.'

'Tell you the first thing to be done, boss,' one of the Squad chipped in, 'find a good hotel and a decent lunch.'

He turned to Pat.

'Where's the best place in this town of yours?' he said.

Pat looked at him steadily.

'There's a sandwich bar at the corner where they do a very reasonable class of baguette,' he answered. 'I've been living on them here for the past month, those and canteen tea, and I'm none the worse. As for a hotel, we'll give you a list when you've settled in.'

172

'Ah, well, mate, in the Squad we take better care of ourselves than chewing on baguettes.'

'It's *Superintendent*. When you're not calling me *sir*.'

'Have it your own way . . . sir. But just tell us where we can get a good lunch. We've been belting up the motorway and we're hungry.'

'That'll do, Marsh,' Commander Rance said. 'Ask someone else, and when you go, be back here in one hour, no less.'

'Very good, sir.'

Rance turned back to Pat.

'Right, Mr Murphy. Be so good as to put me in the up-to-the-minute picture. Your office, if you please.'

★　★　★

Harriet, listening to good wishes and inquiries from officers she knew, could not quell a growing feeling of depression. Not ten minutes earlier she had been experiencing a sense of pure jubilation at being in the big, noise-buzzing room with its phones constantly ringing, its fax machines chattering, its computer screens winking with envelope icons for incoming e-mails. She had been welcomed into the nerve-centre of the operation. It was where she had longed to be able to play a part, however unofficially. But now, even before she had had time to ask Pat what the state of play was and to bring him the titbit she had learnt from Mrs Long about the manning of the gate at the Club, she was acutely aware that the barging-in Londoners were intent on running the whole investigation.

What part can I play now, she asked herself, when it's plain enough that Commander Rance is going to take over, lock, stock and barrel? Look how he pretty well marched Pat off to give him the latest information, the information Pat was going to give to me.

She wondered whether she should simply leave Pat a note and make her way back home. To sit idly. Or go back to days in bed. But, she told herself, in the end that would be to admit defeat. And that was something she was not going to do.

So she accepted an offer of a cup of tea from a DC she had worked with once — Christ, I can't remember his name, I know it and I just can't remember it — and sat where she was. Time passed.

The NCS team returned from whatever lunch they had secured for themselves, a good one it seemed from the aroma of alcohol that swept in with them. She watched them for a little, noting their total failure to mix with the Birchester officers.

Then Commander Rance came down with Pat from his office.

He went straight up to the low platform at the top end of the room.

'Gentlemen,' he called out. 'A few words with you, if you please.'

The voices in the big room fell away into silence, even those of the slighted women officers.

'Now, I have been hearing Mr Murphy's full report, and I have to tell you that I have formulated the way the investigation is to be carried out from now on.'

A rat-tat of a cough, and he continued.

'It is plain to me that all the incidents that have taken place in Birchester, as well as the one in London yesterday, have been planned with just one object by Target. Target, for the benefit of my own officers, is a woman who has been identified by one of the security staff at the Majestic Insurance Sports and Social Club where the first attempt at poisoning took place. Detective Superintendent Murphy, in his cautious way, appears to have some doubts about this identification, and I intend to see the man who made it, a Mr Bruce Grant, myself in the course of today. But in the meantime let me tell you that I see this woman, Target, as preparing to acquire for herself some very large sum of money. Within days now, believe you me, we are going to be presented with the first of her demands. The investigation will proceed henceforth in expectation of that attempt and in taking steps to frustrate it by arresting the perpetrator. Thank you.'

There came a murmur of renewed optimism from every part of the big room. Harriet noted that the Birchester officers seemed to be as much enthused as the NCS team by Commander Rance's pulsing determination. She hardly was herself, but put that down to the knowledge that she was unlikely now to have any part in the hunt.

'One thing more,' Rance cut into the excited murmuring.

Another sudden hush.

'I understand that this room has been referred to throughout the length of this inquiry as the Incident Room. It is no longer going to be called that. Ladies and gentlemen, you are now standing in the Murder Room. The Murder Room.'

And, again, excitement could be seen to run through all present like so many diverse darting electric currents.

Harriet glanced over at the bull-like form of Pat Murphy, just behind Rance on the platform, a silent figure in his bulging, bright blue suit. Nothing at all in his big, round, red face, with the little blue eyes planted in it like currants in a bun, betrayed either approval or rejection of Rance's stagey change of the room's name, nor of his bright-polished new theory.

But rejection of that, or something not far short of it, was what she herself was beginning now increasingly to feel. She was not sure why she was so opposed. The idea was at least tenable. The history of crime was full enough of examples of icy killers attempting that sort of major blackmail. Yet, apart from her own belief, as yet unsubstantiated, that Bruce Grant's identification of the Poisoner as a witch-like old woman was pure make-believe, she could not help feeling that the Poisoner was acting from a quite different motive. Acting, simply, out of that terrible desire to exercise the power of life or death.

But, up on the platform, Commander Rance was getting the investigation on his own lines rapidly under way, body leaning eagerly forward, eyes glittering with the intensity of his purpose. Beside him, Pat stood, a monument to showing no opinion.

For a quarter of an hour or more Rance hammered on. New tasks were allocated. Earlier lines of inquiry were abruptly terminated. Among these, Harriet was pained to hear, were two that Pat must have put to Rance out of a determination not to hold anything back. First, no further steps were to be taken about 'an old man who, I'm given to understand, claims to have seen someone digging at a clump of monkshood plants out at a place called Halsell Common, miles from this city' and, next, 'a scheme for reconstructing the circumstances of the first murder, or murder attempt, which is unlikely to take us any further forward'.

So much, she thought, for the little I've been able to contribute to stopping the Poisoner.

But, before Rance had wholly finished, there came a clattering interruption.

The desk-sergeant from the front hall came in, face flushed with excitement and embarrassment. In his fists he was clutching what looked to Harriet like four or five copies of the *Evening Star*.

'Sir, sir,' he positively shouted out. 'Sir, I think you ought to see this at once.'

It was not totally clear whether he was addressing Pat Murphy or Commander Rance. But Rance did not hesitate to jump down from the platform and stride along the length of the big room, hand held out.

He met the sergeant a yard or two short of

where Harriet was standing, and in his eagerness to snatch the copy of the paper that was being offered him, contrived to send the whole bundle skittering to the floor.

So it was that Harriet, accustomed to the paper's layout, was able to read the headline *The Poisoner Writes to the Star.*

Then, a minute or two later, as Rance apparently absorbed in a single gulp the newsprint in front of him, she learnt why the Poisoner had written.

Rance had swung round and mounted the platform again.

'Didn't I tell you?' he barked. 'Here it is. A demand for money. A demand from Target for one million pounds to halt her campaign of murder.'

Harriet would have liked to snatch up one of the copies of the paper Commander Rance had knocked to the floor. But the desk-sergeant had already bent ponderously down, scooped them up and was setting off towards Pat Murphy.

So it was not until a quarter of an hour later, when Pat handed her one of the copies, that she was able to read in full what the Poisoner had said.

The time has come to say why I have thought it appropriate and necessary to bring to an end the lives of a number of citizens of Birchester, and even to show that I have the ability to send to Hell, where they deserve to languish, a person outside the ambit of this wicked city. The lesson must be learnt. It is time for the wickedness to end. It is time to go back to the old ideals, the forgotten ideals, to regain healthy minds in healthy bodies.

For this reason I chose as sacrificial victims on the altar of probity a woman lying obscenely naked beside a swimming pool, a youth indulging in the grossest passions in a drinking den dedicated to displays of flesh, a young woman wantonly lying in the sun almost unclothed in the very heart of the city, a lady of mature years who yet flaunted scarlet lips and scarlet fingernails in a modest tea shop, and that arch corruptor of all that the city should stand for, Sir Billy Bell, owner of establishments throughout Birchester selling gramophone records of the most raucous music set to the lewdest words, the man who has turned once decent cinemas into places showing the vilest of pornography.

I tell you now that all such activities must cease. If within the next week I am not paid, in a manner I shall indicate to the authorities, the sum of one million pounds by way of punishment, I shall continue to eliminate such offenders as I chance upon. I have the best historical precedents for my actions. In the wars that have ravaged the world many, many sinners have perished. Let Birchester beware lest some hundreds die in much the same way that in the War of 1914–1918 sinners choked to death in their thousands or became victims of almost fatal attacks of vomiting illness.

Then, below, the signature. *Mentor.*

She handed the paper back to Pat.

'So it seems I was obscenely naked,' she said, relieved to find something in the letter she could see as more funny than not.

'That aside,' Pat replied with a hint of a grin, 'what do you make of it all?'

'What do you?'

'Ach, no, I asked you first.'

'All right. Let me see. Right, between you and me, I think all that stuff was written by a man.'

She glanced over towards the platform where Commander Rance was talking emphatically to one of his team.

'We won't go into that just now,' Pat said in a heavy whisper. 'So, you tell me. You're the one who notices the little things, specially when it comes to words on paper or, come to that, on the lips. Tell me about anything you may have picked up.'

'Right then. It struck me at once that whoever wrote that letter is educated, not at all likely to be a wizened old crone out of nowhere. He's educated, perhaps even over-educated. I'd guess he's fairly well on in life and the product of some school at a time when schools laid down the rules, whether of grammar or of behaviour.'

'You're right there, I think. He's certainly someone who believes he knows how everybody should behave. But does that help us one little bit to get hold of the fella?'

Now Harriet ventured on a somewhat daring comment, pleased to find herself capable not only of thinking but of putting her thoughts into the right words for Pat.

'Isn't getting hold of the Poisoner,' she said, 'the task now of Commander Rance and his merry men?'

Pat pulled a face.

'And who's at this moment under the command of Mr Rance?' he said. 'And ought to be up there, listening for orders?'

Poor Pat, she thought.

'Oh, I think you'll be able to hold your own. And if you do need a shoulder to have a little cry on, mine's ready and willing.'

Only to find the remark had been overheard, or partially overheard, by Commander Rance coming sharp-paced towards them.

Pat, having no doubt seen such colour as she had in her cheeks draining away in a moment, made matters worse by coming to her assistance with a mild joke.

'Commander,' he said, 'I think you'd like to meet the lady that Mentor of the *Evening Star* described as *lying obscenely naked* beside the pool at the Majestic Club.'

His quip provoked a response Harriet had not at all expected.

'It's Detective Superintendent Martens, is it? Then, Miss Martens, I have just one thing to say to you. I don't know how you come to be here in the Murder Room where the crime you were a victim of is being investigated, but I have no doubt at all that this is the last place you ought to be. I'll say good afternoon to you, and I trust I will not see you anywhere near here again.'

14

Harriet, feeling moment by moment more depressed and exhausted, found a taxi waiting outside. Sinking down on its back seat, she shut her eyes and let semi-oblivion pour over her.

God, how things have gone wrong. Two hours ago, less, I was more hopeful than I've been at any moment since I heard Mr No-hyphen saying, 'you can take it now that we've pulled you through.' And now I'm even absolutely barred from my own place of work, most likely from all inside news of what's happening. I thought I was managing to push forward a little the hunt for the man who put poison into my drink on that sunny morning, who's put poison into what five other people drank. And now there's nothing I can do to help. I'm barred. It's a total setback. Total.

Tears, the first she had shed since the long-ago days supercharged with emotion immediately after her wedding, began to spurt from her eyes. Unstoppably they rolled down her cheeks.

Only when the wetness penetrated through her shirt on to the tops of her breasts did she sniff herself into calm. Not before time. The cab was at the corner of her road.

It came to a halt. She thrust open the door, staggered out on to the pavement, feeling so weak she hardly trusted her legs.

Behind her the driver called out for his fare. She turned bewilderedly, then remembered that her purse must be in the bag on her shoulder. She found a note in it, fingered it clumsily out, handed it across.

Then she realized the man was holding out her change. She extended her hand like a beggar and watched as he slid some coins into it.

Tip, she thought. I should . . .

She snatched up some of the coins, any of the coins, handed them over.

It was all she could do then to make her way along the path up to the front door. And there, for what seemed minutes, she stood beneath the shelter of the long porch in front of the house, unable to recollect what had to be done to get the door open.

Eventually it floated into her mind that two keys were necessary, and then that they must, like her purse, be in her shoulder-bag.

★ ★ ★

John, coming home at about half-past six, found her lying flat on the bed, still with all her clothes on and fast asleep. He helped her to undress and got her under the duvet. No rebukes. Then, as he was asking her whether she would like some supper, the phone beside the bed rang out.

John picked it up.

'Yes, Pat, she's here. But — '

Hazily Harriet heard Pat's vigorous, Irishy tones saying something she could not make out

'No,' John said in answer. 'No, you'd better tell me, and I'll pass it on.'

Then came that always irritating series of yeses in answer to things being said at the far end. Harriet listened to them, lying flat on her back, unable to decide whether she really wanted to know what Pat was saying or not.

Eventually John dropped the handset down on its rest.

'It's another one,' he said.

And then Harriet knew she did want to hear.

'Another poisoning? Where? Who was it?'

'Well, it was in Nottingham, and on Sunday evening, not very many hours later than the murder at that Gay March in London. But only when it was diagnosed as aconitine poisoning were the police here informed. It was a young man by the name of Tenter, Lee Tenter. A student. It was at that famous pub, supposed to be the oldest in England, the Trip to Jerusalem.'

'Yes, I went into it once.'

She felt energy flowing back into her like a tide creeping across wide, wet sands.

'Well, I gather the place is a big students' haunt, and on Sunday evening, when it was still hot over in Nottingham, there was a crowd of them milling about. And this Lee Trotter, no, Tenter, Tenter, suddenly vomited, in the way we know all too much about. Apparently though, some of his friends had spotted someone putting something into his beer and, thinking it was some sort of practical joke — they're not as aware of the Poisoner as we are in Birchester — they gave chase. But, of course, they lost the fellow. In the end they were able to give the police, quickly enough on the scene when it was realized young Tenter was dead, only the vaguest of descriptions.'

Was it, Harriet thought at once, of a man in a three-piece suit somehow resembling a white rabbit? Was it him really? The Poisoner? So nearly caught.

Or, even though John had said *the fellow*, had it been after all a witch-like old woman, perhaps in some sort of disguise?

'The people who gave chase,' she asked, 'did they say they could have been going after a woman, an old woman?'

'Well, Pat said they talked about a man. But the descriptions were not at all clear. It was getting dark and the area all round the pub was full of people. The runaway was white, it seems, and wearing a cap — though of course quite a few women wear them these days — as well as some sort of nondescript mackintosh. The Nottingham police still hope, when they've questioned everybody whose names they managed to take, that they'll get a better description, though Pat doesn't seem to place much reliance on it.'

'Yes, I wouldn't either. But the more I hear the more it seems to me the Poisoner is a man.'

'Yes, Pat agrees with you, more or less. But apparently Commander Rance of the National Crime Squad still firmly believes he's looking for that old woman whose picture was in the paper.'

'If he is right, and it was a woman there, or a mannish woman, say, then Bruce Grant would still be the actual witness to . . . to my murder, or near-murder.'

She was unable to suppress a long shiver.

'I suppose so,' John said, looking down at

her. 'I'm sorry I didn't let you talk to Pat yourself. But you certainly didn't seem to be up to it.'

'No,' Harriet said, 'I wasn't. And I'm not sure I'd be now.'

She told John then how Commander Rance had expelled her from his 'Murder Room' and how the setback had affected her tremulously poised nervous system.

'Well,' John answered, 'I'm in two minds about it all, to be frank. You know that it's true you really aren't fit to go about searching for this man, or this woman. For this monster. On the other hand, if you're stuck here at home fretting, that won't do anything to speed your recovery. I don't know . . . '

'No.' Harriet said abruptly, 'but I do know. Yes, I've made up my mind. I can't take setbacks like the one I had this afternoon. I'm going to have to let it all go. I'll do my best to put it all out of my mind. Let the great Commander Rance get on with it. Let his Target try to get her million pounds, and let Rance catch her when she does, if he can. If she's there to catch. I'm sick of it all. It's too much for me. I've tried, and I've failed. No, I'm on leave, under medical advice. For three months. Let them roll on and leave me in peace.'

Exhausted again by her scarcely controllable vehemence, she let her head fall back on her pillow.

John, looking at her, was faintly smiling.

★ ★ ★

The phone remained silent all that evening and all next morning. But at about three in the afternoon it rang. Harriet, propped up in bed trying to read an Agatha Christie John had given her as being nicely undemanding, thought for a few moments of letting it ring.

But then she realized that Mrs Pickstock would be in the house, possibly in the kitchen replacing things in the cupboards with organic substitutes. She would be bound before long to pick up the instrument downstairs. The thought of her muscling in on whatever the caller had to say was too much for her.

She snatched up the handset, nearly let it drop from her sweaty palm, squeezed harder, spoke the number.

'Harriet? It's Pat. Harriet, come down to Waterloo Gardens, quick as you can. Don't come inside the station. I'll be outside, in the gardens themselves. By . . . by where? Oh, yes, by the pond. You know it?'

'Of course I do.'

190

'Come as soon as you can. Can't talk any — '

At the far end the phone clunked down. And, she knew, she was going to do what Pat had asked her to.

As soon as I can. But, Christ, doesn't he realize how impossible that is? I'll have to get up, get dressed. Drag myself up, try to think what I should wear. And then . . . then what? I can't even get myself round to imagining it.

She allowed herself to sink back on her pillows.

A moment's rest. Just a moment's . . . or a moment or two.

But the tiny voice of conscience put in its word.

No, this was Pat. Pat asking me to come, *quick as you can*. I can't refuse. I must do it. Now. I owe Pat. If it wasn't for him I'd have been lying here day after day, hopeless, helpless. Perhaps never to get back to what it is I do. What it is I am. A police officer. A detective.

No, it was Pat who, against all the rules let me in on the investigation, hauled me back into being what I am, what I should be.

Yes, I owe him. He gave me hope. And he wants me. He wants me now. Wants me for some reason, some reason he plainly could not mention where he might be overheard.

He wants me now, down there by the pond in Waterloo Gardens.

She rolled out of bed. Shakily then she forced herself to her feet. She shook her head and looked around for her clothes.

No. In the wardrobe and the chest of drawers.

I will be able to get out what I'll need. I can put them on, in the right order, the right way round. And to hell with it, anyhow, if they aren't right.

She lurched over and pulled out the first things that came to hand. Jeans. The old jeans she wore only for gardening, had worn when she'd gone with Miss Earwaker in search of monkshood and had found that chopped-off, poison-packed tuber.

Thoughts running willy-nilly through her head as she wrestled with panties, bra, shirt, brought her suddenly to the full realization of what she had undertaken to do. She had pledged herself to get down to Waterloo Gardens as fast as she could. And that meant, she knew it now — had obscurely known it all along — that she would have to take her car. She would have to drive there. All right, it was possible to phone for a taxi, wait till it came, go there in it. But how often, on the rare occasions when she had needed a cab, had she had to wait and wait

192

till one came in answer to her call. Birchester taxi firms were notorious for promising more than they could perform. *With you in ten minutes, madam.* And half an hour later, when called urgently back, it would be excuse after excuse and finally *With you in ten minutes, madam.*

She found she had somehow got herself dressed. Wash and make up? No, fuck washing, fuck pink lips.

So now it was the car.

She realized she had tautened her mouth in a line of too fierce determination.

All right, I'm about to follow through the decision I have made. But unless I can relax about it I'll end up reversing out of the side-gate straight into the path of some oncoming vehicle. No, I must make myself believe this is just a customary trip down to the city centre, something I've done hundreds of times. The convenient way of getting from place to place, from the house over to Waterloo Gardens where Pat will be waiting for me, by the pond.

So now, yes, scribble a note for Mrs P, leave it on the hall table in case she comes offering me camomile tea. And, thank goodness, John's safely at work. No objections to be overcome.

Car keys? Where are they?

Yes, yes, all right, they're in my bag where they've been ever since that hot day when John drove us to the Club to get an early swim. And I took a good swig from my second Campari soda.

★ ★ ★

Without having much of a memory of how she got there, she found herself sitting in her car looking uncomprehendingly at the controls, covered with a layer of fine dust.

But then she thought, *Start, you have to start a car.*

But will it start now? It's been here in the garage for six weeks. I think. Six weeks or more while I've hardly remembered its existence. It may not start. Even if I can recall what to do.

Think.

Yes. Yes, it's my new — newish — automatic. So it's easier than the old stick-shift.

Now, relax. Make myself. Relax, and let my interior autopilot take over.

Then, after a blank space of time, she found the car was out in the road, headed towards the city centre. She blessed the fact that the rain had ceased and, though the trees to either side looked heavy with moisture, the road surfaces were dry. No oncoming vehicle had smashed into her, and the engine was running smoothly.

Right then, this is easy. I can do it. I've done it hundreds of times, thousands even. I'm a driver. I've driven this car and all its predecessors. Nothing to it. As easy as walking.

So, off we go.

Yes. Yes, this is fine. Any traffic coming from the right? No. All clear. Go.

Then suddenly a vehicle.

Where? Where did it come from? I'm on the wrong side. Wrong place. I'm going to be in a crash. It's going to hit me. Kill me.

Christ, it's gone. Gone past. On the other side. I wasn't in the wrong lane. That brief whirr of engine noise and it's gone. Glimpse of the driver, man with a cap. Funny how some men always wear something on their head in a car.

And I'm still going. Going down to the city centre. To meet Pat.

Why? Can't think.

Must think.

Think, thin — Yes. Yes, Pat rang me, said he wanted to see me. Urgently. And not inside the station. In Waterloo Gardens, by the pond.

Red light, come to a neat halt.

Meet Pat by the pond. Circular, circular

municipal pond, tarmac-surrounded. And railings, not very high, green-painted, keep children out of the water, and dogs. Ducks. A few ducks swimming round and round. But why at the pond? Why a secret meeting? And think of how in the end he suddenly banged the phone down. The phone in his office? I suppose someone —

Jesus, the car behind hooting. Hooting at me. Oh God, yes, the light's gone to green. What do I do? Got to go forward. Can't think. Wait, yes, don't think. Do. Just do.

Yes, fine. Here am I going smoothly along again. No hassle at all. People occasionally do go into a dream when the lights seem to stay at red minute after minute. All I did. No one's hooting now. Yes, I'm back to it. Driving. Way I've done for years.

And suddenly ... the screech of brakes. Horn blasts on every side. Was that the shudder of something just biffing the car?

My car? Me? Yes.

Oh God, where am I?

Deep breath. Take a deep breath. Look up, look round, I am in the city. I am near the city centre. Near Waterloo Gardens. Yes, this is Dean Street. I'm quite near the gardens. Which is where I was going. To meet Pat, Detective Superintendent Murphy, Senior Investigating Officer for the Poisoner invest

— No. He's been superseded. By Commander Rance, National Crime Squad.

Oh, and, God damn it, I drifted into the other lane. That's what all the hooting's about. Have I been in a crash? A shunt? Can't hear the engine. Yes, I sort of knew something was wrong. No sound from the engine. It's come to a stop. I'm stuck here, in the wrong place. Christ, what am I going to do?

Think. Think what's gone wrong if the engine isn't going. Don't know. Can't work it out.

Oh, stop that bloody hooting, can't you?

Start up? Start up again? Try.

Yes. Yes, yes, yes. It's going. I got it right. Engine had just cut out. And, yes, if I'm quick I can nip back into my right stream. Before some idiot comes shouting in at my window.

Now.

Into forward. There's the gap. Take it easy. And, yes.

15

Pat, a solitary, bulky, bright blue-suited shape, glancing about almost furtively, had planted himself within a foot of the glinting sun-lit water of the railings-surrounded pond. Evidently spotting Harriet the moment she came within sight, he gave her at once the merest hint of a nod and strode off deeper into the gardens.

Her nerves still jangling from her nightmare drive, Harriet realized that he wanted her to follow, though at once she found he was setting a pace she could hardly keep up. The upper part of her right arm had begun to jerk uncontrollably. She longed to see a bench where she could sit down.

In a whirl of fruitless questions she asked herself what Pat was up to.

Trust him, trust him. It's all I can do to batten down the tumult in my mind.

But at last, when she had begun to be afraid that at any moment she would lose sight of him altogether, he turned abruptly off the dusty-looking tarmac path and plunged, shouldering his way, into a stand of clustered pine trees.

There, in the damp shelter they afforded, Harriet at last came face-to-face with him, and found the muscular jerking in her arm ceased.

He spoke before she could formulate any of the questions she wanted to ask.

'Harriet, sorry about all that. Truth to tell, it's that bugger Rance. He's sitting there just waiting for his imaginary witchy friend to tell him where that famous million pounds is to be put for her to pick up. Then he's all set to mount his wonderful ambush and show the world what clever sods the NCS are. And in the meanwhile he's doing damn all about stopping another poor soul being murdered, just amusing himself criticizing everything I've done since the day your man saved your life with that Agatha Christie book of his.'

Harriet blinked in astonishment. She had never thought to see stolid Pat so hassled

'And that's why we're meeting here?' she asked. 'Skulking under these trees? Pat, I've just had the most god-awful drive down here, the first time I've had the car out since . . . well, since. Pat, I want to sit down. I must sit down.'

'Ah, dear God, I was forgetting. I was forgetting altogether. To hell with spying Rance, there's a nice bench we passed; *In* memory of Mrs Alexander Walker MBE who loved these gardens. Come along.'

★   ★   ★

Seated on the bench, with the metal plaque to Mrs Walker digging a little uncomfortably into her back, Harriet heard at last why in particular Pat had summoned her so urgently.

'This is the way of it. You know the storm we had last night?'

'Did we? I must have slept through it, though I do remember I had another of my nightmares, probably caused by the noise.'

'Well, if you slept through it, I did not. It woke me up. Woke me up to what I'd failed entirely to put in hand because bloody Rance had vetoed it. As I lay listening to the rain coming down cats and dogs, what suddenly entered my head was that this'd be no time to have a half-naked WDC lying out by the Majestic Club pool.'

'And so . . . so you want to do that now, now it's a reasonably sunny day again?'

'No, I've done it. I arranged it all first thing this morning, before himself was there at all in the Murder Room, as he calls it. Still eating his big breakfast at the Hilton hotel, I dare say. You know the whole lot of that team of his has moved in there? Doing themselves

200

damn well, at the expense of Greater Birchester Police no doubt.'

'But your reconstruction? What did you find? How I wish I'd been there.'

'Ach, no. You wish nothing of the sort. You'd never be up to it. I hope I don't see you there beside that pool again, not for months yet. Not till next summer, if then. Seeing that recliner and — '

'Pat, what conclusion did you come to?'

'Yes. Sorry. It was simple enough. From where I was standing at the gate there, pretending to be Grant, to where DC Helen Baggot was lying on that self-same recliner, shivering away in the chill of dawn, poor girl, I couldn't at all see what was happening on the far side of her. I couldn't see that Campari stuff we'd put there. I couldn't have seen any class of a hooked nose on an old woman, bent or not bent. Not if I'd had binoculars clamped to me eyeballs, I couldn't.'

'I knew Grant was making it all up,' Harriet broke in. 'I knew it from the moment he said nothing at all about me being there, all but naked to the world.'

She took a deep breath.

'So surely it's beyond doubt now,' she said, 'that the Poisoner's a man. I thought so the moment I read that letter in the *Star*. No woman uses words and expressions like those.'

'And Commander Rance,' Pat added sharply, 'when he turned you out of the incident room deprived himself of what you, better than anybody, could have told him.'

His big red face creased momentarily in a wicked smile.

'Inspector Fowles at the Meads PS has pulled in Grant for me. And, out of the way over there in just a few minutes' time, I'm going to put that fella through it. I'm going to get a full confession out of him. Then I'll show it to Rance, and we'll see where his imaginary witch flies off to then.'

He gave Harriet a glance of impending triumph.

'What's more,' he said, 'I'm not going to be so stupid as to do it without the benefit of your eyes and ears, Detective Superintendent Martens.'

★ ★ ★

Bruce Grant proved, when it came to it, a tougher proposition than Pat Murphy had counted on. The weapon he fought back with was obstinacy.

Facing him across the strongly lit table of the interview room at the Meads police station, Pat, with a DC from the Meads sitting silently beside him, went in two-fisted.

Harriet, mouse-quiet behind Grant in the darkness beyond the pool of light, was able to watch his every expression in a small mirror which Pat had placed high up on the wall opposite. Together she and Pat had arranged a code of signals to alert him if anything unexpected struck her.

'Right, Mr Grant, we meet again. And I have some news for you. Earlier today I carried out a wee experiment in the grounds of the Majestic Sports Club. I took up position just where you yourself were on gate duty that day when, you say, you saw an old woman put some liquid into Detective Superintendent Martens' drink. The self-same recliner she was asleep on was in the exact position it had been, and DC Helen Baggot was lying on it, dressed in a bikini like the one Miss Martens had on. I stood there and I did my best to see the little wooden table beside DC Baggot with on it a dead identical glass of the Campari soda there on August bank holiday Monday.'

No cough-mixture jokes now, Harriet registered from the darkness.

'Right, I have to tell you,' Pat went steadily on, 'that I was entirely unable to see that glass, never mind how much we shifted it about on the wee table. I could not by any possibility have seen anyone pour anything into it. So what have you got to say to that?'

'Nothing.'

'No, that won't do. I'm telling you that you were a bare-faced liar when you said you'd seen an old woman who looked like a witch put something into that glass. So were you lying, yes or no?'

'I saw her, that's all. Say what you like.'

'I say you did not see anyone, man or woman, young or old, put anything into that glass.'

'I did.'

'No, you did not. You could not have done. You're a liar, Grant. A liar pure and simple.'

'I'm not. And . . . and there's two who could be lying here. I say it's you that's a liar, detective super or not.'

'No, that won't do.'

'It'll have to do. I told you what I saw, and I'm not going to say I never did.'

So it went on for a quarter of an hour or more. Time and again Pat put the facts to Grant, and each time Grant simply denied them. Harriet grew almost tired of looking at his sullenly stubborn features in the little tilted patch of reflective glass. There was a small band of pain across her legs where the taut edge of of her chair's seat webbing dug in at her.

What can I see there that'll give Pat a chink

to push into? Nothing. That damned unchanging look. It says nothing. Nothing, nothing, nothing. Fixed to one compass-point only, the magnetic north of blank denial.

At last Pat switched to broader questions about Grant's life. No lack of intelligence in Pat, she thought. He's aiming to soften up the obstinate bugger. He'll go on along this line till he judges that the ice-core of denial has gradually begun to melt. And then, bang, back will come that plain fact of the invisibility of the glass of red liquid. At that Grant will come out with a fuller answer, a more concocted denial. And he'll get caught up in a mess of self-contradiction.

Time went by. Patiently Pat put question after question about Grant's life from his schooldays onwards, listened with seeming interest to the dulled replies. Harriet, almost mesmerized looking into the mirror on the far wall, kept saying to herself, wait, wait and wait till Pat judges his moment has come.

Yet it seemed as if the waiting was to go on for ever.

Has Pat misjudged it, she asked herself. Was there something earlier that was the right moment? A few seconds ago? Ten minutes ago? Something in one of those weary replies he should have leapt on?

But if it was there, I didn't see it any more than Pat.

On went the commonplace questions, moving painstakingly from detail to detail.

Harriet began to feel her invalid's body yielding to dragging tiredness.

And then . . .

It was not some indication from Grant's latest dull reply. It was a tiny something she had seen, almost without seeing it, in the mirror. It was a tiny flick of hesitation in Grant's right eye that told her — something in the repertoire of tell-tale signs she had acquired in interviews over the years — that a major lie was on the point of being put forward.

She thought rapidly. What had been the last monotonously routine question Pat had asked?

Yes. *So you thought then you'd come up here to Birchester?* The almost meaningless query. So why is Grant lying hard now in his answer? With, yes, rather more fluency than he's yet shown.

'It was a mate of mine in London. He'd gone to Birchester, thought it was . . . thought he'd, like, try his luck here. And he got a good job. Yes, at . . . at the Rovers ground. Not terrific pay, but a good crowd there. And you could go on from one thing to another.

Better money each time. So he wrote to me and said why didn't I try my luck here too.'

'And you got a job — '

But Pat had heard her signal. One small sharp *tink* with a pencil on the metal side of her chair, meaning here's a lie, an unexpected lie.

'No,' he went on with scarcely a break in the rhythm of his questioning, 'put it this way. If he was telling you of a good opportunity at Rovers FC, why didn't you take it? This mate of yours never existed, did he? You came up to Birchester because you were in trouble down in London. That's it, isn't it?'

'I — I wasn't in no trouble. What trouble could I — I mean, why d'you say that? It's not fair saying I'm dodgy.'

A very different response from the monotonous denials of plain fact that he had adopted at the start. And Pat took advantage of it.

'Your mate who wrote to you didn't exist, did he, any more than the woman in the green cloak you told the *Star* all about?'

'Stupid lot there at the paper. Why shouldn't I tell 'em a bit of a tale?'

'No reason, Mr Grant. But every reason why you shouldn't have told me a tale. You were wasting police time, and that's an offence in law. And more than that. You were

207

sending the hunt for whoever was poisoning people left and right all over Birchester off on a wrong trail. You were endangering dozens of innocent lives. Even hundreds.'

'I — ? I didn't. I — I didn't mean to. It was — it was just a joke.'

On and on went the pathetic dribble of justification. But Harriet paid little attention to it. It was rubbish being swept out of the way. Now Pat, with her help, could take the hunt on the right line again, and Commander Rance would have to let him.

She waited till Grant had been led away and then, in triumph, she told Pat what she saw as the situation now.

But Pat stood there silent in the bright pool of light on the interview-room table, his face wearing an unreadable expression.

'Pat, you're not happy with what you learnt?'

'Sure, I am. Clearing up all that business. Why wouldn't I be happy?'

'But you're not.'

A huge sigh.

'You're right, Harriet. I'll tell you what it is. Here at last we've sorted it all out. We've got rid once and for all of that stupid Grant's old witch. And what's it my duty to do? To tell Commander Rance.'

'Who will have to admit that he was wrong

and you were right.'

But Pat's big round face was still fixed in gloom.

'Pat, why not? Why not? You know that's the truth of the matter.'

'I do so. But I'm after working under that bugger . . . '

'And . . . ?'

'And he'll wriggle out of it. I know that. He'll somehow back himself still. He'll accuse me of insubordination for following a line he's said was not to be pursued. Anything.'

Harriet thought.

I must keep Pat alongside. I must. All right, I can see why he feels unhappy. A long-serving police officer, and he thinks he's about to be asked to blatantly disobey an order. But if that's what he'll have to do to stay with me till I see this through to the end, then I'll have to put him in a position where that will be the lesser of two evils, at least.

'Rance has treated you like shit,' she said at last.

'He has that.'

Now Harriet hardly needed to think.

'Listen, Pat,' she said. 'How did you come to learn about that chap digging, out at Halsell Common, in the grey three-piece suit? All right, we've not got a name for him or much of a description. But isn't he very likely, very likely indeed, to be none other than the Poisoner? And you learnt about him through me. And what am I? I'm the woman Commander Rance expelled from the incident room. 'I trust I will not see you anywhere near here again,' he said. I remember. All too well. So, think about it. Is it really your duty to pass on to him now anything you learnt from me?'

Pat thought. Visibly.

'Ach, you make out a good case, Harriet, so you do.' He twisted his great bulk about uneasily. 'It's not the truth of the matter, not at all. But, all right, it'll do. It'll have to do. After all, Rance is a hundred per cent persuaded Grant's witch is the Poisoner, sitting there waiting for her million pounds. And she's not. And we know it.'

Harriet found a big grin had appeared on her face.

'You're right, Pat,' she said. 'In a way it's our duty, your duty and perhaps mine, if Rance is determined to stick to the line we've finally managed to discredit, to pursue our own.'

'Then lead the way.'

'No, but listen. While I was waiting for Grant to be taken away, I gave a little thought, in the light of what we'd just made sure of, to that letter in the *Star*, signed

Mentor. I have a notion that, if more attention was given to that, it might well pay off. I think, in fact, that's our first step. At the worst it'll be something extra to confront Rance with if it comes to a showdown.'

'I'm listening, Harriet. But I ought to tell you that Rance has taken some action there. He had the letter itself sent to Fingerprints, though with no result after all those grubby hands at the *Star* had been pawing at it. But he had it sent, too, to some handwriting expert or other. To be told just what you yourself could have told him. Written in what they call *an educated hand.*'

'And that was all? Just an educated hand?'

'It was, so far as I'm told anything. Rance let the letter go back to the *Star*?'

'Then I'd like to go there and talk to them about it. I've . . . right, I've a feeling, no more than a feeling, that they didn't print every word of the letter. There were oddities of phrasing, I don't know.'

'Okay. There's no reason at all why a lady who was almost killed by your Mentor's activities shouldn't go and ask the *Star* about that letter. Damn it, you've every right.'

'If you say so, Detective Superintendent.'

The smile abruptly left her face. An awkwardness lay ahead.

'Listen, Pat, there's another thing. There's

211

a man I once worked with, an expert . . . well, in point of fact he's a well-known profiler. Now, I know your views on profilers in general, but this man, Professor Scholl from the University of North Essex, known to most police officers, to you too I dare say, as Dr Smellyfeet, is different. And he could tell me a good deal that I'd be — '

'No, Harriet, no. I see what you're after. You want to get him up here, either by me suggesting it to Rance, who'll take no notice at all, or by going behind Rance's back, one way or another. And I'm not going to do that. I'm just not. If I did, and it came out, I'd be in bad trouble, dismissal time very like, whatever the rights and wrongs of it.'

So Harriet parted from Pat on worse terms than they had been only a few minutes earlier. She felt a sharp disappointment. Never in all her time as a police officer had she felt so much in need of friendly and knowledgeable support. And now Pat, who had seemed to be providing that, had blocked her access to the man she had once learned to trust, the man who might be able to tell her things about the Poisoner's mentality that would lead eventually to his arrest.

But at least, she thought, it's been agreed I can talk to the editor of the *Star*. So will I at least learn from him something about Mentor

— I suspect it's there — that will strengthen our case?

★ ★ ★

She got to see Jonathan Whitaker, the paper's young editor, that very afternoon. A certain amount of negotiation over the telephone had been needed. But, newly energized, she found she was able to conduct it with all the necessary uncompromising directness, while even managing to suppress her long-held dislike of the *Star* and all it stood for. So she entered his office secure in an agreement that the paper could have a first-person account of her poisoning from Mrs Harriet Piddock, otherwise Detective Superintendent Martens, but would not get it while the Poisoner was still at large.

'Oh, come on,' Jonathan Whitaker, young as a student in Harriet's eyes, said breezily when straight away she had asked him if Mentor's letter had actually been printed in full. 'Owner's privilege to censor things, you know. Still applied, we felt, even if old Sir Billy was dead. And the letter had some nasty cracks about the paper itself. Those got cut. I mean, we couldn't have the readers getting the wrong ideas, could we? No, our Mr

213

Mentor, or Mrs Mentor, if you're going to go by all that stuff Bruce Grant told us — '

'Stuff?' Harriet interrupted sharply. 'Are you telling me that you printed that witch picture when all the while you didn't believe what Grant was telling you?'

Whitaker smiled, a little slyly.

'Well, let's say we reserved our opinion about the extent of his truthfulness. But with material for a really scary-wary pic like that, we couldn't let it go, could we?'

Harriet bit back the reply she would have liked to make.

From a safe in the wall behind his desk Whitaker now produced, in accordance with the terms of their agreement, the original of the letter.

'Back from the police scientists,' he said. 'I wasn't going to let them keep their dirty hands on it, bet your life.'

Harriet, looking at the sheets as they lay on the desk, noted at once that her guess about the writer seemed entirely correct. The handwriting appeared to be, as the expert had said, very much that of an educated and even elderly man.

A man, she thought, of her father's generation, though the sentiments were hardly his. But, true enough, he might well have used the occasional Latin phrase in anything he wrote.

She looked up at Whitaker.

'I find the Latin bits interesting.'

'Oh, the Latin. There's a lot of that we had to forget about. Or translate, if we could. We did that with — what's it there? — *mens sana in corpore sano*. One of the dreariest of our sub-editors said he knew what that meant. So we changed it to *healthy minds in healthy bodies*. Did we get it right? Do you know?'

'Yes,' Harriet said, 'you got it right. I learnt Latin at school.'

'Sorry you're not sitting at our subs' table then. And how about *alter ego*, where old Mentor talks here about Sir Billy owning porn cinemas, like the Roxy, under another name. We cut it, of course. But what's it actually mean? No one here was sure.'

'Another self,' Harriet said, not without a sigh.

'Then, look, what's this bit we had to leave out?' Whitaker went blithely on. '*Panem et* — Something about circuses, it seems to be, can't think why.'

'*Panem et circenses*. Bread and circuses. What the Roman mob was always thought of as wanting.'

'I get it.' He looked up. 'Come to think of it, it's what our readers want, if you substitute

215

takeaways and sex videos. I suppose that's what old Mentor got himself in such a twist about.'

'It is. And the way he put it confirms my feeling, even when I first read the letter, that the writer is — '

'A teacher,' Whitaker bounced in. 'What we thought too. Silly old moo.'

'No,' Harriet said, 'not quite a teacher, if I'm right. More a schoolmaster. One of the old breed, and, I'd say almost certainly, now retired.'

'Yeah, see what you mean. Dead old-fashioned. Aren't schoolmasters what they used to have in the classy public schools?'

'And still do.'

Harriet, happy with what she had learnt, was gathering her things together to leave when a thought occurred to her.

'One other thing, Mr Whitaker.'

'Just this. I don't want to see in the *Star* tomorrow a big story headlined. *The Poisoner: Is he a Schoolmaster?*'

'But — '

'No, not a word. If you print that, you'll get no firsthand account from me. On the other hand, if you cooperate, then I'll see what I can do to keep you in the game. That suit you?'

'Suppose it'll have to.'

But when she had reached the door he called back.

'Wait, here's another thing that puzzled us. It's right at the end of the letter, one of the Latin bits we cut out altogether. *Et in Arcadia ego*. Well, even I know *ego* means *I*. But what's this Arcadia stuff? Some sort of an arcade?'

'No, not that. The phrase is actually a famous saying, or it used to be. It translates as *And I too am in Arcadia*. Or paradise, as you might say, a nice rural paradise. The only thing is, everybody disputes what it's actually trying to say. Does it mean the person who said it, the I, is having a good time in his paradise? Or does it mean, as a lot of people believe, *I, too, Death, am in the good place?*'

And no sooner were the words out of her mouth than a wave of almost paralysing coldness swept through her. Death in the paradise of Birchester. Death for anyone, however little a paradise they really were in.

16

Harriet had intended to spend much of the next day phoning all the public schools in the area round Birchester to ask about retired staff. But when she woke she found, as had happened to her before, that a burst of energy, successful energy, seemed to have brought about an equivalent draining away of willpower.

Three months, she thought, as she lay there. Three months before I'm free of this repeated cycle of ups and downs. Bloody Dr Dalrymple may yet prove to be right. No, worse, if I find that after any intensive spell of work I have to take time off, even go back to bed for a while, I'd have to resign. Leave the Job. Be finished.

A thicker fog-cloud of lethargy coiled round her.

For minutes, for a full half-hour, she lay where she was. In a pool of misery.

But, once more, the shrilling of the phone brought her back to the world. By the fourth or fifth ring she had gathered enough energy, or enough curiosity, to heave herself up and answer.

It was, of course, Pat Murphy.

'How d'you get on at the *Star*?' he asked at once.

'Oh, Pat, all right. Yes, all right. I got something. But . . . but I don't want to go into it just now. To tell you the truth, I'm pretty well exhausted again.'

'Oh.'

Pat's disappointment came down the line as clearly as if he had been standing beside her, hangdog.

'No. — I'm sorry, Pat. I'm not really as bad as I sound. Were you calling about something?'

'I was. I am. While there's no one here. Listen, one of the things I had in mind to do, before Rance came along and gave me tasks fit for the youngest DC in the force, was to go and see Sir Billy Bell's widow. Condolences, of course, but I wanted, too, to find out about Sir Billy's state of health before he set off to give out the prizes at the Majestic Club that night. Something in what your John told me about the circumstances made me somehow wonder a bit if everything was just as it seemed.'

'John? John told you something about that evening that he didn't tell me?'

'Ach, don't let me come between husband and wife now. Not at all, not at all. It was just a passing thought of his, that Sir Billy's death looked to him more like some sort of heart attack.'

'Well, yes, I think he did say something of the sort to me. My memory's still not back to where it was, you know. I get patches of complete white-out.'

'Right then. So what I was going to ask was: could you go and see Lady Bell for me? A visit of condolence would come well from you, a fellow victim. But if you're not fit . . . '

And, not for the first time, the scent of battle was enough to send the ears of the stabled war-horse pricking.

'Pat, I'll do it, if I can possibly make myself.'

★ ★ ★

Sir Billy Bell's sprawling house, half Spanishy, half white-walls modernist, was, Harriet thought as her taxi drew up outside, wholly a mess. And suddenly the idea of meeting Sir Billy's widow seemed, despite having had a friendly response when she had phoned, to be more than she would be able to manage. She sat there in the taxi, paralysed in inaction.

At last the driver turned round to her.

'We're here, lady. This is the house Billy Bell had built. Where you wanted, yes?'

'Oh, yes, yes. I'm sorry.'

She began to scramble out.

'That's eight-pound fifty,' the driver said, with an audible sigh of *stupid woman*.

Harriet looked into her shoulder bag.

What is it I want? Oh God, I've no idea. No, wait. He asked me something. Wait. Yes, money. The fare. How much did he say? Can't remember. He told me only half a minute ago, and now I can't remember. Oh, Christ, I should never have set out on this . . .

In its proper compartment in the bag she saw her wallet, pulled it out, opened it. There were notes in their place. She extracted one with fingers that seemed suddenly thick as sausages.

She thrust it at the man, turned away.

'Don't you want your change, lady? That's a twenty you've given me.'

'Oh, was it? I'm sorry, I thought . . . I'll just take the ten. Thank you again.'

The taxi zoomed off, with the driver shaking his head in disbelief.

Jesus, Harriet thought, and I'm meant to be talking to Lady Bell, one-time dancer in musicals, to find out under the pretence of offering her my condolences just what was her dead husband's state of health before he set out for the Majestic Club prize-giving.

Right, I've got to pull myself together. Now.

She marched up to the big, panelled front door, put a finger firmly on the bell-push beside it.

A maid in uniform, black dress, white cap, opened the door.

Harriet, looking at her, again found a flick of a vision of something black and white dazzling across her mind.

No, she thought fiercely, I am about to meet Lady Bell. That is what I am doing. I'm not standing here having visions. I'm here to discover what it may have been that made John suspect Sir Billy might have died, not directly from poison, but from a heart attack. If that's what he did suspect, half-suspect. And the answer may get us nearer the Poisoner. It may, or it may not. But the question, under whatever disguise, must be asked.

'Lady Bell is expecting me. Mrs Harriet Piddock.'

She realized her voice had sounded perfectly strong, even a little too forceful.

The girl gave her a little bob of acknowledgement.

'This way, madam.'

The full business, Harriet thought, looking at the prim figure trotting along ahead of her.

I can see Sir Billy wanting something like this, the touch of class. So what about his widow? Much the same?

The moment she stepped into the big room the maid had led her to she began to think Lady Bell was going to be different. She was, in fact, hard even to find amongst a mass of armchairs, large as small boats, and sofa, large as a punt. But at last Harriet spotted her, sitting perched on the stool in front of the grand piano in a far corner, a tiny figure, silver-haired, face a network of wrinkles, dressed in a dark frock that might have been prescribed as mourning for a schoolgirl whose father had just died.

'Come in, dear,' she called across. 'Come and sit near me, if you won't get lost in the huge chair there.'

Harriet went over and sat on the edge of the white silk-covered, gold-trimmed boat.

'Lady Bell,' she began.

'No, for God's sake, call me Kitty.' Raucous tang contrasting startlingly with the minuscule frame. 'Everybody calls me that. Well, bar my poor old Billy. When he got to be a Sir he kept trying to say Katherine. But he almost always forgot.'

'Kitty, yes. I'll try. And let me say at once that I've felt for days that I wanted to offer you — '

She jibbed at the awful formal word *condolences*.

'No need for that,' Kitty Bell put in quickly. 'I knew when you said you wanted to come and see me you had to be feeling sorry for me. But you needn't try to say it now. Whatever anybody says in these circs somehow sounds all wrong.'

Then a little smile flicked over her pale, thin lips.

'And that's not what a detective superintendent's really come about, is it? You want to know more about what I think happened at that old St Aldred's School, don't you? St Aldred's, that's how I always think of the Majestic Social and Whatsit Club. I used to walk past it every day when I was a kid. On the way to the elementary. Posh old St Aldred's.'

It took Harriet a long moment to adjust to this new, sharper version of the woman she had come to see. What price my careful description of myself as Mrs Piddock, she thought. She was on to that in an instant. No, Kitty Bell, getting on in years though she may be, is a very acute lady.

So where do I go from here?

She found the answer was at once clear in her head.

'You're right, there are things I want to ask

you as a detective, although I must confess I'm still meant to be on sick leave. But I do sympathize with you, too. Weren't you married to Sir Billy for years? You're bound to feel an awful blank.'

'Of course I do. And nothing anybody says is going to make a difference to that. But you: I can see you're still in a state, though that attack on you was weeks ago now. Anyone who was as near death as the paper said you were, when it came out with this Poisoner going about with his nasty little thing of liquid, well, they're going to feel all up and down for a long time to come.'

Harriet felt a dart of gratitude. Condolence. It was what she had come to bring to the widow, and instead she was receiving condolence from her.

At once she decided she could only ask, with equal directness, the question she had come to find an answer to, to ask it before she was ambushed by her body once more.

'Kitty,' she said, 'please tell me: was your husband in a poor state of health on the evening he set out for the Majestic Club? My John, who was there as a Majestic executive, wondered whether his death was caused as much by some kind of heart attack as by the sort of poison he saved me from.'

'Yes,' Kitty Bell said.

'You mean, he might have died from his heart condition and not from aconitine poisoning? Is that it?'

'No, it's more than that. From what I made them tell me about the what-do-you-call-it, post-mortem — I wasn't going to stand for any *Spare the poor widow stuff* — Billy, in the last glass of champagne he took, drank something that upset him. But it would have done no more than that, upset him, the poor old boy. It was just some stuff that made him feel awful, like it was someone playing a practical joke on him. Oh yes, it made him throw up all right. But whatever it was that did that, it wasn't deadly poison.'

Then why the hell, Harriet said to herself, did Commander Rance not tell Pat that? The contempt he feels for country clodhoppers, I suppose. As if Birchester, a city of half a million inhabitants, is some piffling village with three and a bit houses in it. Okay, Pat hasn't, so far, told Rance that Bruce Grant was definitely lying about his old witch, but that's not as bad a trick as keeping the post-mortem result from the man who was formerly Senior Investigating Officer for the case.

And then, sweeping that thought aside, a wholly new idea came glimmering into her mind.

17

Kitty Bell, when Harriet had asked if she could use her phone to call a cab, had at once insisted that her chauffeur-driven Rolls was there to be used. Sitting in leather-smelling luxury on its broad back seat, Harriet set out to examine the idea that Kitty's revelation about the post-mortem had put into her head.

Can it really be, she asked herself, that it was not the Poisoner at all who put something in the final glass of champagne Sir Billy swigged down? Was it someone else altogether who did no more than put an emetic into it, rather than deadly aconitine?

Is there someone who, for some devious reason of their own, decided to take advantage of the poisonings that followed the attempt on me? The frightening roll-call: garage hand Robbie Norman, council telephonist Tommy O'Brien, tea-sipping Mrs Sylvia Smythe, as well as Margery Plummer down in London, and the student Lee Tenter in Nottingham? Did this person, in fact, do no more than play a nasty practical joke on Sir Billy — a joke that went unexpectedly, fatally wrong — just in order, yes, to write to the *Evening Star* and attempt to acquire a million pounds?

Or, to judge by the tone of that hate-filled screed, perhaps to do no more really than vent long-suppressed rage at the way the world was behaving, the world of Birchester in particular, the wider world as well? Was Sir Billy's death the work, not of the Poisoner, but of self-styled Mentor with that talk of *sacrificial victims on the altar of probity?*

It looked like it. It really did.

The Rolls glided smoothly onwards.

And then, glancing up, Harriet caught a glimpse of something that just registered in her mind. For a moment she thought she must have had another flicking vision of that something black and white that had troubled her ever since she had come out of St Oswald's. But, no, it was not that. Something else ..?

And then she saw it again. High on one of the lampposts they were now passing there was a large, colourful placard. And it was reproducing the *Star* artist's imaginary portrait of the old woman Bruce Grant said he had seen putting poison in the Campari soda at her side.

At first she thought it must be a wild advertising campaign by the paper. But

Jonathan Whitaker had said nothing to her of any such plan when she had read Mentor's Latin-filled letter in his office, and in any case it would have been a pointless exercise with the *Star* selling every copy it could print. Then she took in the large black letters at the foot of the garish picture: *HAVE YOU SEEN THIS WOMAN?* and realized the posters had been put up all over the city on the orders of Commander Rance, still hunting furiously for the old woman Pat Murphy had shown was simply Bruce Grant's invention.

Oh, let Rance pursue his will-of-the-wisp then. I've got better things to think about.

She sank back again into the yielding seat.

Who, if I'm right about the person who put an emetic in Sir Billy's champagne, is Mentor? How can we trace him? Is he as hard to get any sort of grasp on as the Poisoner is?

And then a new thought abruptly came clamouring into her head, sending her earlier careful speculations spinning away like debris from an explosion.

St Aldred's School. Quite incidentally Kitty Bell had mentioned that the Majestic Sports and Social Club occupied the house and grounds that had once been *posh old St Aldred's*. Posh? Did that mean the establishment little Kitty had walked past on her way to the arched doorway marked *Girls* at her elementary school had been some sort of fee-paying establishment? It must do. It must.

So, yes, it's likely, more than likely, that there had taught at the school where now the Club stands, a master of the old-fashioned sort? Mentor. It could be Mentor, a man who must have known how to sneak unobserved into, and out of, the prize-giving ceremony where Sir Billy met his end.

If this is so, and at this moment I certainly believe it is, then I'm in sight of finding out who Mentor is. And, with Mentor out of the way, will we be able to see how to find that different person, the Poisoner?

But what shall I do about it all?

Right, I'm going to do nothing. Nothing for the moment. I'm not going to go rushing to Pat Murphy, much less to Commander Rance, to say I've seen how the case may be resolved. I am going to get out of the car when it draws to its smooth halt outside the house. I am going to thank that passive, uniformed back in front of me, and I am going to walk quietly to the front door, unlock it and go into the living-room, where I shall sit down and go over my whole train of thought again to see if the idea is or is not logical and sensible.

★ ★ ★

Half an hour later she felt she was firmly in possession of a worthwhile theory. There were, there must be, two separate people putting noxious substances into such glasses or cups as were easily got at. One of them, the Poisoner, she thought with a calmness that surprised her, attempted to kill me. He then succeeded with five other poisonings. But then a second person, the Schoolmaster or Mentor, had intervened, poisoning only, in so far as it was a poisoning, Sir Billy Bell.

For God's sake, she added to herself, I can't see a man like him, an old fogey, his every thought harking back to an almost forgotten code of behaviour, coming up to me beside the pool that day as I slept in the sun and putting poison into my glass. What would he be wearing among all the women in swimsuits and men in shorts? A striped woollen bathing-dress with shoulder straps? Absurd.

But Mentor's intervention had almost certainly had one unexpected effect. It had caused the Poisoner to bring his campaign of killings to a temporary halt. That must be why there had been that lull in his activities. Broken at last when he had gone down to London that hot and sunny Sunday and given Marge Plummer a tempting can of cool drink, and then had immediately travelled up to Nottingham and visited the famous Trip to Jerusalem, where he had had no difficulty in finding young Lee Tenter's neglected pint glass.

So am I as near certain as I can be that this is what, in all likelihood, has happened? Yes, I am. My argument is well-conducted detection.

So do I now go trotting along to Commander Rance, into positively forbidden territory, and tell him what the logic I have used means?

No, I don't. But I can get hold of Pat, and I can tell him.

And at once she remembered the absurd things she had told Pat before. She sat up, heart suddenly beating in fast thumps.

Is, after all, this theory of mine just one more absurdity coming out of a brain I can no longer trust? I didn't think it was, but it could be. It just could be. I am in a state where such wild notions might well blow up in my head, insubstantial as huge air-balloons, as insubstantial but as much able to block out any other view. Only an hour or so ago, shrewd Lady Kitty told me I would be *feeling all up and down for a long time to come.* So how can I be sure I was really thinking calmly and logically just now? Like the detective I believed myself to be? No, like

232

the detective I ought to be?

She realized tears were lurking just behind her eyes.

No. No, no, no, no. No more sorry-for-myself weeping. Once was enough.

Right, I've been in difficult situations before and thought my way out of them, some even since that aconitine got into my system. Look at that Sunday out with Miss Earwaker when those louts surrounded her car. I was in danger then of getting a going-over. That boy, young man, with the red jersey, he would have led them on. I knew it. And what did I do? I thought my way out of trouble. Just that.

She straightened her shoulders.

So, now start thinking again. Think how to test this theory that Pat Murphy may say is just another of neurotic Harriet's wild ideas. Or that Commander Rance will certainly dismiss as not worth listening to.

And, as soon as she did set herself to think, the simple answer came to her. If there are two men adding substances to easily got-at drinks, the real Poisoner and the man I have labelled Mentor or the Schoolmaster, then what I have to do is to find the latter. To find the one about whom I know just a little, the man who was once a master possibly at St Aldred's. It should be possible to trace him. If difficult.

Mrs Pickstock, whom she had vaguely heard clanking about in the kitchen, poked her head in at the door.

'Oh, you're back then, dear. I didn't hear you come in, or I'd have brought you some nice camomile tea. I know you like that.'

'No, it's all right, Mrs Pickstock,' Harriet found herself able to lie. 'I had some tea when I visited Lady Bell earlier, to offer my condolences.'

'Oh, yes, dear. That was nice of you. I know when my Reg was taken from me in that awful sudden way — well, they called it Sudden Death Syndrome, didn't they? — I know what a comfort it was when friends came to call.'

Harriet repressed a shudder, though she could not have said whether it was a shudder of antipathy, however regrettable, or one of something like cold horror at the idea of death being there for someone, for anyone, so utterly unexpectedly.

Luckily, before she had time to frame an answer, Mrs Pickstock swung away and went to peer through the window.

'Yes,' she said. 'Yes, I thought it was. That's Hubby's car just going round to the garage. So I'll leave you two lovebirds together.'

She disappeared into the kitchen, and at

the same moment that John came in at the back door she went out of it.

'I was just saying to your wifey,' Harriet heard her unrestrained tones, 'I'm leaving you two together. I'm never one to be in the way, you know.'

★　★　★

As soon as John had asked her how she was, and had frowned a little when she told him she had on Pat Murphy's behalf been to see Lady Bell, she brought out a question that had arrived in her mind just as Mrs Pickstock had come in.

'John, there's something perhaps you could tell me.'

'So long as it's nothing to do with the Poisoner. Do you know there's more than one of my fellow executives going about expressing admiration for that woman whose face you see on posters up and down the city? Really daring, they say, the way she risks discovery time and again. Or, when they think of her as Mentor, they're apt to say 'There's more than a little truth in what she wrote about the people she's chosen to despatch.' That's how they put it. Despatch. As if that was what happened to those inoffensive people she's murdered. That

235

they've been sent to some convict colony or other. Sometimes I despair of human beings.'

'Yes,' Harriet said, wrenching that round to her own ends, 'in a way that's what I want to ask you about. About, if you like, the Poisoner and Mentor.'

'One and the same woman, yes? So, what is it?'

She took a gulp of breath.

'It's that I don't think they are one and the same, and I know damn well that the Poisoner isn't the woman on those posters. But listen: you yourself said to me that you thought there was something odd, something different, about Sir Billy Bell's death. Right. Well, just this afternoon Lady Bell told me what the post-mortem on Sir Billy had discovered. Something, incidentally, that Commander Rance did not think necessary to inform poor Pat about. It was this: that Sir Billy had drunk with his champagne, not aconitine, but something that simply caused violent vomiting. Vomiting that happened to give him a heart attack.'

John stood there thinking.

'You know,' he said, 'I really had guessed that from what I saw that night at the Club. But I simply couldn't believe two poisoners were at work at the same time. But what you're telling me now is that, because of the two different substances administered, there are two murderers ranging about Birchester? Not to speak of one of them going down to London and over to Nottingham?'

'Yes, I am telling you that. Except that there are not two murderers. There's one murderer, the person who put aconitine in my Campari soda, and there's also a man who just set out to play a nasty trick on Sir Billy Bell.'

John, who had been standing in the doorway, came and sat down opposite.

'All right,' he said, 'I think perhaps you make out a reasonable case. So what is it you wanted me to tell you?'

A spark of pleasure flared in Harriet's head.

So my mental processes aren't as wonky as I feared.

'I hope you'll be able to tell me this,' she said. 'When I was at the *Star* editor's office and read Mentor's letter in its full, uncut version, something became clear to me. The person who wrote it is very likely a schoolmaster, and a retired one. There was a lot more Latin in it than they printed and other things that chimed in with that.'

'If you say so. But what do you want to know?'

'Right, there was something else I learnt by

chance from Lady Bell, Kitty as I was asked to call her. And what a nice person she is, did you know?'

'Never met her. But go on, for heaven's sake.'

'Sorry. What I learnt from her was that the Majestic Club now occupies the house and grounds of what used to be a private school of some sort called St Aldred's.'

'I know that. I haven't worked for Majestic as long as I have without learning a bit of the history.'

'Okay. Good. But have you thought how easy it would be for someone who was once a master at St Aldred's to make his way secretly into the private presentation of prizes by Sir Billy Bell?'

'No. No, I hadn't. But I think you may be on to something there.'

Again Harriet felt a glow of satisfaction. My brain, one to trust again. Sometimes.

'So how,' she said, 'do I get to know someone, anyone, who can remember that place? Perhaps even twenty years ago or more?'

John gave her a broad smile.

'You've just hit the jackpot. I don't think you've ever met a woman called Mrs Upchurch. No reason why you should have done. I knew her when I was at university here, largely because her son was a sort of friend of mine. A naughty lad, as a matter of fact. Into the modest drug scene of that time, and not above obtaining money on false pretences. His mother, who was already a widow, or at least without any evident husband, took to asking me to exercise my influence on him. Which, needless to say, I was quite unable to do. But — and this is what you'll want to hear — Godfrey Upchurch was an ex-St Aldred's pupil, and Ma, I gathered, had a lot of dealings with the school before her precious Godfrey was asked to leave.'

'And she's still here in Birchester? You know she is?'

'I do. I see her about occasionally. We pass the time of day. Godfrey's abroad somewhere, possibly a reformed character.'

'Then I'm off to have a talk with Mrs Upchurch.'

'All right. But not this evening. Too much excitement for one day. It's early bed for you. But I will phone Mrs Upchurch — think I've still got the number somewhere — and I'll tell her you'd like a chat some time tomorrow.'

He grinned.

'Though I should warn you, she's not the easiest of people.'

18

When Mrs Upchurch opened the door of her house, in a part of the Meads hovering between decline and former respectability, Harriet, confident in her oldish but still smart grey suit with the blue shirt she so liked, realized at once why John had said she was not the easiest of people. Mrs Upchurch stood blocking her doorway as if there were invaders to repel.

But mention of the meeting John had telephoned about brought something of a transformation.

'Of course. And so you're dear John's wife? I wonder we've never met. Didn't he tell me you were some sort of policewoman?'

Harriet forced a smile.

'Yes, I am,' she said. 'A detective superintendent actually. But I wanted to have a word with you in a strictly off-duty way.'

'Oh, well, that's nice. I'm not sure I'd want to have official dealings with the police. Or not unless I had occasion to ring them up because of some trouble in the neighbour-hood. I'm sorry to say there are round here

240

some perfectly appalling . . . well, criminals, I call them.'

Like your dear son, John's university friend, Harriet mentally commented.

Mrs Upchurch manoeuvred her way past Harriet to the door, which she bolted top and bottom. She then led the way back down the narrow hall and into what she firmly called 'the drawing-room'.

'Would you like some coffee?' she asked. 'It wouldn't take long to make. Of course, I never have the kind they call — what is it? — instant.'

Hastily Harriet lied her way out of coffee of any sort.

'I really wanted to talk to you about St Aldred's School,' she announced, blandly omitting to say why.

'That place. They ruined my Godfey, you know. I dare say your husband told you that he and Godfrey were great pals at the University.'

No doubt about the capital U there.

'Yes, John recalls him very well.'

'I'm glad he does. But, as I was saying, St Aldred's absolutely ruined Godfrey. When he first went there he was the sweetest little boy you could imagine. But he fell into bad company at that place. I mean, you would never have thought that Godfrey would have actually stolen, not when he went there. But in no time at all they were declaring he had done so. Stolen. And they said that he bullied the smaller boys too, hurt them. Of course, I didn't believe it. But he had made undesirable friends — your John was at the High School, I believe — and they led him astray.'

'Yes. Very sad.'

'Well, of course, eventually I wanted to take him away. But where else could he go? There were no other decent schools nearby, and I couldn't have little Godfrey going all through the city on buses. Buses.'

'I understand. So Godfrey spent the whole of his schooldays at St Aldred's?'

'And I have to say his behaviour went from bad to worse. He was punished, of course. They were always very strict at St Aldred's. But it seemed to have no effect. There wasn't any understanding, simply none. So, I'm sorry to say, he became more and more difficult, even flatly contradicting his own mother. Of course, if my husband had been here, it would have been very different.'

Harriet thought she wouldn't ask about the absent Mr Upchurch.

'I can imagine it would,' she said quickly. 'It must have been a very difficult time for you. Didn't Godfrey find any of the masters at St Aldred's sympathetic?'

Her bodily shift into the direction she wanted the conversation to go seemed to pay off.

'Oh, the masters there,' Mrs Upchurch exclaimed. 'Do you know, not one of them showed any friendliness at all for my poor boy? In the end, and you'll hardly believe this, he had to confide in the school gardener.'

Damn. The gardener. It's the masters I want to know about.

'Yes, that does seem awful,' she said.

Keep on with the right remarks.

'Jamieson, that's the man's name, was very kind to Godfrey, I will say. He knew at once what sort of a boy he was, and did his best to get him out of any scrapes he got into. And, you know, sometimes he gave him some very good advice.'

'That must have been nice.'

Harriet reviewed her stock of soothing placebos. It seemed to be running dangerously low.

'Oh, yes, Jamieson, although of course he was no more than a gardener, is a very good man. That's why, when the school closed — it had ceased to pay its way, I understand — I took him into my employment. The garden here is far too large for me to manage. It needs a man.'

But Harriet had scented a possible

alternative path. Jamieson, that giver of good advice, might well know a lot about the staff at St Aldred's in those days.

'You know,' she said shamelessly, 'I'd like to meet Jamieson. It's not often you come across someone like that. Is he here today?'

'I'm afraid he isn't. I had to let him go. I suppose he hasn't been with me for two or three years. Now, at a very inflated salary I dare say, he's at that Majestic Insurance Club, exactly where St Aldred's used to be.'

★   ★   ★

Harriet had planned, extricated at last from Mrs Upchurch's web of carping and complaints, to ask her taxi driver, still hopefully waiting, to take her straight to the Majestic Club and the long-ago St Aldred's School gardener. But the moment she thought that she would be going to the very place where . . . where someone had deliberately poured the poison from monkshood into her drink, all her get-up-and-go abruptly faded away.

Oh God, she found she was thinking, why can't I just go home and get into bed?

So John, when he came back, rather later than usual, found her fast asleep in her day clothes, and put her, a somnolent bundle, under the duvet. Then, at what she later discovered was half-past nine, the ringing of the phone woke her.

John called up the stairs that Pat Murphy wanted a word, if she was fit to hear him.

'Yeah,' she muttered. Then, more loudly, 'Okay. Yes, okay.'

Get my head clear. I'm Pat's colleague, if a colleague on sick leave. And I'm going to make myself well enough to listen to what he's got to say. It'll be to do with the Poisoner. And I want to know. I want to know.

She reached for the handset.

'Pat? Yes?'

'I'm after disturbing you when you'd gone early to bed.'

'No. Well, yes, as a matter of fact. But it doesn't matter. What is it?'

'It's just this. Something I thought you'd like to hear.'

'Won't know till I do, will I?'

'Sure, you'd never be able to guess. Commander Cleverdick has summoned assistance, psychological assistance. Who's going to arrive in Birchester tomorrow afternoon, or earlier, but one Dr Scholl, known to some as Dr Smellyfeet?'

Harriet blinked in astonishment.

Am I dreaming? No, it can't be that.

245

'Pat,' she managed to say, 'how did this happen?'

'None of my doing, I promise you. No, the notion came into Old Busybody's head, and in two twos he'd called in your man. Simple as that. So would I be right if I was to say you'd like to see him when he gets a few minutes?'

'You would. Tell him any time. Even if I'm still zonked out in bed, as I may well be the way I'm feeling at the moment.'

★ ★ ★

In the morning she found she seemed to possess more energy, though she decided her meeting with Mrs Upchurch's Jamieson could well be postponed. After all, she thought, Peter Scholl may even arrive by eleven and get away quite soon from Commander Rance's initial briefing, and it would be idiotic if I wasn't here when he came. He'll almost certainly have things to say to me more useful than mere talk about past times. Surely if a profiler's any good — and I have to admit he was very useful to me before — he's bound to have insights into the sort of man the Poisoner is likely to be. Let alone what different kind of a man might have been driven to put a vomiting agent into

Sir Billy's champagne and afterwards write that mad rant of a letter.

What I really want him to do in fact is to confirm, or not, my idea of there being two separate people now involved in the inquiry.

However, in the end, she had to wait, till quite late in the evening before there was a ring at the bell and Dr Smellyfeet, as she still occasionally thought of him in a genially friendly way, followed John into the sitting-room, a large bunch of white roses in his hand.

Roses, she instantly saw, that were more artificial-looking than artificial ones themselves. But, poor chap, he must have had to buy them wherever he could, with shops now liable to shut early as people scuttled off to the safety of home in a Birchester under the ever-looming threat of sudden death.

Peter Scholl was almost exactly as she remembered him. As ever, he wore student-type clothes, though the current T-shirt proclaimed, somewhat inexplicably, *DON'T KILL COWS*. His face, boyishly pink as before, was a little more lined, and the curls on his head, touched now with grey, were revealing a slightly larger bald patch.

'Peter,' she greeted him. 'And flowers, such a huge bunch. John, see if you can find a vase for them, before they all wilt away.'

How short, how terribly short, the life of flowers is, she instantly thought, struck into anxiety-ridden silence.

But John had seen her sudden access of dismay, and took charge.

'I'll have a peer into that cupboard under the sink,' he said. 'See what I can find. A good drink of water will revive this lot, if they need reviving at all. And you two can have your chat without interference.'

'Well, Harriet,' Peter Scholl said, dropping into the chair she had gestured to, 'I gather you're *persona non grata* in the Murder Room here.'

'So I am. But perhaps it's a good thing. It means I can do something, strictly unofficially, towards finding this man who's terrorizing the whole city.'

'Yes, I gathered from your Detective Superintendent Murphy that you're not exactly taking things easily, as perhaps you should be. Rest, Harriet, rest is what you want after something as traumatic as what happened to you.'

'It's what everybody tells me. The Force MO said three months' bloody rest. But, Christ, Peter I can't just sit here or, damn it, lie there upstairs, and do nothing. I was the Poisoner's first victim, and I'm bloody well going to fight him back.'

248

'Him? You sound very sure about the gender. Commander Rance, with whom incidentally I've quarrelled, is equally adamant that he and his team, with perhaps some assistance from your friend Pat Murphy, are looking everywhere for a woman.'

'Is that what you quarrelled with him over?' she asked, with a spark of hope.

'Well, yes. Yes, it was. The truth is that Rance had me brought up here, urgently. But when I arrived he simply instructed me that the Poisoner was a mad old woman who was attempting to acquire a million pounds by threatening to continue her activities. All he wanted from me was a run-down of her psychology. When eventually I said that, even with my limited knowledge of the circumstances, I didn't think his scenario was necessarily very likely, he straight away dispensed, as they say, with my services. I'm actually on my way back now. I ought to catch the last suitable London train quite shortly.'

'Right then, don't let's waste time. But at least let me get you something to drink first.'

'No, no. Pat Murphy saw to that, twice over, in his welcoming way. So, do I understand you're absolutely convinced the Poisoner is a man? I must say I had little doubt of it myself after I was shown that letter in the *Evening Post*.'

'*Star*, actually. The *Evening Star*. But I have to tell you, though, like you, I'm sure that letter was written by a man, I don't think it came from the Poisoner.'

'But — '

'No, Peter. What do you think of this? The Poisoner began what you might call his spree when he suddenly saw me as the ideal target on which to exercise the feeling of the power of life and death he'd been nursing, for years, carrying round with him a fatal dose of aconitine.'

'With you so far, and I think it's probable you're right.'

'Okay, but here's where I think things went astray for him. He failed to kill me. And that made him start off to prove he could still use that power of his, which he did on one, two, three innocent people in the city. Then someone else was apparently poisoned in the same way, Sir Billy Bell, former Lord Mayor of Birchester. But the Poisoner had had nothing to do with it. Big shock for him. So he stopped his activities while he sorted it all out. Then, when he had come to terms with having some sort of rival here, he went down to London and back up to Nottingham all on the same day and poisoned two other innocent people.'

'Still with you, at least as regards the Poisoner's likely behaviour. He's plainly sort of inadequate, if I may for once put it in unequivocal language. But I don't altogether see how this second poisoner you've postulated comes in.'

'Right. Well, I believe he's another nutter, as you high-powered psychologists call them, a man who was increasingly impressed by the series of murders he'd been reading about and decided to weigh in himself. Not with aconitine, which he had no idea how to obtain, but with an emetic of some sort. And he chose to give it to Sir Billy, someone he saw as deserving of punishment, a corrupter of holy, innocent Birchester, a man who had a chain of noisy music shops up and down the city, who owned cinemas playing porn films and a newspaper, the *Star*, that panders to the worst side of people's nature.'

'Okay,' Peter Scholl said cautiously. 'So have you any idea who this second poisoner is, and even why it has to be a man?'

'Oh, that's simple. He wrote the Mentor letter, and in terms that only a man would use.'

'Agreed. Or as much agreed as a profiler ever is.'

'Right, well, I think from what he put in that letter, mostly the Latin bits he peppered it with — and there are more of those in the original, which I managed to see — that he's not only a man but that he may have been a schoolmaster once, and a pretty old-fashioned one at that.'

'Yes . . . could be, I suppose.'

'Oh, Peter, I hoped you would say, 'Yes, yes, yes, you're right of course'.'

'So I might have done, if I'd been an enthusiastic amateur and not a hard-headed academic. But you can't have forgotten, I don't work by having sudden, brilliant ideas. I collect evidence, every little scrap I can, and then . . . well, you remember, I look for a pattern, a pattern of behaviour.'

'Okay, what's the pattern of behaviour of the man I've called the Schoolmaster?'

Peter Scholl laughed.

'Absolutely no answer from me,' he said. 'No, Harriet, it's not that I won't help you. It's that I can't. I haven't any evidence to go on. My one and only bit of advice for you is: look at all the evidence you can lay hands on, and then look for a pattern.'

'But what sort of a pattern can I expect to find when the man I'm looking at has committed only one poisoning, and a half-cocked one at that?'

'Then there won't be one. Too bad for you, I'm afraid.'

Harriet looked at him, fury rising in her head.

He may have seen the signs.

'But now I really must say goodbye to your husband,' he said hastily, 'and be on my way, or I'll miss that train.'

★ ★ ★

Harriet may have believed that Friday she had no way of finding a pattern in the Schoolmaster's actions. But almost at once there was another incident of a violent but not fatal vomiting attack, and it was followed by another letter to the *Evening Star* claiming responsibility.

The victim, Harriet learnt in a swift phone call from Pat, was a man called Alastair Ames, a youngish local government officer who had the habit of chasing away the boredom of his working week by spending Friday nights partying at a pub in the Meads, the Three Donkeys, notorious for its loud music. He had suffered his violent vomiting attack there and been sent to hospital, though for no more than one night.

From Mentor's new letter, which Harriet seized on as soon as the Saturday issue of the

Star was delivered, she learnt that it was the pub's loud music that had brought down Mentor's wrath on Alastair Ames. The letter, though short, was every bit as much of a rant as his first one.

I warned a week ago that unless I was paid a penalty sum of one million pounds I would find it necessary to eliminate more of the inhabitants of the wicked city of Birchester. I have, however, taken one more warning step, in simply causing to one who thoroughly deserves punishment a severe attack of vomiting. But, take note, this will be the last time that any other person I find it necessary to visit with retribution will remain alive. As my sacrificial victim on the altar of probity tonight I chose at random one of the noisy louts who habitually render the quiet of that once pleasant part of our city, the Meads, a hell of pandemonium at the public house which goes by the name of the Three Donkeys. I suppose in this age of panem et circenses

Harriet noted, with a wry smile, that the *Star* had now added a translation: [*Bread and circuses, Latin*].

She read on.

few will appreciate the ages-old riddle still extant in that public house signboard. It shows, as it should, a painting of donkeys, but of two donkeys only, it being left to the onlooker to recognize in himself the third donkey. Donkeys of Birchester, now is the time to mend your ways. Now is the time to insist, as affirmation of your repentance, that the punitive fine I have imposed be paid.

And the signature *Mentor*.

Right, Harriet said to herself. It's clear from all that farrago that Alastair Ames was not one of the purely random victims the Poisoner has been murdering. And, yes, the language is absolutely that of the first letter, even if it uses only one Latin phrase. Translated: H. Martens. So definitely, whatever Commander Rance may be thinking, this letter was not written by the Poisoner but by my Schoolmaster.

She glanced over it again.

And something stirred in her mind.

She strode over to the bureau where she kept her various documents.

Yes, here's the cutting from the *Star* of that first Mentor letter.

She read rapidly through the turgid, Latin-spattered column.

Yes. Yes, yes. I've remembered correctly. Here it is: *lying obscenely naked*. How could I have forgotten that description of my bikinied self? And, yes again, that other pub where an aconitine poisoning took place, the Virgin and Vicar, is described as dedicated to *displays of flesh*, and then poor little Tommy O'Brien is said to be *lying in the sun almost unclothed*.

All right, those are Mentor's words, Schoolmaster's words, not, if I'm right, the Poisoner's words. But they have shown me — I think, I think — the pattern in the murders the Poisoner has committed. The sort of unconnected pattern which, just yesterday, Peter Scholl told me to look for. The trivial, on-the-side circumstances linking the three cases are that Tommy and myself, at the time the Poisoner slipped aconitine into our drinks were semi-naked and that young Robbie Norman was happily gawping at the naked strippers at the Virgin and Vicar. Here surely is the pattern that may, one day, point unerringly to the Poisoner.

But, wait. Mrs Sylvia Smythe at that tea shop? She doesn't seem to fit. But clearly two others do, the people murdered in London and Nottingham. Marge Plummer in London was taking part, on a hot day, in a march of gays and lesbians, no doubt flaunting plenty of flesh, the way they always delight in doing in such circumstances. And at that pub in Nottingham on that warm Sunday evening, among a crowd of carefree students wouldn't there have been plenty of female flesh on display too?

And yes, doesn't the letter here say something at least about respectable, middle-aged Mrs Smythe with an e? Not that she was stark naked sitting in that prim tea shop, but something else. Yes, here. Here it is. *A lady of mature years who yet flaunted scarlet lips and scarlet fingernails.* Not much of a crime to have earned her an appalling death, but enough apparently to make the School-master claim she had deserved it.

But the pattern as a whole is surely clear enough. The Poisoner is set off by the sight of naked female flesh. Which, come to think of it, is not unlikely if he's the sort of inadequate Peter Scholl pointed me to.

So where does this tell me the Poisoner could be found? Where you can see naked flesh in profusion. There are enough places in Birchester you can see that, if not out of doors now the weather's changed. And, of course, something that won't be so helpful, there are even more places elsewhere than in

Birchester. If the Poisoner has operated in London and in Nottingham, there's no reason why he shouldn't, if he chooses, go anywhere: to Edinburgh, Cardiff, wherever.

Right, I must point this out to Pat. It may be the key to finding the man who put aconitine in my Campari soda, and into all those other drinks.

Then a hesitation.

Pat's no believer in profilers. All right, he did go out of his way to tell Peter I'd like to see him. But that surely was out of simple kindness to me. No, Pat's pretty unlikely to latch on to any theory that depends on something Peter said. And if I'm the one who passes on that theory, he'll go back to thinking that, ill as I am, I'm not to be trusted.

But I believe it all hangs together. I do believe it. You can't always resolve a case by relying on plain physical clues. You have to make assessments of what your criminal, your murderer, is likely to do, of the way that they think. And I've made my assessment, and I'm sticking by it.

I'm going to act on my belief, at least until some hard fact contradicts it.

Right, first step.

Yes, clear out of the way the Mentor red-herring. If I can prove, beyond doubt, that the Schoolmaster is a totally different person from the Poisoner, then perhaps Pat will take seriously the pattern I have detected in the Poisoner's crimes.

19

So on Monday morning — a decently sunny day — Harriet, sensibly dressed in her oldish but still good lightweight eau-de-nil suit, set out in a taxi for the Majestic Sports and Social Club, place of work for the gardener who had apparently befriended bad-boy Godfrey Upchurch at St Aldred's. And also, as she was fully aware, the scene of her own poisoning.

Her taxi made its way rapidly enough through the morning streets.

Not too far now, she murmured to herself. And at once a flutter of doubt set in.

That August bank holiday Monday. Me there, enjoying life with John. Nothing much going on among the city's criminal fraternity. A quiet weekend in the seemingly unending heatwave. A good swim. Then, stretching out to benefit from the sun, well covered in sunscreen, sipping a deliciously cool, tangily herby Campari soda. And a second one. And John needing a pee. And my eyes closing. And then —

No. No, I can't go there. I can't.

'Driver? Driver, can you just stop a moment?'

'You all right?'

But what is it *just*? Just that I'm suddenly overcome by terror at the thought of going to a place I've been to dozens of times over the years? I can hardly tell him that.

No, I really must be perfectly well. It's nonsense to think I'm not. I am all right, and I've got a task to carry out.

'No, I'm sorry, it's such a nice day for once that I think I'll walk the rest of the way. Do me good.'

'Whatever you like. But it's quite a step to that Majestic Club place.'

'Yes, I know. But I think I will walk it. How much do I owe you?'

And, once she had paid, with a somewhat larger tip than the short ride had warranted, she set out cheerfully enough, feeling she had made an unnecessary fuss.

Walking on at a good steady pace, she abruptly grinned.

All very well to say it's a nice day for a walk, though it is, but the worst part of the Meads is hardly a delightful area for a stroll, however few people there are about at this time of day. The edge of my old B Division territory, where once the Hard Detective, then only a Chief Inspector, had her day of *Stop the Rot* glory. Narrow little houses packed in dull-faced terraces, and the pavement and roadway littered with rubbish of all sorts. To think, not really so long ago, I was on the way in this very area to putting an end to casual rubbish-dumping and vandalism.

And to truanting from school, too, she added, as she caught sight at the next corner of a lone small boy apparently playing some game involving a stubby iron pillar at the kerbside. For a moment or two she stood where she was — just by the Roxy cinema, castigated in Mentor's letter in the *Star*.

And not undeservedly perhaps, she thought, looking up at a huge poster advertising, in a riot of long limbs, almost naked breasts and pert behinds, a film called *Seven Swimsuits and One Murder*.

But now, that boy there. Do I revert to the Hard Detective of old, go stamping down on that little fellow's petty offence?

I would have done, once. But, no, I'm off-duty, on sick leave. Let the little bugger —

Then there came to her ears a sound she knew all too well. The noise of violent vomiting. And she saw that the boy had not been playing with the pillar but clutching it as a sudden feeling of sickness must have overtaken him.

And she ran.

Half of her told herself as she pounded

down the street that she was being ridiculous. Small boys often overeat and are sick. But the other half of her could not thrust away remembrance of the sound she herself had made running with John to the loos at the Club that sun-broiling day.

Ladies or Gents, she thought absurdly as she ran. Can't remember, can't —

Then she was there at the pillar.

One look at the boy was enough to tell her that this was not a case of one ice-cream too many. He was deathly pale, and round his mouth the flesh was puffing up. Between jerks of vomiting his teeth briefly chattered in flurries of castanets.

This was aconitine poisoning. No possible doubt.

She slipped her mobile from her jacket pocket.

9–9–9

Thank God I decided to take this thing with me. I nearly didn't, off-duty.

They're answering.

'Ambulance. This is a life-or-death emergency. Aconitine poisoning.'

She gave the location and her name, preceded unhesitatingly with her police rank. Anything to impress on the operator the need for speed, though with Birchester under siege from the Poisoner every phone operator

263

should know how speed was necessary.

She turned back to the urchin clutching the pillar.

Did I come too late?

Christ, the vomiting's ceased. He's trying to wipe at his lips. The fiercely pricking tingling. I remember.

And I remember something else, too. John's fingers probing deep into my throat, and the life-saving spasms of vomiting they produced.

She grabbed the boy's mop of dirty blond hair, jerked his head back and then plunged the index and middle fingers of her right hand into his mouth, slimy with the vomit he had so far voided, and pushed and pushed.

It worked. The good old method.

Past her fingers she felt a new flush of vomit rushing up. She dropped to her knees — there was a can of Coke in the gutter there — and pulled the boy forward, twisting round to keep her fingers pushing as deeply into his throat as she could get them.

How long she stayed like that, feeling the boy's internal organs jerking and throbbing, she never knew. But it cannot have been very long before she heard the *pan-pon pan-pon* of an oncoming ambulance.

The paramedics, jumping out, were by her side in seconds.

'Listen,' she said, 'this is aconitine poisoning. I know. I was the Poisoner's first victim. Go straight to St Oswald's. Insist on him getting to Mr Hume Jones. Hume Jones. Man who saved my life. Hurry, hurry.'

★ ★ ★

Standing there, hand on the rounded top of the iron pillar to stop herself falling flat on the road, she found herself looking, as if at some interesting museum object, at her suit trousers bedaubed with sharp-smelling vomit.

Well, she thought idly, as though from a great distance, I thought this would be the last time this year I would wear this suit. I'd have probably taken it to the cleaners in any case.

Then a moment of blackness, only just aware that it was her hold on the pillar that was keeping her upright. Dimly from inside the surrounding dark she told herself that she must not faint.

Yes, there's work to do. I am the Investigating Officer, the first officer on the scene of a crime. Right, I take control. She opened her eyes.

No one about, not that I've seen, but there may well have been people who were looking on, from further up the side street here, from a window, from anywhere. I'll get to them in a moment. Next, preserve the scene. All I can do at present is stay where I am, shout out at anybody who comes by to keep well back. Route taken by offender, or offenders? One offender, the Poisoner. It must be him. Aconitine. It's certainly not the Schoolmaster. And there was no sign of anybody near when I first saw the boy. The Poisoner could have gone off in any direction.

Property left at scene?

God, yes, that Coke can.

She forced herself to look down for it. Yes, there, almost at my feet. And, of course, it's been opened. Somebody — him, yes, the Poisoner — almost certainly offered the poor truanting kid a drink. A whole can of sweet fizzy Coke.

Prints? Possibly, though he's always taken precautions up to now. What else? Yes, the vomit. In the gutter. On my trousers. No, they won't be going to the cleaners after all. Bagged up, they'll be going to Forensics. Shoe prints, clothing fibres? Scenes-of-Crime will have to see to them, so long as I've kept back any onlookers. And onlookers will come at any moment; nothing like a noisy ambulance for that.

Now, better ring Pat, if I can get hold of him. My call for the ambulance may not have been passed on elsewhere.

Awkwardly she wiped off most of the slime from her right hand on a cleanish patch of her jacket, and took out her mobile again. Wiping it too as much as she could, she pressed the digits.

But when she got through to Pat she learnt that the operator she had spoken to had done well.

'We know,' Pat said. 'I wanted to come meself. Only you're getting someone else.'

'Rance?'

'Of course. He'll be with you any moment.'

★   ★   ★

Some little time passed, in fact, without Commander Rance arriving. Lost in the criss-crossing streets of this unfamiliar area, Harriet guessed, with a touch of malice.

In the meanwhile people had begun to gather on the far side of the road. So she had the opportunity to cross over and at least ask each of them whether they had seen anything of the boy while he had been clutching the pillar earlier. There one of the aproned mothers told her he was Jacob Welland, known as Jakey.

Nobody, it appeared, had seen him. Or, if they had, in this part of the city where police were mostly thought of as enemy, they were not going to say. So there had been nothing more to do than begin taking names with a view to further questioning. And even this was something of a humiliating complication when she realized that, of course, she had no official notebook with her. At last she had been reduced to using the back of a long-ago shopping list fished out of one of her jacket pockets, writing on it in painfully small letters.

One half-success she did have. Just before a mini-cavalcade of tyres-screaming police cars came in sight, she spotted a familiar figure sliding by at the rear of the small crowd.

'Prodger,' she called out. 'Prodger, come here. I want you.'

Prodger, Prodger Matthews, was an old acquaintance. Arrested for dozens of different petty offences in her B Division days, he had never borne her much of a grudge.

At the edge of the little gathering he slowed his steps — never very brisk — and at a third 'Prodger!' came to a total halt.

'Right, I want a word with you. Did you see Jakey Welland here earlier on?'

Prodger made as if to walk away.

'So you did. All right, what did you see?'

'Nothing. Nothing at all, honest.'

'*Honest.* That always meant you were lying.

268

So, come on, Prodger, just what did you see?'

'Saw a bloke.'

'Good. And what was he doing, this bloke?'

'Nothing.'

'No, Prodger. No.'

'He was talking.'

'Talking to Jakey, that it?'

'Could of been.'

'Did you hear what he was saying?'

'Couldn't, could I? From the corner there? Just saw him give the kid a can o' Coke. Shouldn't have done that.'

'Why not, Prodger?'

'If he was giving away drinks, could of given it ter me.'

'You're damn lucky he didn't. But what did he look like, this mean fellow?'

'Dunno.'

'Oh, yes, you do. You know him by sight? Is that it? And you're keeping your lip buttoned?'

'Ain't.'

'All right then, what did he look like?'

Silent opposition.

For a moment.

'Had a 'tache. Big white one.'

'A big white moustache. And what else?'

'Cap.'

'He had a cap on? What sort of a cap? What colour?'

'Dunno.'

And now out of the first of the three brakes-squealing police cars there stepped Commander Rance. Harriet abandoned Prodger, who could always be picked up again when needed, and went over.

Rance was dressed in full white search-kit. Much of it, Harriet noted, a little too large for him, giving him a touch of the ridiculous. So, it had been equipping himself and his team in this way that had caused the delay in their arrival.

All the better, since it meant I spotted Prodger, who may yet give us a fuller description of that man in a cap with a white moustache. The cap at least links him with the man the Nottingham students chased in vain from the Trip to Jerusalem. So, is this the moment to tell Rance that the Poisoner is, in all probability, not his old woman but a white-moustached man?

But any to-and-fro doubts were chased from her mind by Rance himself.

'So,' he snapped out, 'we have Detective Superintendent Martens getting herself involved once more.'

'Yes, Commander, I am involved. If only by sheer chance. I happened to be walking through the street here, and I saw the boy — called Jakey Welland, by the way — being

270

acutely sick just there where you can see the remains in the gutter. Luckily, from my own experience I guessed he might have been given aconitine, and I called an ambulance.'

Rance looked at her.

Abruptly she was conscious once more of the stains all down the front of her suit trousers.

'So you *happened* to be on the spot,' Rance said. 'Hardly the sort of area, I should have thought, for an officer on sick leave to be taking a gentle stroll in.'

The sod, Harriet thought. He's seen straight away that I wasn't here doing what I ought to be, behaving in a thoroughly convalescent way. So he suspects, does he, that I'm still poking my nose into his case? Well, I am. Little though I want him to know it.

A quick answer bubbled up.

'Yes, sir, it must seem a bit odd,' she said. 'But in point of fact I was sitting there at home and I'd begun to cast my mind back to my earlier days in Birchester. And I thought I'd like to see if my old stamping ground, round about here, was in a better or worse state than when I left it.'

'And is it better? Or worse?'

'Rather worse, I'm sorry to say, sir.'

'Yes. Well, let that be a lesson to you, Miss

Martens. There's no use in putting in hand startling new measures if you don't stay with them and follow them through.'

'No, sir. Though I did gain one benefit from my days here. I found that an old acquaintance of mine, one Prodger Matthews, habitual petty offender, saw someone offering to the boy Jakey that can of Coke I've left *in situ* there. There may be prints, and Matthews may be able to give you a fuller description than I had time to get out of him.'

'May he indeed? And I suppose from whatever description a criminal of that sort produces we *may* be able to make an arrest. But in the meantime I'd like to be able to get on with my investigation into the circumstances here. So I suggest the best thing for you will be to put you in one of my cars and send you back home, where you can get on with the business of making yourself fit for duty.'

'Yes, sir. Thank you.'

20

Commander Rance's advice had, of course, the opposite effect to the one he had intended. By the time Harriet left the car that had taken her home — like a damn delinquent, she thought — she found her mental energy almost fizzing. It fizzed on for the rest of that day, producing at least one odd thought. Commander Rance, could he have known me by reputation before that unfortunate moment when Pat told him who I was and in an instant he sent me packing? Could he, even though we'd never met, have been obscurely jealous of this woman picked out for media attention as the Hard Detective? Most police officers, I know, were divided in what they thought of me in those days. Some, an encouragingly large number, applauded what I was doing. But almost as many believed I was too big for my boots, especially as I was wearing a woman's thigh boots. And they expressed their belief as yellow-spitting jealousy.

So, if that's the case with Rance, then I've nothing to worry about. Or . . . or will I have a great deal to worry about?

She shrugged.

Nothing I can do. Just wait and see.

What she did by way of waiting was, comically she felt, just what Rance had told her to do. She sat in idleness, flipping through a book, yet another Agatha Christie pulled at random from John's packed shelves.

She hardly paid attention to its unfolding story. Only when she suddenly realized that the title, *The Pale Horse*, was meant to send resonating through the alert reader the biblical quotation 'Behold a pale horse and the name that sat on him was Death' did she get up and try, not with success, to squeeze the paperback into its place in the shelves.

Too much of death in Birchester under the ranging presence of the Poisoner.

She dropped the book on the table beside her. Then with a renewed spurt of rage she thought of the way Rance had rejected hearing any details of the description she had extracted from Prodger of the man very likely to be the Poisoner.

Of the man. The man. If the bastard had listened for one moment, the notion he had in his head that Bruce Grant had seen an old, witch-like woman putting aconitine into my Campari must have been at the very least put to the test in his mind. All right, what Prodger said was pretty thin. But he spoke clearly enough of a cap and, more, of a white moustache. And one day . . .

Right, she told herself, tomorrow I am going, come what may, to the Club. And this time I'm going to find Mrs Upchurch's Jamieson and question and question him till either I've satisfied myself that no former master at St Aldred's School was capable of writing Latin-filled moralizing letters to the *Star*, or that I have found a name that fits. And then . . . then, with the Schoolmaster out of the way, I'll be able to prove that the Poisoner never wrote those letters, that he is not seeking the blackmail sum of a million pounds, that he is not the absurd witch Bruce Grant tried to persuade us to go looking for. And that he is a danger still hovering over Birchester, the rider on the pale horse.

The rider on the pale horse: she must have murmured the words aloud because Mrs Pickstock, emerging from the kitchen and, in her customary way, just poking her head round the door, said cheerfully, 'Oh, you've been reading that one, not quite my favourite, but nice all the same. Though I do always think it is a bit creepy really.'

She came waddling further in.

'But you know,' she said, 'it did save a boy's life once.'

Harriet, still caught up in her train of

thought, found herself believing for an instant that Mrs Pickstock must be saying that *Twisted Wolfsbane* had somehow saved Jakey Welland's life as well as her own. Then, as she realized her mistake, a shiver of premonition ran through her.

Jakey: has his life been saved? At St Oswald's has Mr Hume Jones been able to work his magic once again? Did that ambulance even take Jakey to the right hospital?

'Just a moment, Mrs Pickstock,' she babbled out. 'I — I've got to make a phone call, rather urgent.'

John had put a card with the St Oswald's number beside the phone in case of an emergency. With a trembling forefinger she jabbed it out.

Jakey was, in hospital terminology, in a stable condition.

It was all she could learn, and she lacked the forcefulness even to try to batter more out of the woman she had spoken to. But it was enough. Perhaps her fingers pushing down Jakey's throat had given Mr Hume Jones and his team enough of a chance to begin their life-saving procedures.

Sinking back into her chair with a sense of relief that brought the sweat up all over her body, she tried to think what it was Mrs

Pickstock had been saying.

Something about . . . yes, *The Pale Horse*, the old paperback on the table here. She glanced down at it. God, what an awful cover, with that spidery white skeleton lying there like some sort of discarded plaything, instead of riding high, Death himself on his rearing pale horse.

Yes, Mrs P had been saying something about saving a boy's life. Made me think of little Jakey.

'You were telling me something about this book, Mrs Pickstock? I'm sorry, I suddenly remembered I had to call the hospital.'

'Yes. Well, dear, I wonder Hubby never mentioned this to you. There was this little boy, you see, a foreigner of some kind, not that I've anything against foreigners, and his very rich parents had brought him over here when he was on the point of death from a mystery illness. Only even our doctors couldn't think at first what the cause of it was. But in the ward, one of those private ones you know, there was this nurse keeping an eye on the boy, and while she was sitting there she was reading just this book, *The Pale Horse*. And suddenly she realized the words in front of her at that very moment were a description of the exact symptoms the little boy had, and Dame Agatha had said just what the poison was that caused them. Of course, she told the doctors at once, and they soon enough put everything right. Come to think about it, it was just like the way it was with Hubby reading *Twisted Wolfsbane* and saving you, wasn't it? I always say dear Dame Agatha is one of the best writers ever.'

Picking her way through that verbal jungle, Harriet could only reply, 'Yes, you're quite right, Mrs Pickstock.'

But, she thought, in the book there must have been another one at death's door. Like Jakey. Like me.

★ ★ ★

Harriet had aimed to leave the house next day by quarter to ten so as to get to the gardens at the Majestic Club as soon as she was likely to find old Mr Jamieson at work. She had put on the little tub chair the night before the outfit she had chosen, which she felt made her look like someone who could be an acquaintance of difficult Mrs Upchurch: a light tweed jacket and skirt in a shade of pale grey. It had been in her wardrobe for years, seldom worn.

An unexpected telephone call changed her plans.

'Detective Superintendent Martens?'

'Yes?'

What is this? Detective Superintendent Martens is meant to be slowly recovering from an almost-fatal poisoning. No one, bar close friends, should be ringing me up. And I'm damned if I recognize this voice.

'Miss Martens, I'm the almoner at St Oswald's Hospital with special responsibility for child patients.'

Jakey, she thought at once.

Has he . . ? Not dead? Surely not dead. When yesterday they told me he was in a stable condition.

'Yes? Yes, what is it?'

'Oh, no need to worry, Miss Martens.'

Bloody woman. Why can't she just say what she's got to say?

'So how can I help you?'

She let the steely edge show in her voice.

'It's just this, Miss Martens. Little Jacob Welland is a lot better today. He's really making an unexpectedly rapid recovery. Mr Hume Jones worked wonders when he was brought in. And nothing will satisfy Jacob today but saying thank you to the lady who called the ambulance for him and, as he's convinced, saved his life. He's a bright little mite, you know.'

'He wasn't exactly in a condition to show any brightness when I saw him.'

'No, I suppose he wasn't, little thing. But he's bright as a button this morning.'

If he's as well as she's implying, the thought came abruptly to Harriet, I might be able to get a better description from him of the man who offered him that poisoned can of Coke, a far fuller one perhaps than the few vague details old Prodger was prepared to give me. I could even learn enough to make a positive identification.

'I suppose I might be able to come and see him,' she said cautiously. 'Should I bring something more in his line than flowers?'

'Well, yes. Yes, I think that's a very good idea. Perhaps you should bring him some sweets. Nothing difficult to swallow, of course, and nothing too rich.'

It'll not be exactly a bribe, she thought. But . . . but something to encourage talk. A lot of informative talk, if it's to be had.

Her heart began to beat noticeably faster.

Calm down, calm down.

'I could come this morning,' she said. 'As soon as he's ready for me really.'

'Oh, yes, Miss Martens. That's just what we had in mind. It will settle little Jacob splendidly, though of course you should be careful not to over-excite him.'

All right, I will be. I will be. But I'll talk to him for as long as it's necessary, and I won't let any Nurse Bhattacharya or anyone of that sort tell me to leave off.

'So when shall we see you, Miss Martens?'

'In . . . in about half an hour, if that's all right.'

'That will be perfect. Jacob is so eager to see you.'

★ ★ ★

Jakey, as it turned out, was occupying the very same room at St Oswald's that Harriet had had herself. She found him propped up on pillows, looking almost well, if with cheeks more flushed than they might have been.

'Yeah,' he said as Nurse Bhattacharya, none other, opened the door. 'Yeah, that's the one. The one what poked her fingers down me froat.'

Harriet grinned.

'Hope I didn't hurt too much.'

'Nah. Saved me life, didn't yer? That's what Mr Jones said anyhow. An' fanks very much.'

Savouring the *Mister Jones*, ferociously hyphenless, Harriet produced the box of soft fruit-shaped sweets she had managed to buy when she stopped her taxi on the way.

'The doctor I saw downstairs,' she said, 'told me these would be okay for you. But only one at a time, mind, and a big gap between each. So — ' A dart of inspiration. 'No guzzling, not in the way you guzzled that Coke the man gave you.'

Right, she said to herself, pleased with her stratagem, now to see how much he remembers about what happened then.

Christ, though, will I have stirred up terrible memories? That prissy almoner with her warning about not over-exciting him. All right, classical fusser there, if I'm not mistaken. Yet . . . yet what if I do cause a relapse, and . . ?

But she was saved from the possible consequences.

'That what happened then?' Jakey asked, his voice much less bright. 'I been trying to fink.'

'And you haven't remembered anything?' Harriet asked, torn between her desire to know more and fellow feeling for another who had suffered as she had. 'Anything at all about it?'

'Nah. Nuffink.'

Nuffink. Then my whole clever little plan's up in smoke.

'Yeah,' little Jakey was going on. 'I told that Mr Jones about that, an' he said it's what happens most of the time when you've had that sort of accident. Well, that's what he gave out, if he wasn't telling a whopper.'

Yes, Harriet thought, Mr Hume No-hypen is more than capable of telling a whopper, if it suits him. Look at the way he tried to keep me here as his prize patient. You're a sharp little devil, Jakey Welland. Even if you can't be any help to me.

'Yeah, it was a major accident what I had,' Jakey continued, reflectively. 'Major. An' what about you, Miss? You were poisoned jus' like me, weren't yer?'

'Yes, I was poisoned just like you, although I think I got it rather worse. And, yes, I can't remember much about it, even now.'

'Don't yer worry,' Jakey said. 'It'll all come back one day. Least, that's what old Jonesey says.'

Harriet decided this piece of juvenile philosophy gave her the opportunity to leave. Jakey had given her his *fanks*, and there had been, as it turned out, nothing more to learn from him about the man in the cap with a white moustache. So, with a final 'Right, get well soon, you little wretch,' she set off back home.

* * *

For a moment in the taxi she had toyed with the thought of saying once again that she would go directly to the Majestic Club.

But, no. No, I need a bit of a rest. A bit of time to nerve myself up. Enough to be able to see again that recliner beside the pool, the stout little table beside it on which there had stood a tall glass of bubbles-sailing, cherry-red Campari soda.

Yes, a little time.

There flashed across her mind then the still living feel of John's fingers probing and probing, in just the way she had had to put her own down Jakey's *froat*. And then once again there came that momentary inner sight of something black and white.

What . . ? What the devil does that mean? Why? Why do I see it time after time? It must surely be something originating from those few minutes while I was dropping off to sleep on that recliner. But what? What?

Will everything, as Jakey kindly said to me, all come back one day? And what will I learn then?

The taxi drew up in front of the house. And this time she not only succeeded in paying the fare unasked but managed to open the front door without having to stand there and work out that a latch-key and the mortise were needed. In the sitting-room she found the copy of *The Pale Horse* lying where she had left it and, feeling now no need for any anodyne mental comfort, she put it without difficulty into its proper place in its jam-packed shelf. Next to *Twisted Wolfs-bane*.

She ate the lunch Mrs Pickstock had brought her from Organics 'R Go, the Four-bean and Ginger soup, which she now found perfectly palatable, and the soft brown, grains-dotted organic roll. Then at last she felt ready to go to see what she thought of, with a touch of wry amusement, as *the scene of the crime*. To where not only had the Poisoner committed his first offence, but where, too, old Mr Jamieson, once grounds-man at St Aldred's School, might very well be able to identify for her the Schoolmaster, writer of those farrago letters to the *Star* claiming to be the Poisoner. She rang for a taxi — not yet ready to drive herself again — and endured the long wait for it in happy patience.

This time, she found with increasing satisfaction she had no need to call a halt on the way and say, untruthfully, that she wanted a walk. Which, she reflected, was just as well, since a seeping rain had begun to fall once more.

The taxi came to a halt. Still sitting inside in view of the rain and her lack of any protection from it, she paid the fare, tipped to a nicety and got out.

But then, the moment she walked through the Club gates, disaster.

She came to a blank and total halt.

I — I can't walk. I'm frozen into a statue. Locked rigid.

She felt her heart begin to beat crushingly. Cold established itself in all her body, from the soles of her feet to her very scalp. A feeling of nausea swelled within her.

Before long, her breath was coming faster and faster, ever more shallowly. She gasped and gasped. Soon it felt as though at any moment it would be impossible to breathe at all.

She fought against it. But it was too much for her.

Christ, I'm going to die. Death's door.

Christ, the Poisoner's won. Now. Now, after so long.

And it was that dimmest of thoughts that brought her back from it.

I'm not going to let him. He's not going to win. I am going to win.

Gradually her locked frame relaxed. She found she was breathing almost regularly again. Her heartbeats had slowed, the crushing feeling was rapidly leaving her.

She still felt nauseous and she was still cold to shivering point. But she knew she had beaten off the calamity that had seemed to

286

threaten her very life.

No, Poisoner, you didn't win. You didn't win over me, any more than you won over bouncy little Jakey. Yes, the thought of this place, where you tried to send me to death, did put me into a state of wild panic. But that's what it was. That's all it was. A panic attack. Just a more severe panic attack than the one that happened to me on the way to see Mrs Dora Long, who was not after all my witch-like murderer.

★ ★ ★

Still a little shaky, Harriet managed to set off again into the Club grounds. She came to the as yet undrained pool, its blue water pock-marked by the droplets of the steadily descending rain, a few yellow leaves floating here and there on its surface. And at the sight of the wooden recliner in the very same position it had been in August with its table there beside it, she experienced not the least tremor of unease.

So that's where it happened, she thought. As if, a schoolgirl on a tour of the Tower of London, she had been informed by some loudly reciting Beefeater in red and gold skirted uniform that this was the spot where Anne Boleyn had had her head chopped off.

She took one last look and moved on.

At this early hour of the afternoon in the middle of the working week the grounds were wholly deserted. Careless of the by now thoroughly wettened state of her tweed jacket, she went here and there hoping to see an ancient gardener at work. In her mind's eye she actually had him dressed in corduroys tied round with straw at the knees and with a piece of sodden sacking across his bent shoulders.

But nowhere was there any such figure, or any other more likely figure. She began to feel a mounting sense of anger. Wasn't it the man's duty to be at work here somewhere? Who did he think he was to take a day off when, first thing, it hadn't even been raining? When someone urgently wanted a word with him?

Then, as she strode on, head down, the rain-heavy branch of an ornamental cherry tree brushed straight into her face. She cursed it. And cursed again the hard-to-find Mr Jamieson.

Damn it, damn it, damn it, I'm going to have to give up. I'm going home. To take off this horrible old suit and get myself dry and warm.

But, no.

No, she thought, dabbing with a damp

sleeve at the heavy raindrops on her face, I'm here to find that man if he's anywhere to be found. To find him and learn from him the names and characters of every single member of the teaching staff at St Aldred's School at the time the man I call the Schoolmaster was likely to be here.

And, yes, damn it, if Jamieson's not at work in the gardens themselves, where will he be?

The answer arrived, clear as a bell, into her mind.

Why, somewhere round the back of the big house taking shelter, of course.

She swung round and marched off.

* * *

She found old Mr Jamieson sitting comfortably in the shelter of the open door of a shed behind the big house, looking across, no doubt, at the kitchens area. Perhaps, she thought, just inside, there's a store room where, back in August, someone fulfilling an early order reached down a new bottle of Campari. Or perhaps not.

But, placidly smoking a pipe and watching the rain ruffle the puddles and soak into a big heap of white-bleached sweetpea haulms uprooted earlier, Jamieson — it must be him — was not at all the figure from the past she had imagined. No sodden sacking on his shoulders, no straw-bound corduroys. Instead he was enveloped in a shell suit in the brightest of reds.

'Mr Jamieson?' she asked as a formality.

'That's me.'

'I wonder, could I have a word with you?'

'I'm here, and I'm not going to give myself rheumatics going about in this rain.'

Harriet laughed.

'It's probably what I've done, though,' she said. 'I never thought to bring a mac when I started out.'

'Oh, yes? And where were you going then?'

She was taken aback for an instant.

'I was going to find you, Mr Jamieson,' she confessed.

'Well, you found me.'

Is he going to return minimal answers to everything I ask? Am I going to get nowhere for a second time today after little Jakey?

But she persisted.

Keep the conversation going. Don't let him have time to wonder why this middle-class lady is asking him questions. Especially as I'd find it awkward to produce my customary *I am a police officer*.

'I was speaking to Mrs Upchurch the other day, Mr Jamieson, and she told me you had worked for her once, but before that you had been employed here, when it was St Aldred's School.'

'Nasty place.'

He shot up into a sudden stiff-backed position. His shell suit top crackled.

'St Aldred's?' she asked. Harriet felt the trail she had hoped to find go flicking out in front of her. 'It was a nasty place, despite its reputation?'

'I said nasty.'

How to get him a bit more forthcoming?

'From what I heard from Mrs Upchurch about St Aldred's,' she began. And switched, recollecting in a flash how Mrs Upchurch had sharply dispensed with the old gardener's services. 'Though I must say,' she hastily went on, 'she's not a lady I much cared for.'

'Tight-fisted bitch. I could tell you a thing or two about that one.'

It's worked. It's working. Now let's hear his *thing or two* and just hope they lead from bad-lad Godfrey Upchurch to the masters at St Aldred's in its prime.

'I'm interested.'

She made herself look as if, bright-eyed, she would be fascinated by every word he was going to say.

'Had a boy at the school. She tell you that?'

'She did indeed.'

'All right then, I'll show you the other side

of the coin. Young Godfrey, she made him out to be a little saint. I'll bet she still did that to you.'

'Yes, yes. She did.'

'Well, he was a wee devil. I know the St Aldred's masters were a strict lot, some of 'em delighting in it. But that Godfrey — not that they ever called him Godfrey in those days, all surnames then — he deserved everything he got. I don't mind a bit o' naughtiness in a young 'un, but he was more than naughty. He was as bad as bad can be. I tried once to put a bit o' sense into him, took him aside — into this very shed here, as I recall — and told him how if he didn't mend his ways pretty soon he'd ruin his whole life. And you know what he did, the wicked imp of Satan? He went and tried to make his form master, Mr Grigson, believe I'd taken him in here and done what they call nowadays *indecently assaulted* him.'

A grunt of a laugh.

'Of course, in them days nobody got so hot under the collar about a thing like that. So, even if Mr Grigson had believed him, he wouldn't have done anything about it. Delighted in doing his share of assaulting himself, with the cane, from all I heard.'

I wonder . . . Harriet thought. I wonder if, straight away, I've lighted on the very man

292

that I hoped I might.

'This Mr Grigson,' she ventured, 'he sounds like a real teacher of the old school, drumming Latin and that sort of thing into boys' heads or, as you said, at the end of his cane.'

'That's him.'

'And strict about everything, you said?'

He hadn't. Or not explicitly. But that's what I want to know about.

'Oh, yes. Great one for good behaviour was Mr H.F. Grigson — Old Heffalump was what the boys used to call him, on account of those initials — and with him it was all what a gentleman should do and what a gentleman never should.'

With every new revelation, Harriet felt increasingly certain she had found the man she had been looking for, the Schoolmaster, writer of highly moralistic letters to the *Star*, full of threats of punishment for the wicked.

Too good to be true finding him as easily, she asked herself. Am I being absurdly over-eager?

No, even if I am, this ex-schoolmaster ought at least to be eliminated from the inquiry.

'Tell me, is Mr Grigson still alive, still about in Birchester?'

'Couldn't say.'

Is it back to monosyllables now?

'You haven't heard of him at all? Not since the school closed down?'

'Not likely to, am I? Him the gentleman, me the gardener.'

'No. No, I suppose not.'

She thought for a moment. Time to go? Right, it is. I've found out what I wanted, as much as I'm likely to get.

'I've enjoyed our chat,' she said. 'But I see the rain's beginning to ease off, so I'd better be on my way.'

She gave her shell-suited informant a quick, friendly smile and went.

Thoughts racing.

21

There proved to be only one H. F. Grigson on the Birchester electoral roll when at home that afternoon Harriet consulted it. Herbert Fitzwalter Grigson lived in the Meads, in one of the better parts in that nowadays very mixed area, a small enclave at some distance from where Mrs Upchurch was holding out against encroaching yobdom. Its wide roads were still, she remembered, lined by houses named *The Laurels*, *The Hollies*, *The Cedars* . . .

It was, she found, from *Wistaria House* that H.F. Grigson went out to cast his votes, if he ever took part in democratic elections.

All right, she said to herself, so now probably I know where to find the man who has attempted to usurp the Poisoner in order to harangue in the *Star* such inhabitants of Birchester who displease him. And, in doing that, he has seriously hampered the investigation into the real poisonings. But what am I to do about him? Go to Commander Rance and finally tell him what I believe? Should I? Ought I to?

She sat in silence, the computer screen in

front of her glowing with its extract from the electoral roll halted at *Grigson*. The minutes passed.

But at last, with a heave of a sigh, she submitted to what she knew to be her duty, whether an off-sick police officer or not.

She tapped at the buttons on the phone, picked it up.

'I want to speak to Commander Rance of the National Crime Squad. It's Detective Superintendent Martens.'

'Commander Rance has left urgently for London, ma'am,' the man on the switchboard answered. 'Can I put you through to another member of his team?'

'No. No, thank you. But put me on to Detective Superintendent Murphy, if he's there.'

'Here almost twenty-four hours a day, ma'am.'

'Right. But, no, on second thoughts I'll drop in and speak to him face-to-face.'

★ ★ ★

The reward of virtue, Harriet said to herself, entering forbidden Waterloo Gardens central police station and making her way up to Pat Murphy's office. While the jealous cat's away, sick-leave police officers can play.

But her appearance in the office seemed not to be altogether welcome to Pat.

'You shouldn't be here.'

'But who's away down in London? And, now I think of it, what's he doing down there? Has there been some development?'

'Well now, it just so happens that Mr Rance had been looking over the statements the Met people took after that woman, Margery Plummer, was poisoned. And he didn't think they matched up to his own high standards.'

Harriet was tempted to say, *How could they?* But she decided that might embarrass Pat even now.

'Listen, Pat,' she said instead. 'I think I've made a discovery.'

'Of a way to hurry on convalesence, is it?'

'Damn convalescence. No, Pat, it's this. I know now who it is who's been writing those letters to the *Star*. And it's not the Poisoner.'

'And you've come here to tell me all about it, after finding out our Commander Rance is in London. The man on the switchboard had a word with me after you'd phoned.'

He grinned.

'We have our sources of information, you know.'

'Right. And I have come to tell you, rather than Rance, what I've found out, or what I think I have. Who else should I tell, since I'm debarred from taking action myself?'

'So it's action you're wanting?'

'It bloody well is. Listen, you know that as soon as I'd read the original of Mentor's first letter to the *Star* I had my suspicions that it had been written by someone like an old-fashioned schoolmaster. Then when you, you Pat Murphy, sent me to visit Lady Bell I learnt something more, something that advanced my investigation.'

'The lady I unofficially asked you to call on, as a favour, advanced *your* investigation?'

'All right. What Lady Bell happened to mention was that the Majestic Club was once the home of a private school, St Aldred's. And I thought that if Mentor was the man who put that vomiting agent into Sir Billy Bell's champagne at the prize-giving, then he almost certainly would have known how to sneak in there by the back way, and as quickly slip out again.'

'So he would, so he would,' Pat said. 'But I have to tell you, as a matter of fact, when you were poisoned we looked into the possibility of the Poisoner getting to you in that way. But we decided it was not at all likely, not at all. It's a bit of a warren of a place, the back parts of that old house. And we thought anyone new coming in there would find it all but impossible to slip in and out, especially on that busy holiday Monday with kitchen staff hurrying here and there.'

'All right, so you agree all the same it could be a possibility at the time Sir Billy died.'

'I just might, if it's you asking.'

'Okay. So this afternoon I went there, and — '

'Wait a minute. You went there? You went to the Club? To the very place where you were nearly done to death?'

'Yes, I did. I had to.'

'And what happened? What happened when you saw that recliner, there where I'd had it put when I did my bit of a reconstruction?'

'Well, you'll be pleased to hear I saw the recliner, I saw the very table where my cough-mixture soda was, and I didn't turn a hair.'

'Did you not?'

An undertone of scepticism in the question brought her down to earth.

'Well, it's true that I didn't turn a hair when I'd got in as far as that. But actually when I first came to the gate I had a pretty bad panic attack. Still, I got over it and I found the fellow who used to be the groundsman at St Aldred's. And we had a bit of a chat.'

'Did you indeed? I wonder why.'

Harriet was checked by the lightly humorous question. The answer she would have to give Pat was not one he was going to accept very easily.

'You wonder why,' she said. 'Well, I'll tell you. It was so that I could learn something about the teaching staff at St Aldred's in those days. And what did I discover? That there had been a particularly strict master on the staff called Mr Grigson, H.F. Grigson in fact. And just half an hour ago I learnt from the electoral roll that H.F. Grigson lives in a place called Wistaria House. It's in the Meads.'

'So?'

'Well, Pat, I think that H.F. Grigson is, not the Poisoner, but the man who has claimed in the *Star* to be responsible for all the murders, including the non-murder of Sir Billy.'

'Ah, I have it now, the action you're wanting taken. You want me to go harum-scarum over to this house of his, tyres screeching as if Commander Rance himself was in it, and arrest a harmless old citizen?'

'No, Pat, not that, as you well know. But I do want you to go and interview this Mr Grigson. Surely he's worth at least questioning? I mean, he precisely fits the bill as Mentor. And if Mentor is not the Poisoner himself, but someone who's simply taken advantage of all the deaths for his own ends, and I believe that's what's happened, then shouldn't he be eliminated as soon as possible? To clear the field?'

'Harriet, I'm sorry to tell you, but once more you've heaped up a great castle of suppositions, and if anyone so much as touched a stone of it the whole thing would crumble away to nothing, so it would.'

For a moment she just stood there. She guessed she must be pouting like an unjustly reprimanded schoolgirl.

Then she admitted to herself that perhaps Pat's view of it all had some truth in it.

'Okay,' she said. 'If you won't follow it up, you won't.'

Now it was Pat's turn to look at her.

'Harriet,' he said at last. 'I'm going to speak to you like your parish priest, not that you'd have any such thing. But pay attention. 'If you won't, you won't,' you said to me. Well, I'm telling you that *you* won't, either. You will not make a fool of yourself by taking the law into your own hands. It's not your task to investigate the poisonings, and well you know it. So don't. Just go home and tell your troubles to John. And then go to bed, right?'

★ ★ ★

Damn it, Harriet thought to herself as she sat at supper with John. Pat was right. I have been behaving like an idiot.

'John,' she said, riding full-tilt over a long, husbandy explanation of the difference between the detective story and the crime novel. 'John, am I still really not capable of making logical decisions about ... well, damn it, about the Poisoner investigation? I mean, this afternoon I had what I suppose was a panic attack, a full-scale one, when I went back to the Club. I meant to tell you that I wanted to go, but — '

'But somehow you hoped to go without me knowing? You went, and now you're telling me about it because you're suddenly afraid your brain isn't working normally. Which, of course, it isn't. Some of the time. You'd be very lucky if it was. Remember, your Dr Dalrymple said you'd need three months before you were fully recovered.'

'Sorry I broke into your interesting disquisition, darling.'

John grinned.

'No, I wasn't giving you a subtle rebuke. I'm used to having my disquisitions, if that's what they are, rudely interrupted. But, no. I was telling you the truth, as I see it. You're not as fit as, from time to time, you deceive yourself into thinking you are. You really ought not to do anything but take it easy. Fifty or sixty Agatha Christies await. Well, say, twenty really good ones.'

'Thank you, but no. Can't you point me to something not about murder?'

'Hm. Let me see. How long ago was it that you last read *Middlemarch*?'

'Oh, blush, blush, I never have.'

'George Eliot's great contribution to the novel? You should bury yourself in it straight away, even though, now I come to think of it, it does have a murder in it, or a sort of murder. Crime raising its universal head.'

'Very good, sir.'

But even as she sat there, head theatrically bowed over her bowl of kiwi-and-grapes fruit salad, a very different resolve came into her mind.

★   ★   ★

John left the house next morning rather later than usual. Harriet, waiting for him to go before she made the telephone call she wanted him on no account to hear, crept to the bedroom door and opened it to see what it was that had delayed him. It was the visiting nurse who, a few minutes earlier, had gone through her by now customary, almost perfunctory, bedside checks.

Her voice now came floating up.

'You know, Mr Piddock, I think I ought to tell you it isn't really necessary for me to come every day now. Your wife's temperature has been normal for more than a week and her blood pressure's just as steady.'

'Yes,' John was answering, 'I've realized she's been nearly back to her old self for some time. But, you know, the Greater Birchester Police medical officer told her that she shouldn't expect to be fully fit for as much as three months. So perhaps you had better keep coming. But, shall we say, only twice a week?'

'Very well. Best to be on the safe side. And it is always possible that if she gets into a serious accident of some sort, in the car or even just tripping up over something and hurting herself badly, she could be sent, well, right back.'

And on and on the medical platitudes went, pit-a-pat. Harriet, crouched on the side of the bed, did her best to let them go by in patience. But her best was hardly good enough. By the time she heard the front door close definitively behind them both she was in a good, healthy rage.

But she counted to five, and then made it ten, before she seized the phone, still thinking how ridiculously fussy the two of them were, and jabbed out the number of her former station in B Division.

To her deep-running delight she found an old friend, Detective Sergeant Watson, was there in the CID room and not at the moment engaged with anything more urgent than going through the left-hand pages of his notebook to make out his expenses claim.

He was happy to be taken away from that task to meet for coffee at the nearby new Starbucks.

Entering the place, Harriet was at once sharply reminded of how, shortly after her return from St Oswald's, Miss Earwaker, on the way to their first unsuccessful hunt for monkshood, had taken her into somewhere similar, after the noise of the traffic all round the battered little Honda had become too much for her fragile nerves.

Thrusting that unpleasant memory aside, she told Mike Watson she would go and get them caffè lattes. Then, without any other preliminaries, she settled down to telling Watson what it was she wanted him to do. At the end of twenty minutes' careful explanation, accepted much more easily than Pat Murphy had done, he agreed to go with her directly to Wistaria House in the Meads in the hope of finding H. F. Grigson at home and, if it looked as if her suspicion was correct, arresting him there and then.

And at Wistaria House they found him. Watson had agreed that when his notoriously retentive large red ears had recorded evidence enough, he, not being a potential witness, would be the one to make the official arrest. So it was left to him to announce them both as police officers and to flourish his warrant card.

Grigson had opened the door to them himself, shambling and stooped in a shabby brown tweed suit that looked almost as elderly as he did, his dully pallid face marked out by a nicotine-stained grey moustache. Looking at him hard, Harriet detected no sign of anxiety at this unexpected visit.

'So, what can I do for you, sergeant?' he said. 'Has there been more of this loutish vandalism? I had occasion to report something of the sort some months ago, but I hardly expected to hear the culprits had been brought to trial.'

'No, sir. We've come about another matter. There are some questions we'd like to ask you.'

'Oh, are there? Then we had better go into my study.'

He led them, without another word, into a room smelling strongly of pipe tobacco, with a roll-top desk against its far wall, a solitary leather armchair, a carpet so threadbare there was no telling its original pattern or colour, and on the walls sepia photographs of Greek and Roman ruins together with one, above the mantelpiece, of an infantry officer of World War I days.

There was a pair of what looked like discarded dining chairs beside the desk, both piled with ancient, cracked-spine books. H. F. Grigson, the Heffalump, lifted these up, dumped them on the floor and, rather awkwardly, pushed the chairs more into the centre of the room.

Harriet, all this while, had seen no sign in him of any uneasiness.

Have I got it wrong about him? The thought rose up in her mind, a threatening torpedo-ready submarine. Was John right last night? Was Pat right, there in his office? Is my mind still affected by my experience? Have I been led astray by sheer wishful thinking?

Too late now.

Sitting herself on the nearer to the Heffalump of the two chairs, she waited while Watson asked him some preliminaries about his full name and the length of time he had occupied the house — 'Ever since I was a boy, as a matter of fact, sergeant' — and then she came in with her own first question.

'Mr Grigson, I understand you were formerly a master at St Aldred's School here in Birchester. Is that right?'

'Yes. It is.'

A faintly puzzled look appeared on the pallid, wrinkle-marked face as he leant against the back of the worn leather armchair.

'What did you teach there?'

A little deeper puzzlement.

'I was the classics master, though in the school's latter days it fell to me to teach whatever was needed: mathematics, French, a little science even.'

Ah. So he may have known enough at least to concoct whatever emetic he had poured into Sir Billy Bell's champagne and into Alaistair Ames' beer at the Three Donkeys. Perhaps I haven't got it wrong after all.

'I see. So, as a teacher of Latin, you will be familiar with such phrases as *panem et circenses* and *Et in Arcadia ego*?'

Now a look of wariness had appeared in the faded blue eyes beneath the jutting grey eyebrows.

'Well?' Harriet barked. 'Can you translate those phrases for me?'

'What is this? Why are you asking me to perform such a ridiculously easy task?'

'Oh, because they're Latin expressions I read in that first letter in the *Evening Star* signed Mentor. I wondered exactly what they meant.'

'But they never printed *panem et* — '

He came to an abrupt halt as he must have realized what he had said.

'No, Mr Grigson, the paper replaced that phrase with a rather ugly English version, which took away some of the sting, didn't it?'

The Heffalump's slack grey face coloured up into a dull red.

'One more wretched instance of the stupid, ill-bred young idiots in charge of our newspapers,' he spat out. 'It oughtn't to be allowed. There should be a law against it. There should be more responsibility exercised by those whose fortunes allow them to obtain ownership of organs of opinion. Look at that disgusting Sir William Bell. Billy Bell. Billy Bell, he took delight in calling himself. A man not fit to own anything, and he goes about buying up shop after shop to sell those appalling, noise-blasting gramophone records. He acquires a perfectly respectable cinema down here in the Meads and turns it into a place showing the filthiest porno-graphy. He made life hell in Birchester for anyone with any sort of a decent education. A hell, I tell you. He deserved to die. A dose of a good emetic was what he needed, and he got it. He got it.'

The words had poured out in a chaotic, unstoppable, careless-of-everything rush.

And they were enough.

When the screaming diatribe at last came to a halt, Harriet gave DS Watson a nod.

'Herbert Fitzwalter Grigson,' he said at once, 'I am arresting you on suspicion of having caused actual bodily harm to Sir Billy Bell and to Alastair Ames. You do not have to say anything. But it may harm your defence if you do not mention when questioned something which you later rely on in court. Anything you do say may be given in evidence.'

Herbert Fitzwalter Grigson chose not to say a word.

* * *

Pat Murphy, tucking into the large steak that John had cooked for the three-person celebratory dinner he had arranged for Harriet, paused for a moment.

'I think I recall,' he said, 'that DS Watson was one of the team you took down to London, Harriet, when you carried out that corruption investigation.'

Harriet looked at him, smiling amiably.

'Yes, as a matter of fact he was.'

'I wondered where he got that 'from

information received' stuff. You wouldn't think any B Division snouts would have had much contact with an old schoolteacher like Grigson.'

'No. No, one wouldn't.'

'Oh, come off it, you two,' John put in. 'I'm happy to give my wife credit where it's amply due, even if she wants to be modest. And you, Pat Murphy, haven't any need to be so determined to know nothing.'

Harriet put down her knife and fork, leaving almost half her steak untouched, her appetite not very much better than it had been a fortnight after her return home.

'The question is,' she said, 'are you any more inclined now, Detective Superintendent Murphy, to listen to what an officer on sick leave might have to say to you?'

'Don't let her bully you, Pat,' John put in.

'When have I ever?'

'All right. But you're bloody well going to listen now to what it is I've been thinking since, with Grigson charged, I've been able to concentrate entirely on the proper Poisoner.'

'I will so. Never let it be said I don't take heed of anything you tell me, sick or well.'

He raised his wineglass to her.

'Pat,' John said, 'just take a look at what's left on that plate there. Remember, she still is ill.'

'But not so ill I'll let anybody stop my mouth, John Piddock.'

'Okay, say what you've got to say. We know you're going to.'

'All right. This comes from something Peter Scholl told me just after our friend, Mr Rance, sent him packing.'

'If it's that mop-headed fella — '

'Yes, Pat, it is. And you just sit on your prejudices till I've finished.'

'Ma'am.'

'Now, what Peter said to me was that anyone trying to narrow down the hunt for the Poisoner should take a good look at each of the poisonings to see if any sort of a pattern emerged from them.'

'For God's sake, Harriet, what do you think I've been after doing, day and night, ever since this all began? Amn't I thinking and thinking what could be your man's motive?'

'Oh, yes, Pat, I know the sort of hours you've been working, and I can guess how much of that time you were asking yourself what could be behind the poisonings. But what you didn't have, and I'm quite serious about this, was any backing from a forensic psychologist like Peter Scholl. So you weren't actually looking for a pattern not obviously connected to the actual crime, were you?'

'If you're wanting to put it like that, I wasn't.'

'So hadn't you better listen at least when I tell you about the pattern I think I've found?'

'I'm listening.'

'Right. This came to me actually while I was standing outside the Roxy cinema in the Meads, wondering about a small boy who looked as if he was playing truant. The Roxy was advertising a film called *Seven Swimsuits and One Murder* with a huge poster showing a posse of young women hardly wearing any swimsuits at all. Then I suddenly realized that the boy — it was Jakey Welland, of course — was being extremely sick into the gutter, and at once the memory of John lugging me into the loos at the Club came rushing back to me.'

She gave John a wide smile.

'Which was it in the end,' she said, 'the Gents or the Ladies?'

John laughed.

'Do you know, I've completely forgotten.'

'Never mind. Let me tell you the thought I had when I eventually recalled that moment, after the Grigson business had been cleared up.'

'It was..?' Pat asked quietly.

'This. That all but one of the Poisoner's murders had occurred in circumstances

313

parallel to the sight he must have had of all those naked beauties on the Roxy poster.'

'I'm not as familiar as Pat with all the details of the murders,' John said, 'though I can see that naked female flesh did feature to some extent in most of them. You, lying there at the Club in that scanty bikini, darling, and hadn't that young man at the Virgin and Vicar been watching a strip show? And — '

'And,' Pat broke in, 'Tommy O'Brien was lying there in the sun outside the City Hall, all but undressed. I know just how naked she was; I had to go and look at the body. Poor kid. And you could add that lesbian lady in the march down in London, plenty of flesh on show there, the reports said. And, right, at that pub in Nottingham, a very warm evening and most of the drinkers there students. Plenty of nakedness again. You're right so far, Harriet. If this means anything.'

'No, what about the woman who was poisoned at the tea shop out in Boreham?' John asked. 'I can hardly see her sitting there without any clothes on.'

For an instant Harriet acknowledged to herself that the pattern seemed to fail in Mrs Sylvia Smythe's case. But it was for an instant only. Her recent recall at the Meads Starbucks of that awful morning with Miss Earwaker in the coffee shop had brought

314

something back to her mind. Miss Earwaker, in her distress at misunderstanding the noisy young Italian man there, had twittered about how much nicer old-style tea shops were, where they had *ladies* serving and little vases of flowers on the tables. And she had mentioned Mary's Pantry. She used to go there for tea, she had said, while the children she was in charge of had been looked after by some *excellent fellows* at the nearby public swimming baths.

'No, listen,' she said. 'My friend, Miss Earwaker, told me once she used to take children from the school she taught at — perhaps even Graham and Malcolm, John — to some public baths near Mary's Pantry, where years later Mrs Smythe had aconitine put in her teacup. Well, why had the Poisoner gone out to Boreham? To watch, licking his lips, girls parading in swimsuits and bikinis at those self-same baths, yes? But the baths nowadays are closed on September the first. So going there to watch on — let me see — yes, as late as September the sixteenth, he was thwarted. Thwarted, and so went, probably while waiting for a bus, to nearby Mary's Pantry. Where he suddenly saw his chance.'

'All right,' John said. 'Just.'

'No, I want to go on from that. Look, the

315

Poisoner, an inadequate of some sort — Peter said he might well be — is strongly attracted by displays of women's flesh, right? And he somehow couples his feelings about that with exercising his power of life or death, putting what he's made from the tubers of monkshood into the first neglected drink he comes across in conjunction with a display of flesh. And, listen, I can tell you where there's going to be, in the immediate future, a monster display of flesh that the Poisoner knows all about. It's — '

'I know,' John broke in. 'I've seen the posters all over the city. 'Birchester's Biggest Beauty Contest. At the Roxy. Saturday October 27–7 p.m. to midnight — Bring Your Swimsuit — See Seven Swimsuits and One Murder'. Something like that. I suppose you could call it Sir Billy's last will and testament.'

'Yes,' Harriet said. 'I've seen that ad in the *Star*, full page, and I'm certain the Poisoner will have done too. Seen it and taken note.'

'No, damn it,' Pat exploded. 'You mean to go there, Harriet, don't you? But it's all just fantasy, piled up till it's spilling over. And I'm not saying that because I think it's a lot of psychological ta-ra your Dr Smellyfeet passed on to you. No, I'm saying it's just one more of your own special eejit ideas, like the ones

316

you've had in your head ever since you came out of St Ozzie's.'

'No. No, Pat, it isn't. Look, John thinks I'm right. Why can't you judge it all as sympathetically as he's done?'

'Well, remember,' John said, 'I'm no more than an insurance company executive. And Pat's a senior detective. You can hardly expect him, with all the experience he has, to kow-tow to my off-the-cuff judgement. In fact, if there's any kow-towing to be done, it ought to be the other way about.'

'No.'

'Well, I'm sorry, darling, but I feel it's actually yes. Thinking it over, I have to admit I was being rather too sympathetic towards you when I seemed to endorse your idea. All I really did was to jump in and add a few extra bits.'

Harriet, at this betrayal, felt an almost overwhelming impulse to get up from the table and storm out. With an effort she checked herself. Storming out would only underline the frailty of her mind.

Wait till I get John to bed tonight, she thought, letting a lava trickle of anger run through her head.

Until she abruptly remembered that John had not shared their bed since he had brought her home from St Oswald's in that expensive ambulance. And, too, that she had felt no desire, in all the weeks that had gone by, that he should do so.

Perhaps, she thought then, I am really still far away from my normal state.

An ever-thickening sense of dread entered into her.

Perhaps John, and Pat too, has justice on his side. Perhaps I really have failed to be rigorous enough in sorting out the logic of what's happened, the logic of what's been going on in the Poisoner's head. Perhaps I have done no more than seize on an attractive idea and then build it up into —

Into another of those castles of suppositions that Pat rebuked me for claiming were real.

'Yes,' she said at last, making the least concession that she could. 'Yes, I suppose it is possible that I've allowed myself to be carried away. And, as you said to me when we talked before, Pat, I am in the habit these days of building up towering castles that can be toppled just as easily. So, thank you for knocking another one down.'

Pat raised his glass to her again.

'Fully admitting,' he said, 'that in the last instance Castle Grigson turned out to be built solid.'

So they parted friends.

But in the solitude of the night Harriet had fully to acknowledge that she was not now the Hard Detective any more. She was for the time being only, she hoped, the Soft-headed Detective.

22

Yet again Harriet was woken by the clamour of the phone beside her bed. Blearily she looked at the little green figures of the digital clock.

Good God, 9.57. John must have gone hours ago.

She clamped the earpiece to her head.

'Yes? Yes, what is it?'

And to think that for years I never answered the phone except with our number and no more. Yes — the ugly fact fleetingly came back to her — I am, now at least, the dangerously Soft-headed Detective.

'Miss Martens?'

'Yes. Yes, it is.'

I've heard that voice somewhere before. And bloody irritating it was.

'Miss Martens, it's Mrs Woodruff, children's almoner at St Oswald's, again.'

Christ, bouncy little Jakey wanting another visit? Finished his box of fruit-shaped sweets? Ridiculous woman.

'Miss Martens, I'm afraid it's bad news.'

Then she knew. Not a box of sweets. No, Jakey must be — It couldn't be anything else.

'Jakey's dead. It's that, isn't it?'

'I'm afraid it is. Mr Hume Jones says that, though he wasn't expecting it, it could have happened at any moment. He called it Sudden Death Syndrome. He said after a major trauma it does sometimes occur.'

Harriet managed to mutter something, perhaps 'Thank you for letting me know,' before she dropped the handset on its rest and let herself fall back on her pillow.

For a long time, fifteen minutes or more, her mind stayed perfectly blank. Then, one by one, thoughts presented themselves to her.

This must not have happened. It must not.

It's intolerable. Intolerable.

A boy like that. An innocent, for all his street wisdom.

He should not have died. He should not have been poisoned to death.

The poor little bastard, he didn't deserve it.

He was a nice kid. A bright kid.

What we want in this world is kids who'll grow up into people who do things.

Christ, yes, even if he turned out, with his background, to be a clever housebreaker.

No, cheeky little devil, he'd be a con man.

Or, other side of the coin, in the police.

Yes, make a first-class detective, an eye for a lie, Mr Jones.

Poor little sod.

Damn it, he's gone too far this time, the Poisoner.

He's gone too far.

By God, I'm going to get him. I will. I will. I will.

★ ★ ★

A few minutes before seven on Saturday evening Harriet marched into the Roxy, eyes alert.

Though how, in God's name, I'll know him when I see him I can't think. I haven't even any mental image of the Poisoner. An inadequate? Very possibly, if Peter Scholl's off-the-cuff judgement is to be relied on. But what the hell does an inadequate look like? On the other hand, although I didn't have a name for the Schoolmaster, I suppose had I seen an old fellow in an elderly brown tweed suit somewhere about in the city I might have wondered about him. Might even have followed him and eventually got on to H. F. Grigson. But any retired schoolmaster might well have a nicotine-stained grey moustache and —

Two sudden thoughts came into her head, jostling for preference.

Prodger. Prodger at the scene of poor Jakey's poisoning; hadn't he said the man who gave Jakey that Coke had a white moustache? About the only thing I managed to screw out of him before Rance and his brakes-squealing cavalcade arrived.

And, equally insistent, a flashed vision of something black and white had appeared. Flashed and, this time, flashed and flashed again.

My malfunctioning brain? No. No, something telling me that as I lay there at the Club on that slightly uncomfortable wooden recliner about to fall asleep in the sun, someone, a man, came towards me . . . or, no, had stood not far away looking at me. A man, not very tall, with, yes, a full white moustache and, oddly in contrast, a head of tufty, black-as-black hair.

Him. It must have been him. The Poisoner.

She pushed her way further in through the crowd of young women and their noisy boyfriends, the girls almost all scantily dressed on top of sometimes visible bikinis.

Where will he be? Here? Can't see anyone answering that description, though I have him in my mind's eye all right now.

Push further in. Where it's most crowded. Where he's most likely to be looking for his prey.

The bar there. Plenty of glasses about, hardly guarded.

She fought her way into it, eyes probing. Black hair, black-black hair, anywhere in sight?

The dozens of patrons' backs clamouring to be served.

Then, as one of the lucky lads swung blunderingly away, a beer-spilling pint glass in each hand, a head turned in anger. And revealed . . . him. The man with the puffy white moustache and that tufty, grease-gleaming cap of black, black hair.

Even as she squeezed and pushed her way towards him another answer came into her mind.

He's an albino. What did that old man out at Halsell Common say? Yes, *like one o'they pet rabbits, the white 'uns.* Yes, it fits. That thick white moustache, that all too plainly dyed black hair. And, yes, though most albinos — one in every 20,000 of us, didn't I once read somewhere? — deal with their lack of one normal pigment well enough, for a few it will be a burden. A burden turning them into — Peter's word — inadequates.

Yes, the Poisoner, the man who perhaps even as a white-haired oddball schoolboy, listening to Keats read out in class, found the words 'neither twist wolfsbane, tight-rooted, for its poisonous wine' had lodged in his head. He's here not seven or eight yards away from me.

But those few yards are an almost impenetrable jam of pushing humanity.

And, if I do manage to worm and fight my way through to him, how can I deal with him when I get there? Christ, I was a fool to set out alone. I could have asked Mike Watson to come with me again. No, no. No, I couldn't. He's already risked a lot of trouble arresting Grigson for me. But Pat? Surely I could have persuaded Pat, in the light of day this morning, that I'm right. Or could I? Probably not. Almost certainly not.

No, I have to stay here where I am and keep my sights on that black-headed, white-moustached figure until it's nearly time for the show and the crowd here clears.

No sign of that yet.

And, damn it, with all the pushing and shoving up against the bar, it's impossible to watch those hands of his at every instant. A few moments ago, even, if he'd been slightly less jammed in, he could have slipped from his pocket whatever he carries his monkshood juice in and tipped it into one or the other of that blundering man's slopping pint glasses.

Wait. If I move a bit to the left, I may —

He's doing it. He's hauling his arm free. He's going to plunge it into his trouser pocket, pull out . . .

Must get to him.

She put her head down and, without consideration for anybody, man or woman, torpedoed her way forwards, eyes fixed on the hand of the arm now freed from its jammed-up position.

Dimly she heard protests. A man swore at her.

But the packed bodies were yielding.

No, his hand's still in his pocket . . .

Push, push.

Must get here. Must. Will.

And, yes, I'm right. His hand's out now, and in it . . . what? A metal tube? No, something silver, small as a pencil stub.

Get there. Get there. I must. He's picked a

target. Glass on the bar? Anything.

I know. It's a scent-bottle. Victorian. We had Granny's one back at home. Memento.

And I can't get to it. I'm too far off.

'Out of the way!'

She had screamed it.

And had been obeyed.

There was a path now, narrow, jostled from each side, between her and the bar. And, yes, he was wrestling with the tiny glass stopper of the phial inside its silver casing, a finger and a thumb attempting to twist and twist.

And out. The tiny stopper out. The poison ready to tip.

A plunge. All but a dive.

At full force she shot her arm out ahead. Her stretching fingers just connected. The little silver scent-bottle went scuttling across the drinks-wet surface of the bar.

The Poisoner wheeled round. And, it was plain, he had set eyes once more, after long months, on the woman he had failed to kill on that sun-blazing day when the impulse to murder, kept in delicious check for so long, had at last burst through. His unnaturally pale face was contorted in tensed-up rage.

He hurled himself into the gap Harriet had created with her frenzied scream.

Unbalanced, she could do nothing to defend herself.

She was on the point of actually falling into his seeking, clawing arms.

And she was knocked flat to the floor.

She sensed a heavy foot thumping down almost right beside her head. A thick blue shape shot over her. The Poisoner was enfolded in two massive arms.

Then she heard a familiar voice.

'Begod, it's Fredericks, Leon Fredericks, no less. I had you as a Peeping Tom maybe twenty years ago, and now I've got you as a poisoner.'

A Few Words of Explanation, If You Need Them

Leon Fredericks, under questioning, confessed with almost embarrassing readiness. It turned out that Harriet's lightning guess, as she had fought her way towards Fredericks in the jam-packed Roxy cinema, was pretty well correct. He had been fascinated as a much-bullied schoolboy by Keats' lines about poisonous wolfsbane, read out aloud in class. He knew that the plant, under its name monkshood, grew in his parents' little garden — the one thing that flourished there. And he had experimented on, of course, the family cat. Thereafter he had gone about always with

328

the scent-bottle, which he had picked up somewhere, filled with poison. On August bank holiday Monday, sneaking through the back of the house that had once been St Aldred's School to glut himself on the female flesh on display round the pool, he had seen Harriet half-asleep on her recliner, stretched out and defenceless. The sight of her had at last converted long-hugged temptation into action.

Envoi

Pat Murphy had insisted that it was his turn to hold a quietly triumphal dinner. He had chosen to incorporate it in his family Halloween celebration out at his house in Boreham, a place he rented from the Police Authority after they had bought it from the widow of the senior officer who had been murdered in the road outside.

So round the table there, while in the darkness outside fireworks exploded and trick-or-treat youngsters shouted and screamed, were seated Pat, his wife Maire, and their two neat-headed boys, a solemn eleven and twelve. Solemnity a little spoilt by murmured objections when they saw Maire bringing in the first course.

'Oysters, yuck.'

Their mother quickly shushed them.

'If you don't like the thought of oysters, you'll have to make do with the good soda bread there beside you. But dear knows what protein you'll be getting tonight. You know what follows on Halloween.'

The younger boy's eyes glistened.

'Did you ever eat — ' he began to chant.

His brother unceremoniously clamped a hand over his mouth.

'You mustn't ever say it till it's come to the table.'

'So what's this all about?' Harriet asked, sipping at the glass of creamy Guinness Pat had poured to go with the oysters under their topping of glowingly orange cheese sauce.

'Ah, you'll have to wait along with the youngsters for the answer to that.'

Pat looked at John then, with a sliver of doubt in his embedded blue eyes.

'Sure, I hope you'll care for it when it comes,' he said. 'As you'll maybe have gathered there's no meat to it at all.'

'Well, at least Harriet's good friend Mrs Pickstock would approve of that.'

Soon enough Maire left her chair and re-entered the kitchen. She came out clasping an enormous bowl of green-flecked mashed potato, a deep little well in the middle of the mound swimming with rich yellow melted butter.

'Off you go then, boys,' Pat said.

And off they went, chanting verse by verse one after the other.

Did you ever eat colcannon
When 'twas made with yellow cream,
And the kale and praties blended
Like the picture in a dream?

Did you ever take a forkful
And dip it in the lake
Of heather-flavoured butter
That your mother used to make?

And now Pat and Maire leapt in.

Oh, you did, yes, you did,
So did he and so did I.
And the more I think about it
Sure, the more I want to cry.

God be with the happy times
When trouble we had not
And our mothers made colcannon
In the three-legged pot.

Much to her surprise — grimly bitter kale was a pet hate of hers — Harriet found that the big helping on the plate in front of her seemed to be disappearing more rapidly than anything she had eaten in all the months since she had swallowed that last drink of Campari soda.

Either it's some sort of Irish magic, she thought, or I must be rapidly getting better.

Evidently the two youngsters were as eager colcannon devourers as she found she had become herself. In no time their second helpings had disappeared. Bowls of delicious blackberry mousse vanished yet more rapidly.

'Oh, the secret of it,' Maire said, in answer to John's lip-licking inquiry, 'is you have to pick the blackberries at their very best before they get nasty and woody or, as we say at home, before they have the devil in them.'

'Right, boys,' Detective Superintendent Murphy commanded when the very last traces on their bowls had been scraped up, 'it's bedtime for you this minute.'

And, like well-drilled cadets, the two of them, voicing polite goodnights, were on their way upstairs.

'So it's really over now,' Harriet said, the moment she saw the door shut.

'Yes,' Pat answered, 'we'll not hear much more of Leon Fredericks. He's so far off the scale of normal behaviour, the wretched fella, he has to be classed as mad. Almost to a certainty he'll be put away safe for the rest of his days.'

'Over indeed then,' Harriet echoed. 'No one armed with death hovers now above the good citizens of Birchester.'

She gave a bit of a laugh.

'But will they be aware of all the other ways death may come to them with no warning?'

'No, they won't,' John answered cheerfully. 'After all, who is aware of that? Look at how we contrived, when we thought World War III was going to break out almost any day, not to go on thinking from dawn to dusk about the atomic bomb. Probably, you know, when all's said and done that's the best way to deal with all such threats. Just to get on with things.'

'Sure, let's drink to that,' Pat said, taking from the sideboard a bottle of whiskey — Irish, needless to say — and pouring generous measures.

'But what I want to know,' John went on, 'is why, Pat, after everything you'd said the other evening at our place you still decided to go down to the Roxy and, yes, save Harriet's life?'

Pat grinned.

'Didn't I say that night, too, that she could be right in her castle-building, occasionally? Like when she fixed on that poor fella Grigson, who's likely to be another one found unfit to plead. Sure, I knew well she'd go down to the Roxy that Saturday whatever I'd said. And the thought that she might be right about your man being there niggled away at me, till suddenly I decided to take a look. Simple.'

'Simple, but wonderfully good of you.'

Harriet's turn now to raise her glass.

She had prudently declined whiskey but found her Guinness was once more full to its deep-white frothy head. More Irish magic.

'And what I want to know,' she went on, 'something I've never found a chance to ask you, Pat, is just what did Commander Rance say to you before he went buzzing off back down to London?'

'Ah, I can tell you that. It was few enough words at parting. I think I have them right. 'I told you, Mr Murphy, that this wouldn't take long to clear up.' '

'Let's all drink to that,' John said.

★ ★ ★

Harriet, who had contrived not to take too much of her Guinness, slid into the driving seat of John's car when at last they had said they ought to be on their way. It was a very different trip from when she had gone, on her own, to meet a rebellious Pat by the pond in

Waterloo Gardens. Fifteen minutes, swift, efficient and smooth, saw her putting the car neatly into the garage alongside her own.

She slept that night, John beside her, without any hint of a nightmare. And at seven in the morning, her usual time, she woke to find she knew with simple inner certainty that she was back again to her old state of health.

Gone the Soft-headed Detective, no longer near death's door. Back in place, ready to go, the Hard Detective.

THE END

We do hope that you have enjoyed reading this large print book.

Did you know that all of our titles are available for purchase?

We publish a wide range of high quality large print books including:
Romances, Mysteries, Classics
General Fiction
Non Fiction and Westerns

Special interest titles available in large print are:
The Little Oxford Dictionary
Music Book
Song Book
Hymn Book
Service Book

Also available from us courtesy of Oxford University Press:
Young Readers' Dictionary
(large print edition)
Young Readers' Thesaurus
(large print edition)

For further information or a free brochure, please contact us at:
Ulverscroft Large Print Books Ltd.,
The Green, Bradgate Road, Anstey,
Leicester, LE7 7FU, England.
Tel: (00 44) **0116 236 4325**
Fax: (00 44) **0116 234 0205**

Wat
ST.
BM.